MOMENTUM LOST

Endurance and Survival at Sea

Momentum Lost

ENDURANCE AND SURVIVAL AT SEA

Jeffrey E. Denning

To Emily

I am here today through the grace of yesterday.
This is a backstory and a way to know who I am.

Inspired by true events.

My gratitude goes to Patricia Mariano Denning.
Without her, there may not have been a story.
Without her encouragement, this book may not have been.

For the complete synopsis, reviews, and backstories, visit
WWW.JEFFREY-DENNING.COM

ACKNOWLEDGMENTS

"Make sure your story is credible and accurate,"
advised industry experts who helped make it so.
Thank you for sharing your expertise and experiences!

Bruce Brown—Bruce Brown & Associates

Barrett Canfield—Southcoast Yachts

Dave Costello—President, Avalon Rafts

Chris Gil—Chief Engineer—Oil Tanker, Middle East

Capt. Robert Harding—Atlantic Coast

Capt. Michael Wescott

Sherry Haines—R.N., California

US Coast Guard

TABLE OF CONTENTS

WHAT IS IT?

Abbreviations Used in This Story

AB—Able Seaman – a rank on a merchant vessel indicating a mariner with a variety of skills that make the person proficient in duties such as steering, lookout, and ship maintenance and repair. The list of duties is long, and the mariner is able to perform all the duties well and at a moment's notice.

AIS – Automatic Identification System – a marine navigation safety system that allows boats to automatically exchange information with other boats and shore-based systems. It allows mariners to "see" other vessels beyond radar range.

ASA—American Sailing Association – an organization specializing in sailing education, providing a wide range of courses for sailors of all levels to build their sailing skill.

BOAT – Bring on Another Thousand (B.O.A.T.) – a humorous acronym for describing the cost of boat ownership.

BVI – British Virgin Islands.

EPIRB—Emergency Position-Indicating Radio Beacon – an automatically activated emergency communication device that uses satellites to relay the position of an object—such as a boat.

ETA—Estimated Time of Arrival – the time (and date) of anticipated arrival at a specified destination.

FRB—Fast Rescue Boat – As the name implies, an FRB is fast and used for rescues. In this story, it is a twenty-two-foot durable, inflatable boat with a hard hull and single outboard engine, equipped with emergency gear that can be quickly deployed from a tanker in emergency situations.

MOB Button – Man Overboard – a button on a boat's navigation system that, when pressed, records the boat's longitude and latitude and is used to help locate a person who has fallen overboard and cannot be seen.

PA—Public Address System – a "loudspeaker" system that allows someone on a ship to communicate to everyone aboard at the same time.

PFD—Personal Floatation Device – similar to a lifejacket or life vest but can be inflated automatically or manually. A PFD is considered more comfortable than a lifejacket or vest because a PFD is not bulky when not inflated.

PLB—Personal Locator Beacon – an EPIRB for individuals.

PTSD—post-traumatic stress disorder, a mental health condition that typically results from experiencing or witnessing a terrifying event, or indirect exposure to such an event through the traumatic experience of a family member.

RPM – Revolutions per Minute. It is a measure of speed. The higher the RPMs the higher the speed.

UHF – Ultra High Frequency (handheld or stationary) radio used for short range communication, usually less than six miles.

Terms Used in This Story

Bare Poles – sailing with no sails set, as during a violent storm.

Beam – the widest part of a boat.

Beating (to Wind) – Sailing (or pointing) at an angle into the wind or upwind. Since sailboats cannot sail directly into the wind, "beating" is the closest course to the wind they can sail – usually forty-five degrees.

Bulkhead – an upright partition (wall) separating compartments.

Davit – a crane arm that projects over the side of a ship and is used to raise and lower boats or cargo.

Head or Marine Head – a boat's toilet or bathroom facilities.

Heave-to / Hove-to – a way of slowing a sailing vessel's forward progress, as well as fixing the helm and sail positions so that the vessel does not have to be steered. A maneuver frequently used as a storm tactic in severe weather.

In-Irons – a term that refers to a stalled boat when it is pointed into the wind or in an area known as the "no go zone." If sailors find themselves in this place, the boat will stop and is said to be "in irons."

Lazarette – a storage locker used for gear or equipment a sailor would use around the deck on a sailing vessel. It is hinged for access and doubles as a seating area in the cockpit. *Momentum* has four.

Lee Cloth – a piece of fabric that acts as a safety net to keep a sailor in their bunk on a boat, especially during rough seas or long passages.

Mooring – any permanent underwater structure to which a vessel (such as a boat) may be secured. It takes the place of an anchor.

Old Salt – an experienced, weathered sailor.

"On the hard" – an expression that describes a boat being out of the water, usually in a boatyard or on dry land where they can be placed for repairs or maintenance.

Painter – a rope used for securing or towing a small boat (dinghy) or life raft.

Raw Water Pump – a pump that pulls seawater in to cool the engine. Water is pumped by an impeller which looks and acts like a miniature watermill used in the colonial days. Over time, it wears out and can cause engine overheating.

Safety Harness – a combination of a strap and buckles to tether a person to part of the boat. Many PFDs have a built-in harnessing system.

Significant Wave Field – An average measurement of the largest one-third of waves. It gives the mariner data about the power of waves since larger waves are more "significant" (important) than smaller waves.

Sole – the floor of the cabin or cockpit on a boat.

Station Bill – a list of the crew and their duties in case of fire and other emergencies that is posted in the crew's quarters or another conspicuous place on a ship.

Thru-Hull – a device that is secured to and creates an opening through the hull, to which a pipe or duct can be attached allowing water or fuel to pass in or out of the boat.

Wave Field – the area taken by a wave. Gives mariners a sense of wave energy.

Wavelength – the distance between the crest (highest point) of waves and is one of the factors in determining how the energy of a wave will affect boat performance.

FROM THE LOG OF A MARINER

I haven't seen land in eleven days. Don't know if I ever will again.

I came to face my fears and become an equal among mariners. When sailing at night, I feared I would steer us into a lethal collision with the unseen, that we would be attacked by whales, or I would misread a squall that would splinter our boat. When piloting in storms and high seas, I feared making an ignorant move that would compromise the boat and we'd be swallowed. I feared falling overboard while alone during night watch and that my screams for help would go unheard. But then those fears vanished. Was it because I was too busy, or merely because I grew weary of being afraid?

I used to think seasickness was nausea that preceded puking. I wish it were that simple. I spiraled helplessly into its depths— seeing things that weren't real and wishing for death. I saw a phantom ghost ship and a burning freighter. It's impossible to make good decisions through a veil of hallucinations.

Before coming out here, I thought I understood the meaning of humility, acceptance, and forgiveness.

We are four diverse personalities crammed on this speck of a boat. Earning respect has required more than good seamanship.

I've had to navigate through the rough waters of competitive testosterone, ego, and mistaken perception. At times, arrogance and pride have been the most menacing of threats, and facing those has evoked more fear than what brought me here in the first place.

From the beginning, we have been haunted by a colossal storm system that grows stronger and darker as it thunders toward us with wind that can snap our mast, and waves too mighty for our boat to climb. We've hove-to. We've run. We've been blown a hundred miles off course. The plotlines on our chart memorialize our futile attempts to evade this deadly beast. Our boat systems have failed. Tensions have frayed nerves. Dehydration and debilitation have obstructed reason.

I am now preparing for what we have been madly attempting to avoid.

From the personal journal of Nelson Sharpe
APRIL 30, 2010—34° 30'10"N, 075° 12'10"W

DELIVERANCE

Dead flat was the sea. Not a zephyr to push even a ripple. Sleep, ocean, sleep. The sun sat moments below the horizon—ready to spray its rays across a new day in grand fashion. Color came to life, changing second by second. The sky reflected a rose-colored glow over the water, blurring the line where sky and sea meet. It was a scene of minimal simplicity—the kind a person could watch endlessly, but cannot because it is fleeting. It defines aloneness where a person can lose himself in thought or, if stranded, to insanity.

The oil tanker *Moley Ann* was on her last leg of a twenty-day voyage from the eastern end of the Mediterranean en route to the Port of Philadelphia. She was approximately two hundred twenty miles southeast of Cape May, the gateway to her destination. Watch Officer Hunter stood on the starboard side of the bridge, gazing out over the stillness. He looked astern where the only movement in the sea were two bow wake waves streaming at forty-five-degree angles away from the ship. The wake stretched behind them for miles in a straight, undisturbed line and vanished over the horizon. Inside the bridge, the mood was subdued by the rare sea condition. The humming of the engines sent a peaceful "all is well" vibration throughout the vessel.

The captain sat sipping morning coffee, smacking his lips in savory delight. He looked like a confident captain—well-groomed gray hair and beard, crow's feet at the corners of his eyes. Seasoned by salt, he was "the old man," the mentor, coach, and paternal figure for most of his officers. He engaged in quiet conversation with the chief mate, Westcott, to discuss the daily activities. Hunter's watch partner, Able Seaman Rodrigues, busied himself monitoring the plethora of gauges that measured all that needed to be observed. The bridge was the ship's heartbeat for steering, navigation, engine control, and all communication.

Watch Officer Hunter made one last sweep of the horizon before stepping inside the bridge when a small orange speck off the starboard bow grabbed his eye. It appeared as a faint flicker in the early sunrise. He hesitated, squinted, and shielded his eyes for a better look. Surely, something was out there—far off and indistinct. Hunter could not tell if the object was an escaped crab trap, a pallet, or a container that had fallen from a cargo ship. He stepped inside to retrieve his binoculars.

"Captain," Hunter said. "I'm seeing an orange conical object broad on the starboard bow."

The captain picked up his binoculars. "That looks like a cone, all right. Could be a life raft. It's too far out for a positive ID though... Rodrigues!"

"Sir!" came a crisp response from Rodrigues, who stood over the ship's steering control table.

"Come right to 0-0-0 degrees."

"Aye, captain. 0-0-0 degrees." Rodrigues reset the autopilot to a due north heading. The captain moved to the chart table and recorded an entry in the ship's log, noting when the orange object had been sighted.

SHIP'S LOG—MAY 4, 2010—0620 HOURS—37° 05'01"N, 072° 32'05"W

"Hunter, keep a close watch on the object as we approach. Advise when you can confirm what it is."

"Sir."

"Rodrigues, get ahold of Stevens and tell him we need him on the bridge. Hunter, anything yet?"

"No, sir. It's still about eight miles away."

"Hunter, did you spot that with your naked eye?"

"Sir, I did."

"Good eyesight, officer! Get someone to go forward and watch from the bow. Keep me advised."

"Aye, sir."

Five minutes passed. Hunter radioed the captain. "Sir, confirming the conical object is a life raft. I don't see any activity."

"Try to establish contact." Hunter switched to channel sixteen. "Orange life raft, orange life raft, do you read me?" He waited fifteen seconds before repeating his hail. "Captain, I'm not getting a response."

"Rodrigues, give a long blast and then alert crew over the PA that we are pursuing a possible rescue."

The ship blasted its booming voice across the morning sea. No signs of life on the raft.

Third Mate Stevens appeared on the bridge. "Stevens," the captain said. "We have positive ID on an orange conical life raft about four miles dead ahead. No one aboard is responding if there is anyone on board at all. I know this isn't your watch yet, but you're the ship's medical person in charge, and if anyone's on that raft, they may need your help. Take an AB with you on the FRB and investigate. Westcott, I'd like you to oversee the FRB launching. Rodrigues, full stop when we're two miles from the raft. Hunter, keep your eyes on the life raft. Maintain contact with Stevens as he heads over to it. And I'd like you to extend your watch until Stevens returns."

"Aye, sir."

"Serrano, check in."

Moments later a voice came over the radio. "Serrano here, captain."

"We're launching the FRB for a possible rescue. Check the station bill, assemble the team, and prepare to launch with Stevens and a cadet."

The captain called the Coast Guard on the satellite phone. He identified his ship, gave their position, and reported the situation. He asked if they had picked up any active distress signals in the area. Negative, responded the Coast Guard.

"We're preparing the FRB for launch to take a look," the captain said.

"How are the seas, captain?" came the monotonic voice from his Coast Guard contact.

"Dead flat."

"Do you have an ETA on the FRB to the life raft?"

"Launching within twenty minutes. ETA on life raft is thirty minutes from now."

"Please render whatever assistance you can and, when available, provide an update on any survivors."

"Will do."

* * *

Third Mate Stevens and Chief Mate Westcott met one of the cadets at the FRB on the open deck. Bosun's Mate Serrano had already initiated FRB launch procedures. It was a twenty-two-foot Zodiac durable, inflatable boat with a hard hull and single outboard engine, equipped with emergency gear. It sat in a mounting cradle and was tethered to its own launching winch. A sea painter, attached from amidships of the tanker, would keep the FRB close to the ship and aligned with the davits once in the water. Stevens, Serrano, and the cadet donned personal flotation devices and helmets and climbed into the FRB, and mariners on deck lowered it. When it was in the water, Serrano started the outboard motor and ensured all attaching cables and lines were free. The FRB headed for the life raft.

"What do you think we're gonna find?" Serrano asked.

Stevens shrugged. "Can't say. We'll find what we find. That raft looks like something you see in a disaster movie with ominous music playing in the background. I don't think we're gonna find anything good in it."

The FRB circled the life raft. Stevens spotted a long floating line attached to the raft with a large loop at the bitter end. He pointed and said, "Steer clear of that painter. We'll need it intact for the Coast Guard." The life raft appeared to have taken a beating from the elements. Its rubber pontoons had deflated significantly, and the protective canopy was limp and torn. The raft looked deserted. Stevens hailed the raft but received no response. The cadet secured the raft to the FRB. He unzipped the canopy, stuck his head inside, and was jolted back by a mixed stench of vomit, urine, and what he thought was the smell of death.

"There are two people in there," the cadet said. "I can't tell if they're dead or alive. There's no movement."

"We gotta retrieve them," Stevens said. "It's not going to be easy. It's the dirtiest job we'll ever have, so let's do it and get it done. Let me have a look."

"Can we at least let it air out for a few minutes?"

"In this calm, I don't think it will air out that much. We'll get used to the smell."

"How would you know that? Have you done this before?" the cadet asked.

"I grew up on a chicken farm. Believe me, you'll get used to it."

They opened the canopy, and Stevens and the cadet shuffled equipment on the FRB to accommodate the victims. They prepared a bed on the deck of the boat and opened thermal blankets.

"I need to confirm if they're dead or alive," Stevens said. "The captain's waiting for that information."

Stevens partially climbed inside the raft. "Man, the stench! I'd be surprised if they're alive."

The victims were lifeless, ragged, and smelled putrid. They were sprawled across the flooded sole of the raft like they had been cast inside in a heap. "How did they get so tangled up?" the cadet asked.

"If they were in here during a storm with high seas, they could have been tossed all over. They may have been dead by then or knocked out."

Stevens attempted to straighten out the bodies. He heard a faint sound. "I think one of them might be alive!" he exclaimed. "I think I heard one moaning." He crawled over the bodies, trying to be respectful while feeling around for any sign of life. Neither victim had a pulse that he could feel, but he was sure he heard something from one of them. He placed his ear close to the victim's mouth, hoping to feel air. "This one's alive!" He moved back to the second victim—hoping to find the same. But no pulse. No breathing. He climbed back to the FRB.

"Captain, this is Stevens, over."

"I'm here, Stevens. What do you have?"

"Sir, we have two victims. I can confirm that one has no pulse. The other survived. I can't find a pulse, but there's very shallow breathing. We need to transport and stabilize the survivor."

"Can you transport them to the FRB?"

"Yes, sir. It's gonna be a struggle, but we'll manage."

"When you return to the ship, tow the raft with you. Did you find anything inside?"

"Negative, sir. That's the odd part. There was nothing inside except the two victims and a backpack. There is no emergency equipment. No water. No food. No flares. No paddle. Nothing."

The FRB slowly returned to the ship, towing the raft—partially deflated, ripped, discolored, and severely defeated by the sea. The ship had stopped and was a hundred yards away. The davit lines hung from the crane on the deck down to where they would connect to the FRB. The crew watched from the deck and gangway rails. Water streamed from a bilge pump. The 340-meter-long ship was a view Stevens had seldom seen. "It looks much bigger from down here," he said as they approached.

The FRB pulled alongside the ship under the davits. The crew quickly secured the raft to the davit lines. Stevens watched as the limp raft was being lifted, noting that it looked like a deflated hot air balloon as it drained. The FRB was next. While rescue and recovery was a new experience for most of the ship's crew, they all seemed to know what to do, and each did his part to carefully remove the victims. During the process, not a word was spoken. Silence was the most reverent gesture they could offer.

Two able seamen stood nearby holding stretchers. The victims were carefully placed on them and covered.

"Let's get them to the infirmary immediately," Stevens told the crew. He put his hand on the cadet's arm. "Please go to the bridge and ask the captain to meet me in the infirmary."

In the infirmary, the captain stood with Stevens over the victims. "This is the one who has a slight pulse and is barely breathing." He pointed to the second victim. "I get nothing from him. He's gone."

The captain stood with his hands on his hips. He sighed and rubbed his hand over his chin. "Good job, Stevens. Keep me updated. I need to update the Coast Guard."

"Captain, allow me to do that," said Stevens. "They're gonna want to know about the victim's status and I haven't determined that yet."

"Good idea," said the captain. "I'm heading for the bridge. We gotta get underway."

A long blast came from the ship's horn. The ship resumed its westerly heading to the Port of Philadelphia.

Stevens turned to the cadet standing by to help. "I want to examine this body and see if there are any obvious clues about the cause of death. After that, would you please move the deceased into the ship's walk-in cooler until we receive instructions from the Coast Guard?"

Stevens hooked the ship's medical laptop monitors to the patient and called the medical hotline. After introducing himself, he gave the particulars about the ship, the rescue, and anything else the doctor would need to know. "I have two victims. One is dead. The other is in critical condition, unresponsive to verbal or painful stimuli, temperature is ninety-one degrees Fahrenheit, shows signs of severe dehydration. Heart rate is rapid. Pulse is weak. Breathing shallow and slow. Vitals are being transmitted to you as we speak. Patient has sunken eyes and cheeks, and tenting is noted on back of extremities—mainly hands, arms, feet. I covered the victim with warm blankets and administered O₂ and turned the heat up in the room. The patient looks to be average height and weight, age mid-to-late fifties. From what the recovered raft looked like, they may have been adrift three or four days without food or water. Request permission to begin administering Ringer's lactate IV."

"Proceed with the IV. Administer two liters rapidly—open drip—which will empty two bags in thirty minutes. It's an aggressive dosage, so keep an eye out for respiratory distress overload and back off if needed. If your patient is going to come back, you should see it in about two hours. You're going to have to sit close to your patient. Watch for a rapid increase in blood pressure, abdominal swelling, and coarse crackling during breathing. We're here for you. Don't hesitate to call. Stevens… be prepared. There's a high probability that you will lose your patient. Have you contacted the Coast Guard?"

"Not yet, but I owe them an update."

Stevens began the IV and tucked the warm blankets more closely around the survivor.

He turned his attention to the deceased person. He examined the body, making notes about his observations.

The cadet appeared in the infirmary doorway, holding the recovered backpack. "Stevens, there are some interesting documents in this backpack you recovered."

"Not now. Look, I need you to take those blankets over to the laundry and warm them all up in the dryer. Bring me one at a time as soon as they're hot. We have to keep this person warm. Please bring the body to the cooler. I'll look at the backpack later."

Stevens tended to his unconscious survivor. He could do nothing more except wait, watch, and hope his charge's life did not slip away. He sat back. It was a good time to update the Coast Guard. Learning that the victim's condition was critical and there were no punctures, fractures, or a broken skull, the Coast Guard agreed with the doctor's assessment and that their best action would be to wait and reassess in an hour. They placed the patient on one-hour status updates.

"Have you had a chance to examine the body?" asked the Coast Guard voice.

"I did. I couldn't find anything. No broken bones. No cuts. Only a few contusions. My guess is he died from exposure."

Stevens sat back, sighed deeply, and rubbed his face. He shifted his eyes to the backpack. It reeked of death and vomit. He opened it and spread out its contents. Charts, a personal journal, trip papers, and the ship's log—all had been individually wrapped in ziplock baggies and managed to remain protected from the elements. A small, flooded flashlight rolled across the table. Stevens found a Swiss Army knife stashed in a separate pocket.

Three hours later, he contacted the doctor. "Doc, the survivor is stabilizing. Blood pressure is slowly increasing, breathing is improving. I can't hear any gurgling in the lungs. Pupils are responding to light. I think our patient is going to be OK. I sure appreciate your support."

"Good work, Stevens. Advise if there is any change."

The cadet returned with another warmed blanket. "I need you to stay here and continue changing out the blankets," Stevens said. "Warmth is essential. I'm going to the bridge to brief the captain and show him what's in this backpack."

* * *

"This is gold," the captain said as he pulled out the chart and ship's log and spread them on the chart table. He opened the log to the last entry. "The last entry was April thirtieth at 1630 hours." The captain pointed to a spot on the chart. "This was our position when we first spotted them. Assuming they drifted downwind at forty-five to fifty miles a day and they were out for three days, that means their boat probably went down somewhere around here," he added, pointing to another place on the chart. "I think I'll give the Coast Guard another call to see if anyone called this in. These logs and the chart will make their investigation much easier. The log lists the names of four crew members, yet only two were in the raft. I wonder what happened to the others. Someone knew something big was coming to be this meticulous in protecting the documents, but I wonder why there are no passports or other forms of personal identification in here. Right now, I need to contact the ship owners. Stevens, you're working way past your watch, but since you're the only medical officer on board, you'll be sleeping in the infirmary chair. Chief Mate Westcott will cover for you on your 2000–0000 watch."

Stevens left the bridge and stepped outside. He walked to the starboard side, leaned on the rail, and looked out. What a day. His four-hour shift had turned into three back-to-back shifts. He looked at what was left of the day. It seemed like just moments ago he had been summoned to the bridge, and now it was 1800 hours, twelve hours later.

Reflections pinged in Stevens' head. He imagined his wife standing on a cliff looking out to sea when he was away. *Does she become the paperback icon with her long hair and dress blowing sideways while shading her eyes from the late-day sun? The sea gives me a sense of gentleness, of comfort, and terrible aloneness. What does she do to ease her anxiety?*

Stevens walked down the deck to the galley. He turned on the light to the walk-in cooler and stepped inside. A body lay covered in blankets. When the spirit leaves the body for a different world, it leaves behind a stillness and an emptiness that commands wordless respect.

He put his hand on the deceased's shoulder. "Who are you?... What happened out there?... Was it you who kept the log and the journals?... Was the backpack yours?... Why wasn't there any ID in it?... What were your last thoughts?... Did you feel fear? A sense of peace? Did you leave someone behind who's waiting for you to come home? God, I wish I could know your story." Stevens patted the body and lowered his head. "Goodbye, my friend." He left the cooler and headed back to the infirmary.

* * *

Stevens took his patient's vital signs and detached the depleted bag of IV fluids. Two liters had dripped into the patient, and soon he could hope for some sign of life. An hour passed. No movement. No encouragement. Nothing. Although he was a trained emergency medical technician, none of his actual field work involved victims clinging to life by their fingernails. Yes to scratches, cuts, bruises, abrasions, burns, and even a good head bonking by a low-hanging pipe or a bulkhead door, but he had never brought a person back from the brink of death. None of his prior patients in the tanker's infirmary ever asked, "Am I going to die, Doc?" For the first time as a medical officer, Stevens felt the intense pressure of exacting diagnosis and timely medicine. And it was all on his shoulders. "Did I do right by you?" he whispered. "Did I save you? Was I even supposed to? I guess if you had no plans to come back, you'd be gone by now, right? So are you leaving or staying?"

His patient lay there. Quietly. Saying nothing. No movement except for a rising and falling chest. "OK, I get it. You don't want to talk. I'll just sit here and keep you company and make sure you don't die. You know, I delivered you from death today. Have you nothing to say about that? Like, 'Oh, thank you, Third Officer Stevens, I really appreciate that,'" he said nervously through his fatigue. The long hours and life-or-death struggles had taken its toll on him.

A small undercabinet fluorescent light gave the only light in the cabin. Stevens wiggled around in a sterile and functional chair, attempting to find comfort. He studied the breathing of his new charge. It looked exaggerated in the dimly lit room. He thought about his first-time experience with rescuing or recovering anyone. He wondered, *Does it get any easier with more rescues? If I'm supposed to feel whole for saving a human life, why am I sitting here feeling so empty?*

"Stevens, are you still up? Captain here."

"Sir, Stevens here."

"How's our patient?"

"No change, sir. Still unconscious but stable. We pulled off a miracle."

"You did, Stevens. Look, I thought I'd give you a FYI on my conversation with the Coast Guard. I gave them the name of the vessel and the last coordinates in the ship's log. They confirmed they had not been notified of any incidents involving that vessel. All we can hope for is that our patient comes around and has a good memory. Get some rest, Stevens."

He sat—watching and keeping safe the person he had brought back to life. The humming of the engines sent a peaceful "all is well" vibration throughout the vessel. Stevens' breathing slowed, his eyes fell heavy, and he drifted off to sleep.

THE RECKONING

San Diego Harbor, California
February 6, 2009

The marinas on San Diego Harbor Island were under siege. The meteorologist's promise of a strong Pacific weather front had been delivered on time. A lone man, covered in yellow foulies, struggled against strong wind gusts as he pushed a dock cart filled with gear duffels down a ramp and onto the dock. Rain shot sideways. The man hunched over to protect himself from the pelting and to make himself a smaller target. The wind muscled him, shoving him around like a playground bully, trying to knock him off balance.

Boats yanked on their dock lines, trying to work themselves loose to wreak havoc throughout the marina. The distinctive sound of rigging slapping against naked masts sent a stereophonic warning to anyone pondering the foolish thought of venturing out. Wind vanes mounted atop masts pointed stiffly windward with a sense of purpose, leaving no mistake about the strength and direction of the winter storm cell. Business signs flapped, waved, teetered. A seagull, struggling to keep control in the erratic wind, looked more like an airplane trying to land in a crosswind than the agile aviators those seabirds are.

The man reached the end of the long dock. He stood looking at the boat, *Ms. Sera*. She was a sleek, forty-foot, single-masted sailing sloop. She was well kept with no signs of rust or tired lines. Teak toe-rails, grab rails, and hatches looked freshly oiled. The hull was white and algae-free at the waterline. Dock lines were properly wrapped around cleats, with the remaining bitter end of the line adeptly coiled to prevent sailors from tripping. There could be no question—*Ms. Sera* was loved.

He tossed the contents of the dock cart onto the boat and climbed aboard. He shielded his eyes and looked windward, hoping that the violent wind gusts would soon diminish and become more manageable for sailing. The grimace on his face was not a shield from the weather but a reaction to messages from his stomach telling him what he was about to do was a bad idea.

The man sighed deeply and went about preparations to cast off. It appeared he was ignoring Mother Nature's admonitions.

The wind had pressed his boat to the protective fenders on the lee side of its slip, and the wind against the mast caused *Ms. Sera* to list a solid ten degrees downwind. The man looked to the top of the mast and around the marina to other boats responding the same way. He was the only person on any of the docks. It felt unnerving. He began questioning the wisdom of going out, and that pleased his stomach, which had been shrieking, "Abort! Abort!"

It was not enough to convince him to find a warm fire, a good book, and an overstuffed chair.

He started the motor and loosened the lines. Knowing that the mechanics of prop action while backing out of the slip would keep his boat pressed against the dock, he rigged a line to a dock cleat in a way that would counteract the force of the wind and improve his control. The boat overcame the grip of the wind and began backing out. He could feel that the storm was going to make sailing, or even motoring, a challenge. The fairway channel was the main artery to and from the harbor, but the man had it all to himself. He had maneuverability and took advantage of it. He stowed the fenders and coiled the dock lines, making them ready for his return. But the wind—that gusting element of nature whose breath could stack boats high and crunch them together in a corner like kindling—had not given up. It had quickly pushed the boat leeward and uncomfortably close to the rocky lee jetty. Without immediate evasive action, *Ms. Sera* was on a fast course of running hard aground. He turned her away, but its force continued to put him back in harm's way. The man looked around—now certain he had made the wrong decision. "This isn't gonna work," he said, wiping rainwater from his face. "I don't know what I'm doing and I'm going to get hurt. Badly. I need Logan."

He returned to the dock. The brunt of the storm cell was quickly passing. The weather was taking a breather until the next cell moved in. The wind subsided and the rain continued but without its stinging jabs. Pulling into the dock slip was much easier than what he experienced pulling out. Whitecaps in the harbor vanished. While storm conditions were more forgiving, the thick layer of fast-moving clouds warned sailors to become neither complacent nor comfortable should they venture out. The man walked to the dock entry toward a charter office. He was still the only fool out at the marina.

"Morning, Maria." A woman behind a desk looked up and around her computer. Reading glasses sat at the end of her nose, and her curly hair was wrapped in a hair tie behind her head.

"Nelson! I saw you go out. Looks like you wised up and packed it in."

"Not really. Do you have Logan's phone number?"

"What do you want with him? Anything wrong with *Ms. Sera*? If there is, Logan won't be here until tomorrow to fix it."

"She's fine. Logan told me one time to give him a call if I wanted to go out wave plunging. Today looks like a good day for it."

"You guys are nuts, but here you go."

Nelson pulled the hooded foulies off his head and removed the outer jacket. He was a silhouette in the window, looking out while rubbing his face and running his fingers through his wet hair. He was average height, average weight, clean shaven. With his thinning, gray, way-over-his-ears scruffy hair, he could have passed for a mad scientist or even Einstein.

Nelson moved to a quiet corner and made the call. "Hey, Logan. Nelson here at the charter office. Yeah. Yeah. Everything's OK with *Ms. Sera*. I was wondering if you'd like to go wave plunging. Yeah, today. Yeah, now."

"I'd love to, but today isn't a good day for it," came Logan's disappointing reply.

"The seas are up," said Nelson.

"Yeah, and so are the winds. I saw reports this morning that wind gusts will get over fifty knots, and they'll be just as strong or stronger as other storm cells move through. I'm sure there are small-craft warnings, so there's no sense in trying to get out of the harbor. Have you checked with the Coast Guard?"

"No."

"You might want to do that before wasting your time getting out there. Have you ever been out in that kind of wind?"

"No."

"Were you planning to raise the sails?"

"Yeah, I thought third reef would be enough to keep control."

"Nelson, third reef is way too much—especially near Ballast Point. You can be blown over even with bare poles. What are you trying to prove?"

"Prove? You once told me to call you to go wave plunging."

"Well, that was with five-to-six-foot waves, *and* we could get out of the harbor. The waves out there today have gotta be ten feet or higher. Add storm winds to that dend there's nothing fun about wave plunging. You'll get tossed all over, banged around, soaked, cold, spent, and you'll put undue stress on *Ms. Sera*. Why do you want to go out? And don't think I believe it's to wave plunge."

"I want more experience with heavy weather."

"Sorry, Nelson, I don't buy that. The conditions out there today are the kind you want to avoid, not go looking for. Do you have some sort of death wish? Who's going out with you?"

"I'm solo. I started out, but the winds kept pushing me toward the jetty."

"That right there should have been enough to tell you to sit it out. If you can't handle wind in the fairway channel, you certainly won't be able to handle the harbor or go outside. Nelson… are you still there?"

"Yeah, I'm here."

"You still haven't told me why. Or maybe you don't know. Look, we've known each other for about five years. I think you trust me. Help me understand why you really want to go out there."

Nelson hesitated and sighed deeply. "OK, I'll tell you." He cupped his hands around the phone, looked around for unwanted eavesdroppers, and continued in a soft voice. "In one of my scuba classes, a new student asked me what my biggest fear was in diving. I told him it was panicking. Why? Because panicking is an overpowering fear that totally incapacitates a person. You toss aside all your experience, all your training, and all your sea-savvy and run right into whatever it is that wants to hurt you…"

"Nelson, we're talking about sailing, not scuba diving."

"I know, I know. Let me finish. I fear panicking more than anything. Heavy weather sailing is right up there next to panicking. The last thing I want to be known for is being the sailor who craters when conditions deteriorate. What does that say about my competency?"

"So let me get this straight… You're afraid you'd panic in heavy weather, so you picked one of the worst days of the winter to go out and face that fear? It's like saying, 'I want more sailing practice in stronger winds,' so you go looking for a hurricane. When a person is afraid, they usually run the other way. Why do you want to go toward it now? That makes no sense to me."

"I really don't want to go out there today, but if I keep avoiding it, how will I ever overcome my fear? I suppose at times we have to put ourselves in harm's way to gain the experience of dealing with it."

"In ten-foot waves and fifty-knot winds? Isn't that jumping in a little too far? I get that you want more experience. Look, you're the kind of guy who usually thinks things out, but this doesn't sound like you. Or maybe there's something you're not telling me."

Nelson hesitated. "I'm leaving myself vulnerable here."

"I promise you'll be more vulnerable out there."

"I want to be a respected mariner. I've taken all the sailing courses, but I'm still afraid of sailing in anything but fair weather. It embarrasses me."

"You're already respected. If you go out there today, you won't be gaining heavy weather experience. You'll be getting plenty of practice being in harm's way. Nelson, there are other ways to do this. I can help you, but not today. It's unsafe. Promise me you'll put *Ms. Sera* to bed. Work on her if you want but keep her tied up. I'll work with you, OK?"

"OK, I will," Nelson said.

*   *   *

"So what did Logan say?" said Maria as she studied Nelson.

"He can't make it."

"You still taking *Ms. Sera* out?"

"I might. Depends on storm cells. It looks calmer now, but I'm sure another cell will hit us."

*   *   *

As Nelson walked toward the back door, he passed Brad and Nate, dock workers who were staying warm inside the charter office. "You're not going out, are you?" Brad asked.

"I might," Nelson replied, continuing toward the door.

They watched him walk down the dock to his boat. "Do you know him?" Nate asked.

"Yeah. He's been a club member for quite a while. He bought a thirty-four-foot sloop a few years ago and put her in the charter.

That's when I first got to know him. Last fall he traded up to a forty-footer, the one down at the end, *Ms. Sera*."

"Do you know what he does, as in work?"

"I think he's retired. He comes down here during the week when the boat's not out on charter. Other than that, I have no idea what he did or does. He seems like a likeable guy, not a jerk like many boaters who come to party and act like they own the world. He treats folks with respect."

"Does he know what he's doing… like when he's sailing?"

"He does a lot of solo sailing. Anyone who can handle a cruising sailboat that large single-handedly has got to be a competent sailor. He doesn't pretend to know everything. He's not afraid to ask questions. When he puts his boat to bed, he makes sure the lines are tied properly, and he leaves the boat thoroughly cleaned and ready to go back out."

"That's because the boat's his. He probably wouldn't be that way if he chartered."

"Oh-h-h, yes he would. You're new here. You'll see the kind of stuff he's made of. When he rented, he always returned the boat as clean as if it were his. I wish all charterers were half as conscientious."

* * *

Nelson started the engine and prepared the boat for shoving off. He sat on the lazarette, looking around at the calmer conditions. He saw other people on nearby docks walking about, some looking as if they, too, were preparing to go out. Logan's counsel rang in his head. *He urged me not to go, but that was when the boat's wind gage showed fifty-knot wind gusts. Now they're down to twenty. I can manage that. I could go out, keep an eye out for another storm cell, and hightail it back here when I see one coming. Maybe I should wait… I'll be OK. I'm going.* Nelson slapped his knees, his mind made up. He released and secured the dock lines and pulled his boat away from the slip and out to the channel fairway.

Instead of turning left toward the harbor, he turned right to give himself more running room to hoist the sail without worrying about other boaters. Nelson may have left in a lull in the weather, but there was still a twenty-knot fresh breeze, the strongest he had ever experienced in the fairway. He stowed the fenders and secured the dock lines to the boat's safety lines. With no other boats to share the fairway, Nelson turned *Ms. Sera* into the wind, hoisted the mainsail and jib partway so as not to be overpowered, and headed toward the harbor. The sails snapped to attention in the breeze, and *Ms. Sera* heeled to the right and rapidly gained speed. Even with the sails set on the third reef, about one-third unfurled, *Ms. Sera* responded rapidly to a broadside wind, or "reach." She raced down the fairway. Exhilaration cloaked Nelson.

As he trimmed the sails, he could feel the boat become one with the water—sailing in the groove, as sailors call it. He could feel the soul of his boat by the shape of the sail, the lack of luffing, the position of the telltales on the sails, and the sound of the water sliding under the hull. This was what sailing was all about—nirvana.

Nelson would normally shut down the engine once the sails were set and his boat was underway. He had his thumb on the shut-off button, but the fickle wind told him to leave it on until he was out in the harbor—just an added measure of safety.

Ms. Sera approached her first turning point. Nelson steered her toward a smaller marina on the lee side of the mouth of his marina. He studied the wind, his position, his speed. He calculated the precise moment he would have to "come about"—turn her so that the wind would come from the opposite side of the boat—and change direction. He wrapped lines around winches, loosened other lines, and held others in preparation to come about. It normally took three tacks to get into the harbor. Nelson thought he could make it in two, using a maneuver that would require him to sail uncomfortably close to the row of tied-up boats in the small marina, which he was now rapidly approaching. "Playing chicken" with stationary objects had been part of an advanced training exercise he'd gone through to learn about boat performance, responsiveness, and the effects of being pushed sideways by the wind—leeway. He knew what his boat could do, so there was nothing to worry about.

With *Ms. Sera* ready, he drew closer and closer to the tied-up boats. "Wait! Wait!" he shouted, echoing his former sailing instructor. When he realized he had not allowed enough leeway for the force of the wind, his bliss shriveled instantly. He was sliding into an unavoidable collision. His heart pounded with a ferocity that he could feel in his ears. Adrenaline pumped. He had miscalculated the precise moment of coming about, and he was well into the trouble zone. "Now! Now! Helm's alee!" he yelled as he turned to make the tack. *Ms. Sera* began to turn, but stalled when the bow was head-to-wind. A wind gust pushed her back, and she began sideslipping toward the stern of three or four boats. Nelson pulled on the wheel, but she was already hard over and didn't respond. He knew that a sailboat cannot sail when pointing into the wind and cannot be turned without water moving over the rudder.

Ms. Sera was dead in the water. All she could do was drift. And wait. Nelson was powerless. He slipped into a surreal moment—all movement became slow motion, and his reactions were even slower. He visualized the crash. He heard the loud crunching of his boat against others. He heard the clashing of masts and rigging. He saw litigation not only for damages, but for reckless and negligent actions. He wanted to be recognized for competence, and this would bring him harbor-wide recognition as the mariner who could not control his boat. Finally, he saw himself being hurled into wreckage, crushed or mangled beyond medicine's capacity to repair.

Nelson desperately lunged at the engine throttle and pushed it to full forward. *Ms. Sera* trembled with vibrations. White foamy water churned up behind her. Nelson released the jib and let the mainsheet loose. "Turn! Turn!" he yelled as the loosened sails flapped and snapped like bedsheets on a clothesline in a gale, producing their own explosive, thunderous voice. Spilling wind from the sails reduced its power and gave him the precious milliseconds he needed to save his boat. *Ms. Sera* responded and turned through the wind. Nelson held his breath as he watched the starboard stern miss the boats by mere inches.

Ms. Sera flew across the mouth of the marina. Nelson was preoccupied with bringing his boat under control while untethered sails sent their securing sheets whipping erratically, looking for a face to scar, an eye to poke, or a head to knock. Furling the sails became a priority. An uncontrolled sail quickly becomes vulnerable to self-destruction. Nelson turned head-to-wind and pulled in the mainsheet, and the mainsail settled down. Moments later it was securely furled. Then he furled the jib. He motored past the fuel dock. A handful of people stood huddled together—watching him. His near miss with other boats had brought spectators. When bad things happen to good people, a crowd gathers to watch. Nelson pursed his lips. He had brought attention to himself. Unwanted attention. "Don't look at them. Don't acknowledge them. Don't wave," he murmured through clenched teeth.

With the wind at twenty-five knots, controlling his boat within the confines of a harbor remained a nailbiter. Nelson's experience with breezes while in open water had been exhilarating. His yahooing could be heard for miles. But he felt no jubilation this morning.

The events of the morning sped through his head like electricity. He had escaped disaster and now had a decision to make: return to the safety of his slip or resume his "mission" and sail out of the harbor. He felt an increase in wind velocity. In his experience, increases in wind speed were usually ushered in with wind gusts. Sometimes a wind gust is short-lived. Sometimes it stays as the new wind speed. Nelson kept *Ms. Sera* head-to-wind and motored at idling speed to keep from making headway. He turned his thoughts back to his near miss. *Man, what happened back there? Your inexperience blindsided you. You should have anticipated the wind would be more of a factor. You nearly lost a quarter-million-dollar sailboat. If you had collided with other boats, you probably would have been flung into them and crushed. Sharpe, I hope you appreciate how close to disaster you just came. Did you learn anything about sailing? Or were they lessons in dogged stupidity?*

Nelson looked to the southwest, where a darkening horizon was approaching. There was a well-defined gray line between the clouds and the sea. Rain. Hard rain. Sideways rain. Heading his way. The wind was already picking up as whitecaps formed around him. *Turn around, fool. You're done for the day. Well, let's see if we can beat the rain back to the dock.*

* * *

Getting into his slip became a worrisome thought—especially if the storm cell hit just as he attempted to turn into it. When and how fast he would approach it shot through his mind with the complexity of calculus formulae. He knew that once he turned up the fairway to his slip, he was committed. There would be no turning back, because there was barely enough maneuverability on a calm day. Getting into his slip would be like trying to thread a needle in the wind. All Nelson's negative head talk, all his overthinking the "how" of what he was facing, would almost guarantee a crash landing.

He hesitated at the entrance of the fairway and weighed his options. Racing the storm to the slip was his least risky option. He turned *Ms. Sera* up the fairway. The wind was considerably less of a factor than he had anticipated. Then suddenly, the storm cell arrived with a burst of sustained high wind . Rain came sideways, almost blinding him. He increased the boat speed to compensate for the resisting wind. When it was time to turn into the slip, he calculated how far to overshoot it and allow the wind to push him back as he turned in. *Ms. Sera* was halfway into the slip when a wind gust captured the vessel and thrust her sideways. She became wedged with her bow pressing against one side and her amidships jammed against the end of the slip on the other. Throttling up the engine did no good. Just as Nelson was about to jump off *Ms. Sera* and pull her in by her dock lines, Brad appeared and pulled her bow forward with just enough force to get her unstuck. Moments later, they had her securely tied to the dock. Brad ran for cover.

* * *

With *Ms. Sera* secure, Nelson sat out the storm cell in the salon of his boat, updating his ship's log and journal. Strong wind gusts caused the boat to heel over just by the force of wind on the mast. Rain blasted the boat, creating an omnipresent sound of hissing and hammering as it assaulted the hull and sole. Nelson felt a sense of comfort in knowing he was out of harm's way. He appreciated Mother Nature's force even while sheltered from the wind by the higher ground of the marina parking lot. He turned his attention back to his ship's log and journal to memorialize his experience and feelings.

Entry in *Ms. Sera* Ship's Log—February 6, 2009

I screwed up. I cast safety aside. I ignored my gut. I lost my focus. I almost lost Ms. Sera*… and me. Today there was no lesson in fear. I could not have panicked, or* Ms. Sera *would have been lost. My weak link is an inability to anticipate and read the conditions. There are smarter ways to become competent. Today's experience was not among them.*

Time passed. The storm cell subsided. Nelson had repacked his gear and had it ready to toss onto the dock. The wind settled back to a steady twenty-five-knot-strong breeze. *Ms. Sera* sat upright in the slip. Nelson adjusted and furled the dock lines and readjusted the fenders. He found a dock cart and schlepped his gear to his truck, which sat alone in the abandoned parking lot. Wind pressed against him, and he could see a new storm cell rolling his way. *Ms. Sera* had been put to bed and Nelson was ready to leave. He stopped in the charter office to check out with Maria.

"I was concerned about you going out today but didn't say anything because *Ms. Sera*'s your boat and it's not my place to tell you what to do," said Maria. "Logan called back not long after you left. He thought you had decided not to go out. You have some explaining to do with him. Anyway, he wanted me to write this down and give it to you."

Nelson looked at the note, where Maria had written down the website of a business specializing in yacht deliveries and the URL of an article titled "How to Join a Yacht Delivery as Crew; Building Sea Miles and Gaining Experience."

"Thanks, Maria, but I don't think I'm qualified enough to be a crew member on deliveries."

"I wouldn't be too sure of that. There will be plenty of opportunities for shuttling boats out of the Caribbean up the Atlantic before hurricane season. I'd check it out. Talk to companies. Let them decide if you're good enough. What do you have to lose? I think you're ready for that, and I'm sure everyone around here who knows you would say the same."

"Thanks for your vote of confidence, but I'm having a hard time convincing myself that I'm good enough. Why do you think I took all those ASA courses? People think I'm better than I really am, and I feel like I'm deceiving them."

"You gotta stop listening to all that self-doubt talk and give your supporters… us… a little credit," Maria said as she moved her arm in a circle to show inclusiveness.

Nelson leaned over her desk and pointed out to the harbor. "Maria, I almost destroyed a quarter-million-dollar boat today, and all those classes I took didn't help me avert a near disaster."

"You can tell me that story another time." She looked out the window to the end of the dock. "*Ms. Sera*'s secure and safe. Whatever happened out there, you musta done something right. If you took a crew job on a delivery, you'd be working side by side with very experienced sailors, and that would push all that stupid talk out of your head."

Nelson sighed and gave Maria a tender look. "You're a real supporter. I'm glad you're on my side, and now you've given me a reason to check out deliveries. Thank you. I'll do it."

Maria's can-do enthusiasm inspired Nelson. The wheels began turning in his head. *Crew on an Atlantic passage? Hmm. That could be exciting. But am I good enough? I guess I'd find out. I could come back as an able mariner for sure.*

The seeds had been sown.

THE MESSAGE BOARD

British Virgin Islands
January 2010

Nelson and Quinney's chartered thirty-six-foot sailboat bobbed and swayed at the end of the dock in Road Town, Tortola, British Virgin Islands. "Welcome to BVI sailing!" the rental agent said as he issued Nelson and Quinney boat keys, a handheld radio, and a tourist map.

The dockmaster met them at the boat, where they made the requisite "walk-through" and signed off the paperwork. It was official: The boat was going to be their home for the next seven days. "Any questions?" the dockmaster asked.

"I have a few," said Nelson. "The contract says that first-time charterers may have to be checked out by a licensed captain before you release a boat to them. How come you didn't do that with us?"

"The day ain't over," the dockmaster quipped with a gleam in his eye. "The sailing résumé you sent in with your application was comprehensive. We get charterers here with basic ASA certification who have never sailed anything larger than twenty-one feet. Your certifications and experience go way beyond the minimum requirements. We'll watch the way you handle the boat when you leave. If we think you lack the right skills, we'll come and bring you back. What's your second question?"

Nelson unfolded a large navigation chart they brought and

spread it out. He pointed to Peter Island, six miles due south. "Before coming, we read about a restaurant in this corner of the harbor. Can you tell us anything about it?"

"Oh, that's Great Harbor. That restaurant might not be open. Some days it is. Most days it isn't. It's been hit by hurricanes and hard times, but it has good anchorage. Quiet. No bars. No nightlife. You'll have the place to yourselves."

Nelson and Quinney motored out of Road Town and hoisted the sails as soon as they felt the easterly trades. "Any chase boats coming after us?" Nelson asked.

Quinney looked back. "Nope. They must think you know how to handle a boat."

Then she said, "What do you think about what he said about that restaurant? Want to bypass it and find another anchorage?"

"We're provisioned for a week, so we don't really need any restaurants, but let's go take a look."

Quinney held the safety lines as she worked her way to the bow. She clung to the shroud rigging and felt the wind in her face. She looked back to the helm and sent Nelson a glowing smile. She was definitely in her happy place.

* * *

They had met in a grocery store in Nelson's neighborhood where Quinney worked as a cashier. Nelson was a "get in and get out" shopper who didn't commit to a checkout line until he had inspected the carts of the people in front of him to see how full they were. When the store wasn't busy, cashiers stood at the checkout entrances, inviting shoppers to their stands. Quinney stood solidly, all five feet, four inches of her, with her fingers intertwined in front of her. She looked around, greeting everyone. Her body seemed to be always in motion, as if she were dancing to a song playing in her head. Her light brown hair was usually pulled back in a clip, giving her a sophisticated look. His mind wandered through the realm of curiosity. *Grocery cashiers take a lot of abuse—impatient and angry customers, theft, bad hours, stolen life. How can a person exposed to that kind of environment, day in and day out, possibly have any dancing going on in her head? How can she perpetually wear that awesome, disarming, intoxicating smile?* She had a gleam in her eye that said, "I know something you don't." And Nelson felt compelled to find out what it was.

Through numerous yet brief check-stand interactions, she delivered preparation and cooking instructions with his purchases. One time she sent him back for a George Foreman grill to cook shrimp. When there was a line behind him, their conversations ended abruptly—she handed him the receipt, smiled, and said, "Have a nice day." Somehow they discovered their interests and passions were similar. He checked out her eyes—Caribbean blue. They sparkled. He became butter. Captivated, blubbering, and unable to break the spell, he resorted to flirtatiousness. She flirted back. He ran.

Then one day his workday ended late. He raced to the store. She was not in her usual check stand. "Where's Quinney?" he inquired of another clerk.

"Her shift ended. I think she left."

He slumped with the disheartening news. He had just taken a deep breath to evict his disappointment when he caught a glimpse of her leaving the building at the far door. Nelson dashed out to intercept her. "Are you in a hurry to get home? Coffee? We can go to the coffee shop next door or to my house. I live only a few minutes from here." Quinney agreed and followed Nelson to his house in her car.

"Make yourself at home while I change."

When he returned, Quinney was gone. *She left. How discouraging.* He wandered out the back door and found her bent over… pulling weed sprouts from potted plants. Nelson took Quinney's ease as a sign of a woman secure and comfortable with herself.

They moved back into the kitchen, talking for a while as she sorted through a basket of seashells on the counter. He walked her to her car and stood close without the check-stand barrier between them. He leaned over and gave her a gentle kiss. He stood watching as she drove off in the dark. He smiled and nodded. *Weeding? Guess I'll be seeing her again.*

* * *

They had been forewarned by veteran sailors about the shortage of moorings in the British Virgin Islands during the winter "season." The ratio of boats to available moorings was about three to one. Boaters not on a mooring by early afternoon had to sink a hook in the mud. First come, first served—reservations not accepted. Long before sundown, cocktail pennants went up and boaters sat enjoying the entertainment as late arrivals raced to unclaimed moorings, hoping to not miss grabbing the mooring ball. If they did, they were condemned to circle around for another attempt, but most certainly someone else would have already snagged it—all to the delight of the spectators working on their second martini.

Moorings take the place of anchors. They consist of an eyebolt set into the seafloor, a line to the surface, and a floating pickup ball. Moorings are preferable to anchors—particularly in crowded harbors and during stormy weather where anchors can drag. Picking up a mooring ball is much less work and takes a fraction of the time it takes to set an anchor—an important consideration, because cocktail hour commences immediately after the boat is put to bed. The art and science of grabbing a mooring is learned by doing. The task seems simple enough—approach slowly, hook the mooring ball, pull up the rope, secure it to a boat cleat, prepare cocktails.

Mooring proficiency takes practice, patience, and teamwork. The helmsman steers and controls boat speed. A grabber hooks the mooring line with a boat hook that quickly sinks if dropped. As the boat approaches the line, it becomes impossible for the helmsman to see the mooring from the helm. Hence practice, practice, practice. Wind, current, miscalculations, and bad communication all contribute to missing the mooring ball pickup. Success is the result of anticipation and constant course correction while approaching the target. The helmsman and grabber must have a communication plan consisting of hand and arm signals. Ninety-three percent of "missing the mooring" problems are attributed to the helmsman, yet the grabber receives one hundred percent of the blame, which is one of the reasons many men boaters give grabber duty to women. Missing the mooring line results in colorful expletives, inappropriate hand gestures, and name-calling. Not a good way to begin "happy" hour. Moorings have their disadvantages.

Not wanting to become the late-afternoon source of amusement for other boaters, Nelson and Quinney had practiced mooring ball retrieval for months. Quinney had a good feel for the boat and was given the honor of helmsman. Day one of practicing challenged the relationship, but by the time they left for BVI, Quinney had become a master helmsman who made mooring ball retrieval easy.

* * *

Great Harbor at Peter Island was just ahead. Its wide mouth faces north. Nelson pulled out the binoculars for a close-up view of the harbor and to mentally prepare for the impending competition for a mooring . Something was out of place, though—no boats, no competition for moorings. Perhaps what he thought was Great Harbor was actually someplace else. Inside the harbor, they found dozens of unoccupied moorings and a small group of outbuildings in the southwest corner.

"We must be in Great Harbor, but there's no one here to watch us show off our mooring skills," Nelson said. "All that practicing. Let's put the boat to bed and take the dinghy over to see what's in that corner. If we're in the right harbor, that should be a restaurant."

Great Harbor was among the secret treasures of the British Virgin Islands for its solitude and safe harbor. It could easily have been included on the list of most secure anchorages in BVI. A mountainous ridge to the east quelled the twenty-knot easterly trade winds, sending a soft breeze to swirl and cool boat cabins. It gave boaters a chance for a good night's sleep without the worrisome fret of dragging their anchor.

On the charts, the place in the corner was called a yacht club, but as the dockmaster had pointed out, it looked as if too many storms had hit it hard and the owners were struggling to bring it back to life. What at one time may have been an attraction for boaters had become a rickety dock on sticks and a shack with hinged pieces of plywood that covered the bar at closing time.

"Happening" beach bars attract partyers—young and old alike. Before heading to the islands, fellow sailors from San Diego had given Nelson a list of "must-visit" BVI bars. This yacht club bar had not been among them. A "happening" bar is defined by bright lights, loud reggae music, an armada of boats anchored just off the beach, young and talented bottle-tossing bartenders, and artery-clogging fried food. Without such characteristics, the most "happening" beach bar could be a quiet, hidden shack in the corner of the harbor.

They tied their dinghy to the floating dock. The dock wobbled, and they crouched to avoid being pitched into the water. "We're not on a pier. We're swinging on a Himalayan rope bridge high above a canyon in a strong wind," quipped Quinney.

People scurried about—young children, mothers carrying babies, teenagers, and men—some bosses, some laborers. They all appeared busy with assigned tasks, yet wherever they were going, all eyes were on the two visitors.

"I know what's going on," said Quinney. "These people aren't boaters. They all work here. They're probably all family members."

Nelson and Quinney climbed a short flight of stone steps to an open deck devoid of tables, chairs, weather covering, or railing at the edges. They strolled around, inspecting. When they concluded it was closed or out of business, a woman wearing a server's apron quietly approached from behind.

"Good afternoon," came a crisp greeting. "How may I help you?"

They turned to her in surprise. "Hi! Are you folks open for supper?" Nelson asked.

The woman looked around. "Well, it doesn't look like it with all these guys running around here, but of course we can take you for supper."

"We'd like to return to our boat, rest up, and come a little later, maybe around sunset, if that's all right," Quinney said.

"That's OK," the woman said as she handed her a menu.

Quinney looked it over. "Everything looks mouthwatering. It's going to be hard to choose."

"I have an idea," the woman said. "When you return, I'll have a surprise for you."

Quinney looked around. "It looks like you've taken quite a beating from storms."

"Yes, hurricanes and tropical storms have been unkind." The woman pointed as she spoke about what used to be where and the vision of its owners to restore and improve the bar, restaurant, and dock. All it would take was money and a compassionate reprieve from the storm gods. There was hope.

And Quinney learned the name of their gracious host… Atabei.

As they left, Quinney leaned into Nelson. "This place is perfect!"

They returned as late-afternoon shadows covered the western corners of Great Harbor. Nelson and Quinney chose to drag the dinghy to the beach rather than cross on the Himalayan rope bridge. "Let's not make any judgments about this place or the food," Nelson said. "It might look like a crab shack, but we're in the islands—right where we wanted to be."

They stood on the deck of the "dining room." It was large enough for a banquet, capable of catering to hundreds of people, yet there was a lone table in the center. The table was small and square with a white tablecloth, its fringes flapping in the breeze. There were metal utensils, cloth napkins, a small vase with a single red hibiscus, and an oil light waiting to be lit. Smooth rocks placed on the corners of the table kept everything from blowing away. Quinney and Nelson were alone at the restaurant that was sometimes open but mostly not.

They rearranged the chairs—placing them next to each other. They sat in silence, admiring their surroundings, listening to the sounds of Caribbean seabirds and the hush of the late-day breeze. They intertwined their fingers and caressed each other's hands. A bottle of wine arrived with their surprise dinner—a platter filled with bite-size morsels of almost everything on the menu. A toast to proud and beaming Atabei and to the absolute dumb luck of stumbling onto the most unlikely eating place in the islands. They sat in the realization of their dream—to just sail, just feel, and just be. When the moon peered over the east mountain, it was a crème brûlée dessert. The yacht club staff gave them the entire place—low lights, solitude, ambience. Their host could not have been more gracious, and her kindness, along with the rest of the staff, could not have been more genuine.

"Nelson, I've been meaning to ask you something," Quinney said. "I know you took sailing lessons in 2004 and bought your first sailboat, and then the big forty-footer. As soon as I came into your life, you invited me aboard. The first time we really heeled over, I screamed. You snarled, saying there was no screaming in sailing. You helped me get over my fear and taught me how to sail, and here we are in this storybook corner of the world. I never thought I could experience this kind of adventure, but I never asked you what drove you to take such a big step. Tell me how this happened."

Nelson reached for the wine bottle and refilled their glasses. "My interest in sailing began long ago on a summer pond in a flat-bottom boat with a broomstick for a mast, a bedsheet for a sail, and a childhood fantasy of what could be. It made a terrible sailboat, but it was the birthplace of my crazy dream that one day I could own a real sailboat. Fast-forward fifty-some years. I took my mom to dinner to share what I was about to do. She told me I was nuts. 'Why in the world would you want to do such a foolish thing? What has gotten into you?'

"I leaned across the table. 'It's part of a longtime dream,' I said. 'It will take me to new places, give me new challenges and experiences, open the door to learning many new things, and allow me to share my dream with others.' Even with her being so critical, she seemed to come to life whenever I took her out sailing."

"Any regrets?"

"None except for the financial drain. I put the boat in the charter to defray costs. *Ms. Sera* became the sweetheart of the fleet. She's in great demand, and she has made good money for both the charter company and me. Nothing lasts forever. Everyone wants to sail the newer, shinier boats. In a few years, *Ms. Sera* will no longer be the pride of the fleet. Eventually, we'll be asked to leave the charter, and all the costs will become mine—much more than I can handle. But in ten or twenty years from now when we no longer own a boat, no one will ever be able to take away the memories—memories like this."

They lingered and sipped the last of their wine as dusk became nightfall.

Nelson secured money on the table with a rock. The amount was double the ticket. The yacht club had earned it. They stood and thanked their host, bowing back and forth as if they were in a foreign country with a language barrier. Back in their Zodiac, they slowly motored to their boat, surrounded by billions of moonbeams sparkling and reflecting off the water.

* * *

Nelson and Quinney awoke to a crisp day. The easterlies began early and churned up Sir Francis Drake Channel—the main body of water between southern Tortola and many of the smaller BVI islands—including Peter Island. They plotted their course and set sail for The Baths, one of the top tourist destinations on southern Virgin Gorda. The Baths is known for its large crop of granite boulders at the waterline that form natural tidal pools, tunnels, arches, and grottoes that are open to the sea. Thousands of tourists would imagine themselves wandering through the maze of boulders—becoming one with nature and saturated in boundless romanticism. And then the hordes would arrive.

It was ten nautical miles to The Baths. The direct route would be directly into the wind—something a sailboat cannot do. Getting there required tacking, or zigzagging. Nelson reduced the sailing area by "reefing" the sails and pointed the boat upwind. The morning sun cast a silver sheen on the choppy water. By the time they reached The Baths, they had zigzagged twenty miles. Every other boater heading to The Baths had gotten the same message—get there early before the moorings are gone. They had thought ten o'clock would be early enough, but all moorings had been taken. Latecomers circled the area like feeding sharks. Boaters had abandoned all etiquette and safety. Sailboats tried and failed to outsprint a powerboat to a just-vacated mooring. Paddleboarders took their lives into their own hands as boats sped around in search of an available mooring.

Nelson and Quinney motored around the fringes, assessing the futility of finding an opening without transforming into an aggressive beast. They headed a hundred yards north to Spring Bay, where they found plenty of room to drop anchor. Behind the island was dead calm. The anchor fell straight to the bottom and held the boat in place by its sheer weight. No worries about anchor dragging on this jaunt.

They motored the Zodiac to The Baths. There was no room at the dinghy tie line, and The Baths, that romantic and picturesque granite formation, was crawling with hundreds upon hundreds of tourists. "We saw The Baths in the tourist magazines," Quinney said. "I don't think seeing it in person is going to be any better. Let's forget The Baths and explore the beach by our boat."

The warm sun, barren beach, two-inch surf, and cool, crystal-clear water quickly distracted them from any disappointment of not being able to get near The Baths. Laziness lured them into a short nap.

Unlike the morning "beat" to the wind, the return voyage to Peter Island had the makings of a "let all the sails out" Jimmy Buffett kind of sailing. "Maybe we can't show off with our anchoring skills, but we can show off with a little wing-to-wing sailing," Nelson said.

Quinney looked around. "Yeah, why not? The wind is just off our port stern. How can we prevent the mainsail from jibing?"

Nelson chuckled. He set the autopilot and scavenged through the lazarette under the seats. He stood, waving coiled-up line. "Ta-da! A preventer!"

Moments later, Nelson had the line rigged to the boom, wrapped around a forward cleat, and secured to a winch in the cockpit. He eased the mainsheet and let the sail out as far as it could extend to the right. He then maneuvered the boat to catch the wind in the jib on the port side. There was a hush as the boat blew with a twenty-knot tailwind on the jib on the left and the mainsail on the right. It was as though the boat had wings—wing-to-wing. Nelson inspected his work to ensure the wind could not get behind the mainsail and send it flying to port—a combination that could injure people and cause damage. He sat back behind the wheel, feeling like he was riding on a kite.

Suddenly, through the speakers came Bob Marley's "Is This Love." It was the kind of reggae music that is impossible to sit through without moving, swaying, smiling, singing. Quinney emerged from the salon. "I thought this would be a fitting song. It's on repeat, so if you get tired of it, let me know." She sat on an adjacent seat and wore the expression that said she was, once again, in her happy place. Moments later she discarded her swimsuit top and leaned back to feel the full glow of the afternoon sun.

"I remember you told me about the time you were looking over the rail on a cruise ship in Charlotte Amalie just as a sailboat went by with three topless damsels baring it all on the back deck. Remember that? Remember what you said?"

Nelson smiled innocently, waiting to hear.

"You said, 'I gotta get me one of those.'"

"That sounds chauvinistic. I think I said I wanted an unafraid girl like that."

"Be careful what you wish for." Quinney leaned her head back and laughed.

The sun vanished behind a low and distant storm cloud. Very dark and ominous with stabbing lightning and the promise of driving rain and wind. Squall. They come fast, rain hard, and leave fast. It can be concerning to a sailor with sails fully out, and more so when sailing wing-to-wing.

"Do we need to worry about that squall?" Quinney asked.

Nelson watched it move. "No, it will be way north of us by the time we get there."

Reggae music continued.

* * *

A week had passed. It was time to sail back to the Road Town marina. They radioed the charter-master and were told to meet a crew member at the end of the first dock who would take over the boat and bring them into their home slip. Quinney was ready to turn the helm over to Nelson, but he insisted she remain at the wheel. She approached the dock slowly. Using a maneuver she had learned back home, she made sure the boat quickly slowed, and the stern turned slightly and kissed the dock. The crewman stood with his eyes and mouth agape and made a comment to his helper. Women don't usually bring boats home, and most boaters seldom bring them in that smoothly. "Ma'am," said one of the dock workers. "Meaning no disrespect, ma'am. I ain't never seen a woman bring a boat in like that. You're some kind of sailor."

"Oh, I'm no sailor, but I can sure steer a boat."

Once secured in the slip, Nelson and Quinney worked like a cleaning crew on an airplane, preparing it for the next flight. Everything they were to bring home, discard, or turn in to the office fit into the blue dock cart. Quinney sorted out the cart's contents while Nelson turned in the electronics and boat keys.

"Let's get a sandwich," Quinney said as they walked by a large open-air restaurant. The land moved—they had yet to regain their land legs. Lunch consisted of deep-fried greasy deliciousness. Having been deprived of unhealthy food for a week gave them a renewed sense of appreciation for the kind of sustenance that was bad for human consumption in every way imaginable.

They paid the bill, tossed gear over their shoulders, and took one last look at the marina. "Hey, there's something I want to show you before we leave," Quinney said in a giddy tone. They walked over to the marina bulletin board. Quinney tapped her knuckle on a notice and pointed to it with her eyes. Nelson approached it with his nose inches from a message. His eyes lit up and a broad smile grew on his face.

Quinney resumed walking, laughing, and swaying her hips to tease him. "You owe me. You owe me big-time."

Nelson copied information from the message.

The notice on the bulletin board had not been there long. It had not faded with the sun, and the edges had not yet torn or curled.

NOW HIRING

SAILBOAT CREW FOR BOAT DELIVERY

ATLANTIC PASSAGE—USVI TO CHARLESTOWN, MD, USA

SAILING DATES—APRIL 16–24, 2010—9 DAYS AT SEA

QUALIFIED SEAMEN MUST HAVE RELEVANT ASA CREDENTIALS AND

OVER 1,000 HOURS' EXPERIENCE ON SAILING VESSELS 40' OR MORE

INTERESTED SAILORS SHOULD CONTACT CHRIS AUBREY AT 555-8692

RESUSCITATING A SCOW

THREE MONTHS LATER

St. Thomas, U.S. Virgin Islands—only thirty-five hundred miles from home. The first leg of the journey was a late-night flight, and subsequent connections were tight. The plane sat on the tarmac, delayed by some unknown mechanical mishap. If they missed their connection, Nelson and Quinney would have to wait another day for another flight. Boats don't wait either. Once they were in the air, the jet stream was kind, and the plane recovered the lost time. In St. Thomas, a taxi shuttled them halfway around the island to Red Hook. Helpful dockhands directed them to the end of a long pier.

Momentum, with bow facing the pier, rocked rhythmically from remnant ocean swells. There were no finger docks along the sides of the boat, which meant access required climbing over the hundred-pound anchor, over a pulpit, swinging around a furled-up genoa, and navigating through a mishmash of safety lines and rigging. Such a feat might be easy for twenty-year-olds, but for two "old folks" in their fifties and sixties, it took planning, deliberation, and prayer. The boat pitched with the rolling sea, sending its bow up and down. When getting on and off the boat, timing was everything.

"Ahoy, *Momentum*!"

A man emerged from belowdecks. "Ahoy!" He was tall and thin, and the muscles in his neck made him look ocean rugged. His hair blew over his square face and pronounced jawbones that looked tough enough to cut bolts. "You must be Nelson and Quinney. I'm Blake—your captain on this passage. Toss your gear and come aboard."

Come aboard? How? Nelson and Quinney stood looking at the bow, contemplating how they were going to get beyond all the obstacles without a bullfight with the anchor or being swatted by the pulpit.

"How am I going to get on the boat with my squatty body?" Quinney said.

"Don't worry. You'll do fine," Nelson said as he studied the challenge. The bow was knee high one moment and chest high the next. "I'll go first. You watch what I do. When the bow drops, put your foot on the anchor and grab that lifeline stanchion. Do *not* let go. Got that? The captain may be watching, so make it look like you've done this hundreds of times. If you can't get on board, you can't sail."

Moments later Nelson was up on the boat. "Toss me the gear."

Quinney timed her first step, grabbed the stanchion, and soon stood on the boat looking back at the anchor. "I don't know what all the fuss was about."

They stood on a solid-looking forty-seven-foot sloop with rigging, winches, and gear for the serious sailor determined to wring out every knot of wind. The mast could be bent to adjust sail performance to tame the ficklest of winds. "This boat makes me feel like a novice," Nelson said as he looked up at the mast in awe. "It makes our boat look like a toy."

In the cockpit, their expectations of a glistening seaworthy sailing vessel were splintered. What they saw was a worn-out, unkempt boat that looked as unloved as an abandoned animal in the pound. Nelson gulped. Quinney's jaw dropped. She looked around, mystified and in disbelief. Strewn across the deck were boat parts, greasy rags, service manuals with pages fluttering in the wind, and a collection of coffee-stained Styrofoam cups—some of which doubled as ashtrays. One of the four jib winches was in pieces with irreplaceable parts balanced on the gunwale, where one small bump could send them into the deep. The mechanism for adjusting the backstay rigging was disassembled, with nuts and bolts rolling in circles on the deck. A myriad of rusty and useless-looking tools was everywhere. Fix-it projects littered the vessel. Everything seemed to be half started or half finished. Nothing looked like it was anywhere near done. Most bothersome was the thought that neither the captain nor whoever was responsible for the chaos found it unacceptable enough to take action.

"What have we gotten ourselves into?" said Quinney, reeling from the shock of the complete entanglement of disorder and trash. "This boat looks like it's been ransacked."

Belowdecks was equally bad. At least there were cabinets and drawers to hide things. Mariners tend to be strict "neat freaks" who devoutly follow the "home rule" mantra, "A place for everything, and everything in its place." On a boat, storage is tight and the discipline for order can make the difference between life and death, or mutiny. Mariners appreciate the significance of muscle memory when they reach for a needed something, knowing that it will be there. But not on *Momentum*, where apparently, finding something was always a search-and-recovery mission. Most American kitchens have a junk drawer—a home to all things miscellaneous and homeless. Ignoring the "home rule" allows disorganization to proliferate, resulting in cramming and finally… protruding junk. A junk drawer on a boat is as insidious as dry rot. On *Momentum*, it seemed, all drawers were junk drawers. All cabinets, as well. *Momentum* had become dry rot.

Sleeping quarters were ample. Beyond the companionway was the main salon replete with storage, tables, and seating—all a golden varnish on teak. Styrofoam cups were breeding in great numbers and looked as if they had been stand-in petri dishes for science experiments. Someone had once delighted in Chinese takeout and pizza. The sink was a garbage bucket. Food in every form—rotten, dried, spoiled—and dirty plates littered the galley table and counter space.

Blake told them they could take any cabin or bunk they chose except his. Quinney immediately chose the cabin with a door—it offered privacy and the most neatness. Their cabin had more books than a small library, all held in place by side pressure. Clothing was squeezed in closets, and stuffed drawers were unopenable. The bunks, however, were ready to be used for sleeping.

*　*　*

Chaulee was the St. Thomas caretaker for *Momentum*. He was the "captain" and had overall responsibility for the boat while the boat owner was in the States. He talked to himself a lot. Actually, he mumbled indiscernibly. Privately, Quinney asked Nelson if Chaulee was talking to himself or others, or if what he said had any meaning at all. Nelson swore Chaulee spent much of his life smoking brown weeds or taking too many shooters of bad tequila. To Chaulee, a good repair always involved a lot of duct tape and a lot more talking.

With all his shortcomings, Chaulee had a heart of gold—not a bad bone in his body. Always seemed eager to help. His smile could disarm a raging rhino. Chaulee didn't know much about boats, but he knew people who did. While hopeless with sentence construction, this islander was resourceful, which came in handy. As he doled out names, he told Nelson, "Tell them Chaulee sent you."

"Hey, Chaulee, are there any places around here where I can find a small rigging knife with a marlin spike?" Chaulee directed Nelson down the dock. In the marine store, a behind-the-counter worker looked at Nelson and gave him a tired "you're here to bother me, aren't you" look. Nelson mentioned Chaulee's name. The attendant jumped. "Anything for Chaulee!"

Within an hour, Quinney had a clean galley, a reorganized icebox, sorted and stored provisions, and germ-free dishware. Nelson put his hands on his temples and stared in amazement. "Wow! Look what you've done. You've gone and resuscitated a scow." On her crew application credentials she had listed scuba diving, bungee jumping, skydiving, and traveling. She had confirmed that she wasn't afraid to lose sight of land. For her sailing experience, she had listed "galley slave." She'd been hired.

Nelson assigned himself the ship's navigator. He brought charts, a piloting atlas, a ship's log, and an assortment of charting tools. Blake explained the float plan—wiggle through a maze of small islands and make a straight 345-degree heading up to Chesapeake Bay. Nelson turned to his tools to chart the course and set up the ship's log. He enjoyed the challenge of blending precision and deduced reckoning when compensating for current and wind. Taking the initiative for this important task was a good start at establishing his credentials as a competent seaman. When he finished, though, Blake dismissed it, explaining that charting the course would be unnecessary because they had a working GPS. *What if we lose the GPS?* Nelson thought. *What if we have to change direction because of a storm? What if, what if, what if?* Nelson's navigation training had come from an officer on a naval warship. Blake's kind of navigation was vastly different from Nelson's. Blake was the captain, and his word was law. Nelson decided he would keep daily charts and logs if only as a trip memento.

Blake contacted Peter, his meteorologist in New Hampshire, who was one of the best in the States at deciphering weather maps and who had a knack for reliable forecasting. He advised that a strong low-pressure weather front was forming above the Great Lakes, and if *Momentum* didn't leave as planned, she would lose her weather window. It was settled… *Momentum* would sail in the morning.

Nelson and Quinney had a problem—a big one. Comparing the condition of *Momentum* to their near-obsessive discipline with keeping *Ms. Sera* looking her best was mind-boggling. Even though Quinney had become a whirlwind cleaner, they could not scrub the negative first impression out of their heads.

"We're out of time," Nelson told her. "If we don't speak up now, we'll be heading out into blue water in a boat we think is unseaworthy. We have a choice… Either we get off now, right here, or we pray she'll hold together until we get to Charlestown."

"I agree. You know, Blake is gonna freak out if we bail on him now. What are your thoughts?"

Nelson looked around as if to reveal a secret. He pulled Quinney into their cabin and spoke softly. "Blake doesn't seem to think there's a problem, which tells me he must know something we don't. I really want to make this passage, and I don't think he'd deliberately cast off if he thought we were heading into trouble on a bad boat. His focus on leaving is so strong, I wonder if he even sees what a mess this boat is, or cares. I don't know where his thinking is. I vote for putting off the decision until we talk to Blake."

Nelson found Blake in the cockpit. "Blake, is this boat ready to go?"

Blake looked around. "Are you concerned about something?"

"There are still parts all over the place. The winch is in pieces. I haven't seen Chaulee all day, so it may not be fixed by the time we leave. We're really uncomfortable with the overall condition of this boat—so much so that we're considering getting off. I know that isn't what you want to hear, but it's how strongly we feel about it. We agreed that we wouldn't decide until we'd talked to you, so here we are."

Blake sighed deeply. Nelson thought he might be searching his mind for the most convincing response. "Let's talk about happiness—*Momentum*'s happiness. She's happy when everything works—the GPS, the motor, the autopilot, the sails, the lines, everything that keeps her afloat and moving. *Momentum* may be untidy, but she's seaworthy, and that's much more important. If that winch isn't ready, it's no big deal. We have three more. Chaulee said all the safety equipment had been checked out. My concern is missing the weather window. There's a storm front north of the Great Lakes. It's heading southeast—right where we're going. Miss the weather window and we could be contending with a strong weather front. We *must* obey the weather window. That's why leaving at 0600 hours tomorrow is important. Relax, Nelson. *Momentum* is happy, so I'm happy, and you should be, too. Does that answer your concerns?"

"I wish it did, but no," said Nelson.

"Well, get it out then."

"This boat does not look ready for a nine-day blue water sailing expedition."

"So, what does looking ready look like to you?"

Nelson waved his hand around to allow the chaotic mess to plead his case.

"OK," Blake said. "You've made coastal passages in your boat, right? What do you do to prepare that we haven't done here?"

"That's my problem. It looks like there's been no preparation. With all the piles of messes we cleaned up and the complete lack of organization, I get the impression no one really cares about the boat operation. On my boat, I have a checklist to make sure I don't forget things. I won't go through it all, but I make sure the oil is clean and at the right levels and we have a supply of it. I check for spare parts like impellers for the raw water intake pump or the valves for the head. I make sure there's no water in the bilges. Then I make sure our systems all work."

"How do you know that hasn't already been done?"

"Has it?"

"That's Chaulee's job, and he assured me it was all checked out."

"Looking at the way he takes care of things, I wouldn't trust him with anything. His idea of a good repair is talking about it, wrapping duct tape around it, or kicking it."

"Look, Nelson. Your concern is based on what you see, and I agree *Momentum*'s untidy. It's embarrassing. It *does* reflect badly on the rest of the boat, but you haven't checked out any of the systems, and you don't know if any of us have. We just went over this. Either you have faith that *Momentum* is fit for sea, or you don't. If you don't know, then, if I were you, I'd check it out… all those systems you mentioned you check on your boat. You have a responsibility to be comfortable. Either check it out and be OK with it or get off this boat right now. I told you *Momentum* is happy. I'm the captain and you should trust me on this. Lesson number one on a boat: Trust one another. I'm not about to sail off knowing she's not ready. You're concerned about boat tidiness. I'm concerned about everything working, and it does. We're leaving at 0600 hours tomorrow to stay in our weather window. So what's it gonna be?"

Nelson and Quinney looked at each other and nodded. "We'll be ready to cast off at 0600," Nelson said.

Entry from Nelson's personal journal—April 16, 2010

Instead of leaving at 0600 hours, we didn't get underway until 1400 hours. Had to wait for a sail the owner wanted transported. Chaulee arrived at midday with an overstuffed sail bag we couldn't stow below. I lashed it to the deck in front of the mast but discovered once we were at sea that I had trapped working lines under it and had to go forward to straighten them out while the wind blew cold spray across the bow. Got soaked to the bone. Idiot! We were out for an hour when the autopilot failed. Returned to port for repairs. Lost the day. Weather window shrinking. What's a weather window?

Chaulee was unable to repair the autopilot and called in Zeke, another islander, who lived on a ketch with no sails and green algae climbing up the rotting mooring line. He arrived in a very seasoned gray inflatable dinghy filled with weatherproof boxes carefully stowed from bow to stern. His long straggly ponytail brushed his belt. He was cordial, eager to please, and told stories from his heart with a thick southern drawl that eased the tension from frustration over a delayed departure.

Zeke was the local "go-to" electrician. That meant *Momentum*'s autopilot problem had been diagnosed as electrical long before anyone had taken a look at it. Discomforting.

Electrical problems could be anywhere. On boats, electronic devices are interconnected, integrated, and dependent upon something else for them to work. It challenges the troubleshooting process. Checking out an electrical problem requires $15,346 worth of diagnostic equipment. Zeke had the tools—more than enough to qualify him as an expert. They were all protected and well organized. He knew exactly which box to go to. He retrieved his electrical testers and quickly eliminated the possibilities. Then, he announced that the problem could only be with the one remaining component, the autopilot motor. It was below the cockpit in a cargo hold behind the steering-wheel well and integrated with the steering mechanism. Access seemed like it would require double-jointed agility.

Zeke opened the hatch and poked his head into the cargo hold. "There's a bunch of fuel tanks in the way. They all gotta come out."

One by one, enough five-gallon fuel containers were brought up to the cockpit to give Zeke access to the mechanism. He vanished into the hole and reappeared with the motor in hand. He precariously balanced it on one of the boxes in his dinghy and raced off to repair it.

A half hour later Zeke returned, smiling and declaring victory. "Works now!" he proclaimed. *Thirty minutes was way too quick for a repair*, thought Nelson, but it was not his place to question. Zeke admitted he had been unable to make it fail, which meant the unit was never repaired. If a unit does not fail, there is nothing to fix. So goes island reasoning.

April 17, 1800 hours—*Momentum* once again set sail, but without wind. Two hours out, the autopilot failed hard. Nothing intermittent—it was not working at all, and it was not going to. Blake held his first staff meeting with Nelson and Quinney. "The autopilot is dead. We can continue the passage and manually steer the next sixteen hundred miles. Are you up to it or do you want to turn back?"

Quinney wore an "I'm game if you are" expression. Nelson said, "You know our skills. If you believe we're up to it, let's go."

"That settles it then," Blake said, slapping his knees. "We keep going. Nelson, you take the first watch. Steer to 3-4-5 degrees. I'll relieve you in four hours."

Nelson began having second thoughts about so willingly turning his decision over to Blake. Navigating for nine days meant that he, Blake, or Quinney would always have to be at the wheel. The autopilot was like having extra crew. The sea can fight back and suck all the energy out of the helmsman. Blake may have assessed his skills, but he knew nothing about Nelson's or Quinney's stamina or strength. And Nelson didn't know if he had enough strength to last the entire passage without an autopilot.

Nelson looked over his shoulder and murmured, "What am I doing?" The Virgin Islands had become small bumps on the horizon. Soon they vanished—first in darkness and then behind the curvature of the earth, leaving only the faint sky glow from island lights.

Two hours passed, and Blake came bounding up the companionway. "This is insane. I was wrong. We need to turn back. Two of us once made this trip without an autopilot. We were exhausted and began making mistakes. The weather in the north will be difficult. We can't go into it exhausted."

Nelson turned *Momentum* and headed toward the sky glow of the islands.

* * *

They awoke on St. John to the "Ahoy!" from Chaulee and Zeke, both of whom Nelson had hoped to not see again, but how can one not respond to friendly faces and miles of smiles? "We're taking the autopilot to St. Thomas. I know a good mechanic there," Zeke said.

Blake and Nelson kept an eye on the autopilot, which sat precariously on Zeke's dinghy as he and Chaulee motored off to St. Thomas. They looked toward each other out of the corner of their eyes. "Not happy," Blake said quietly.

"You may as well enjoy St. John," Blake added. "We're gonna be here for a while."

"How long is a while?" said Quinney.

Blake looked back toward Zeke's boat. "With the way things have been going with those two, I'm afraid to make any predictions. But if we can't get underway in two days we'll have to scrub the passage. I have another delivery and won't make it back by the scheduled departure date if we don't leave soon. And… sailing outside the weather window is already a concern."

"Well, I have a problem, too," said Quinney. "My employer gave me more time off for this trip than company policy permits. If I'm not back by April 29th, I could lose my job."

Blake rubbed his chin and nodded. "Hmmm. Well then, it looks like we could both have a scheduling conflict, doesn't it?" Blake paused. "Here's an idea. If we have to scrub the delivery, let's spend the rest of our time sailing around the islands. We don't need an autopilot for that."

"I'm for that! I like that idea!" said Quinney with Nelson nodding in agreement.

"Boat delivery is our priority. Cruising around the islands can be our consolation prize. Meanwhile, you two take off and explore St. John."

Nelson and Quinney hitched a ride from Virginia, a woman motoring around collecting mooring fees. She took them two coves up the coast, tied up on a pier, and pointed. "See that path over there? Follow it. It runs along the beaches to a classy resort. When you're ready to return, take a taxi back from the resort."

They headed up the path and were quickly swallowed into a jungle of foliage of all sizes and shapes—all shoving each other for the limited real estate and grabbing for all the light rays they could get. "Look at the size of those leaves!" Quinney said as she pulled one down and in front of her. "That one could work as an entire cover-up. How do I look in this color?"

A steep side path led to a narrow beach. Nelson saw a wooden sign nailed to a tree: HONEYMOON BEACH. They took it. The beach was hidden, hard to reach, private. They tested the water—still cool for April, yet refreshing.

They resumed their hike along the path, close to more secluded beaches, and up a road where they saw a sign to the Caneel Bay

Resort, a high-end getaway. Nelson stood with mouth agape. "My parents came here in the dead of winter in the 1950s. Back then it was called the Caneel Bay Plantation. They came to escape the winter and Ma needed a kid break. When they got back home, they were different—especially Ma. For months, she danced around the house to the calypso music they brought back."

They ate lunch, drank wine, walked around the property taking pictures to show Ma, wandered around the leftover stone buildings from the sugar plantation days, and grabbed a taxi back to Great Cruz Bay, where, they hoped, their boat was ready to go.

*　*　*

"The autopilot is fixed. We're getting another crew member. Be ready to shove off as soon as he arrives. This is maddening," said an agitated Blake within a minute after Nelson and Quinney had climbed aboard from the water taxi.

"Did we hold anything up?" Nelson asked.

"You? No, the autopilot has been installed for hours. Now we'll be stuck here until midnight waiting for our fourth crew member. Let's move the boat to the fuel dock. If they let us tie up there, we can shave an hour off our departure time."

The security officer at the fuel dock intercepted *Momentum* as Nelson jumped off to tie her up. He had the cold black eyes of a shark. Tying at the fuel dock at night—not permitted. Period. No exceptions. Rules are rules. Nelson approached him and nodded—universal language showing respect and recognizing a person's space. The guard looked through him. Didn't even move his head—the universal language of disrespect. He was the most unfriendly, callous, unfeeling, coldhearted, insensitive, unsympathetic, thick-skinned-looking soul Nelson had ever encountered. When Nelson told him Chaulee had sent them, the security officer morphed into a pleasant, smiling, welcoming islander. "Anything for Chaulee! Dock's closed so you can tie your boat here."

Nelson sat with Blake, who looked ahead without blinking. Something was on his mind. He wore a tension that Nelson had not seen in him before. An angry captain affects the entire crew. He was a bomb that needed defusing.

"Blake, how many times have you made this crossing?"

"Huh? Oh, I've done this about a dozen times." He paused. "Yeah, a dozen times."

"On *Momentum*?"

"This is my first time on this boat. I've made trips to Newport, Rhode Island, several to Chesapeake Bay, out to Bermuda. Most from here. In November after the hurricane season, we're busy bringing the boats back down to the islands for the winter."

"You've been using the term *weather window* a lot, and I'm not sure I know exactly what it means. I've done quite a bit of coastal cruising and never thought about the weather window."

"Technically, a weather window is a limited time interval when weather conditions can be expected to be suitable. In our case, we need nine sailing days to get to Charlestown, Maryland. That's what I told the meteorologist. After studying the weather charts, he told me that if we left on the morning of April sixteenth, last Friday, we would have a good chance of arriving at our destination ahead of the weather front bearing down from Canada. That was our weather window. And now, by the time we get six days into our trip, that strong weather system could be waiting for us in the Atlantic. A weather window looks at the conditions during the entire time of our passage. We've already squandered three days. That's why I'm concerned. We need to get underway now or scrub the passage. I know we're gonna get some weather, much more than if we had left on the sixteenth. Does that make sense?"

"It does, but I pulled the information from a flier in BVI some months ago. How can you know the weather window that far ahead?"

"Normally you can't. April is predictably the most favorable sailing month up the Atlantic. Most of the storms that come through are weak or fizzle out. As that can change, we have to alter our plans.

The meteorologist warned of a potentially powerful weather front that could meet us as we approach Chesapeake Bay. That's why it's important to obey the weather window."

"I have another question. This may sound like an interview, but it's more in the category of getting to know your captain. What's your biggest pet peeve in your job?"

Blake waved his hands around the boat. "This. This boat is a mess, like we talked about the other day. The port winch doesn't work. Half of it is missing. The backstay tensioner was in pieces. Nothing has a home. No one has been taking care of the boat. I have no idea what shape the steering cable is in. When you go below and see how all the cabinets and drawers are stuffed, you have to wonder about the reliability of all the boat systems."

"Wait, didn't we already have a conversation about *Momentum*'s happiness? You didn't mention anything about these things then. Why now? Didn't you know this boat was turned inside out before you came?"

"My boss worked all this out with the owner, who assured him that this vessel meets all US Coast Guard safety standards. I'm just the delivery boy. I didn't like the mess any more than you, but none of those bothersome things have anything to do with *Momentum*'s performance. She can be an absolute mess and still be a happy boat."

"So, we have no reason to question our sanity about staying on the boat?"

"Nelson, the autopilot is repaired. *Momentum* is in good enough condition to travel safely on the sea. She's a seaworthy vessel and fit for the passage. *Momentum*'s happy. Look past the mess. Quinney already cleaned most of it up. Be happy, Nelson."

Nelson had a sense that his concerns were being dismissed and he was being placated. But he trusted Blake.

"OK, here's a question that has nothing to do with the boat. What's your pet peeve when it comes to hired crew?"

"My biggest one is if a helmsman falls asleep at the wheel, especially at night when they're alone. That infuriates me."

"Has that ever happened?"

"Once. I caught the helmsman sleeping. He said he wasn't, but how can you deny it when you're slumped over sideways? I was so angry with him, especially after catching him red-handed *and* lying. I wanted to throw him overboard. I truly did."

"Wow! I guess there's a message there."

"Do *not* fall asleep on your watch. A person who does puts the boat and everyone on it in danger. It may be wide open out there, but you never know when there's something big to hit. Every now and then you come across a shipping container floating a foot above water. Hit one of those and you could lose your boat."

"Aren't things like that hard to see at night?"

"Yes, very hard. Impossible if you're sleeping. With all that's floating around out there, it's enough to make you want to heave to and sleep till dawn. But then again, even if you're stopped, what's preventing something from bumping into *you*? And it's only getting worse with more transatlantic traffic from the Mediterranean. If you have any fears about night sailing, this passage will cure you."

Nelson had been with Blake for days now. He was better than average at reading and sizing people up. He was learning more about what Blake wanted and how he operated. One thing was for sure: Do not fall asleep on one's watch. What Blake had told him was not an idle anecdote.

Entry from Nelson's personal journal—April 19, 2010

Blake has eyes so piercing, they can see through lead, and they command the same trembling fear I remember seeing in Gregory Peck when he played Capt. Ahab in Moby Dick. *His smile, though, is a dead giveaway for a different person within. When he's smiling, teeth appear all over his face. His leanness accounts for his energy. He has springs in his feet—always cocked and ready to go.*

* * *

"Hi, I'm Frank." The new crewman stood in the companionway with hands in his pockets, rocking on his feet. He was average height and stocky, with large, hairy arms. He was clean shaven, with a round face, receding hairline, and straight salt-and-pepper hair. Something about him made Nelson suspicious. Nelson looked past Frank's wire-rim glasses to study his eyes. One was caring and the other… cunning. The latter looked like his dominant eye. Quinney stepped out of their cabin to greet the face behind the new voice. There was a sudden change in Frank's demeanor. His eyes shifted from her face to her chest. Nelson bristled at the disrespect.

When Frank turned to size up Nelson, his line of questions stuck to sailing experience, training, and boat ownership. Frank interrupted Nelson's responses with another question. Either Nelson was long-winded, or Frank wasn't interested. Either way, Nelson became reluctant to open up to a seemingly judgmental person he had met only moments before.

Frank apparently needed no further introduction to Quinney. It was plain she had the credentials—an engaging smile and large breasts.

Blake poked his head down the companionway. "Stow your stuff. We gotta go. Let's move!" Nelson had assessed Blake as an easygoing person but wondered if he had misjudged him. *Maybe Frank is one of those guys who makes everyone around him inexplicably coarse.* Frank appeared unaffected by Blake's impatience and ambled about the boat, deciding where to stow his belongings. Urgency didn't seem to be in his lexicon.

Nelson joined Blake on deck and stepped onto the dock. He quickly untied and coiled the bow and stern lines. He untied a third line amidships and kept ahold of it around a cleat until told to cast off. They pulled away from the dock and headed toward open water. Lights from the island interfered with night vision. Nelson clipped his safety harness to the safety line and announced, "I'm going forward to keep an eye out for boats."

Quinney came out of her cabin and was met by Frank, who leaned his arm on the doorway, loomed over her, and began engaging in conversation. Quinney gave a polite but brief smile and pointed to the cockpit. Frank stepped aside.

Blake's agitation increased exponentially. He began cursing quietly, jumping around the wheel, cupping his hands, and yelling down the companionway, "Frank! Let's go! I can hear waves on the shore. We're too close. The cabin lights are blinding me. Turn them off and come up now!"

SHIP'S LOG—APRIL 20, 2010—0010 HOURS—18° 19'50"N, 064° 51'05"W

They were underway four days later than planned. Clearly, they had lost their weather window.

THE BULLY ON BOARD

SHIP'S LOG—APRIL 20, 2010—0200 HOURS—18° 30′19″N, 064° 51′9″W

"Come on back to the helm," Blake called. Nelson had spent an hour with his arm around the mast, watching for other boats in the channel and in between the islands. He worked his way to the cockpit. With two harness lines, he would always be attached to the boat while reattaching the loose harness around a stanchion, the "post" holding the lifelines. While cumbersome and slow, it was one of those safety procedures a conscientious mariner dared not sidestep, especially at night.

A small instrument light shone from around Blake's foot at the helm. With his eyes accustomed to darkness, it may as well have been a spotlight.

"On my boat, the engine instruments are down low like that and hard to see," Nelson said. "I have yet to understand why the ship builders put them there."

Blake glanced down and shrugged. "Are you up to taking the wheel for a few hours?"

"Can do."

Blake pointed to a button on the console. "This disengages the autopilot. Our course heading is 3-4-5 degrees. Just keep to that heading and you won't run into any land for at least another five days. I need some sleep. Frank should be up in a few hours. He's down below, sacked out."

Nelson sat at the helm. The boat was his. It was his first night watch on *Momentum*.

On top of the console sat the ship's compass, backlit with a soft red lamp that allows a person to see instrumentation without affecting night vision. It emitted a faint glow around the cockpit so Nelson wouldn't accidentally trip over something and tumble overboard. This was not his first night sail. It was, however, his first where there was no sight of land or sky glow from city lights. He was immersed in darkness. There is something unnerving about plowing through nighttime waters at seven knots and not being able to see beyond the ship's mast. Sailors place a great deal of faith in boat instrumentation—GPS, automatic identification systems, and radar. Telling the difference between sea and sky was easy—both were black, but the sky was dotted with billions of stars that were equally as bright on the horizon as they were directly overhead. The Milky Way stretched across the sky as a distinctive ribbon of light that could easily trick the observer into believing that they weren't stars but magically lit-up clouds. Through binoculars, a different story emerged. Nelson placed his hat over the compass and kicked a towel over the instrumentation near his feet to create total darkness. The source of all light seemed to be gone, but he could still see the entire cockpit, the mast, and the rigging lines. Even in the deepest and darkest of nights, somewhere there remained a light source. He looked to the heavens. There it was… the uncountable, endless ocean of stars.

Nelson thought back to his boyhood days when his older brother woke him at midnight, took him into the fields on the farm, and set a camera on a tripod to take a time-lapse picture of stars circling around the North Star. "As long as you can see the North Star," he said, "a person can never be truly lost."

In seventh-grade science class, Nelson learned that sunlight refracts as it travels into Earth's atmosphere and its wave fronts graze the upper atmosphere and bend light downward. He gazed deeper into the heavens and could see their immenseness, knowing there was no end to it. As long as he had vision, he could always see at night—no matter how faint the omnipresent light.

Consumed in his fascination with darkness and the vast population of stars, he fastened his safety harness to the lifeline and worked his way to the mast. Things were different forward. The constant humming of the engine at the helm had been dampened by the serene sound of the boat gliding along on the flat sea.

A school of dolphins paced the boat, leaving contrails of blue phosphorescence. They surrounded the boat, then took turns swimming close for a better look. He could hear the sound of spewing air when they surfaced for a fresh breath. Even to a casual observer, these creatures could be nothing less than magnificent. Nelson took the encounter as a good omen. He felt privileged.

The engine suddenly went silent, startling him. The boat quickly slowed. Something strange was happening, and it was happening on Nelson's watch.

"Nelson! Nelson!" came a piercing yell from the cockpit. Nelson was shaken out of his euphoric mood and looked around the mast toward the helm. Blake's flashlight darted around the cockpit, the sea around the boat, and in the distance where reflective marks on Nelson's PFD would make him easy to spot. Blake held an orange life ring, poised to cast off.

"I'm up here, captain."

Blake's flashlight washed Nelson with light. "Come back here." Nelson went back to the cockpit.

"Jeez, Nelson! I thought we'd lost you over the side. We need to talk. Look, the cockpit is the safest place to be on a boat. Out where you were, there's too many things to tangle or trip you up—especially at night. A ship's rule is to never go forward after dark unless it's an emergency and there's another crew member on deck. I know you're hooked onto the lifeline, but if you were alone and fell overboard, you could be dragged and drowned before anyone would know. You gave me a scare. Please don't do it again. By the way, your watch is over. Anything happening?"

Nelson gave a quick briefing, apologized for startling Blake, went below to record their position in the ship's log, and joined Quinney in their cabin.

* * *

SHIP'S LOG—APRIL 20, 2010—0943 HOURS—19° 07′63″N, 065° 05′54″W

Nelson awoke to the sound of the winch grinding on a sheet, and moments later the boat heeled to port, rolling him toward the hull. Then the engine stopped. They were under sail power! No time to waste—Nelson was up and scurried to the cockpit.

The seas were choppy. The easterlies blew at fifteen knots. The sky was cloudless. The midmorning sun felt good on his face. Nelson gave a 360-degree sweep. The water was deep blue in all directions. There was no sign of land, not even a hint from that milky-white hue that hovers over landmass. For Nelson, this was a first. Without the sun or a compass, it would be impossible to determine direction. Even with it, the disorientation can make a person dizzy. Nelson thought, *How did Columbus do it on cloudy days?*

"Hey, sleepyhead!" came Quinney's smiling morning greeting from where she sat at the helm. "Look at me! I'm steering. Frank's giving me lessons. There's coffee and a bagel for you down below."

Frank sat beside Quinney with his lecherous half smile, saying nothing. He sat closer to his student than necessary. Nelson bristled and thought, *He's teaching you how to steer? You already know how to steer. You don't need steering lessons from him.*

Blake concentrated on fine-tuning the sails to maximize their power. With each adjustment the boat heeled over slightly by another degree or two, and the boat picked up speed.

Nelson went below in search of the promise of breakfast and returned to the cockpit with a bagel smeared thick with cream cheese. Quinney joined him from the helm and watched him stretch his neck to study the sails. "If you're looking for birds, you probably aren't going to find any way out here."

Nelson laughed. "I'm trying to get a feel for the rigging."

"OK, I have a question. Back home you talk about standing and running rigging. I never got all that rope stuff straight."

"Ah! Opportunity for a refresher," said Nelson.

"You taught me how to maneuver the boat, not sail it. When it came to adjusting sails, I was just doing what you told me. You think I knew what I was doing?"

"OK, rule number one—don't ever call a line a 'rope.' A rope is a line without purpose except for anchors. If you call it rope, be prepared for mocking looks and scoffs. Anyway, see those lines up there that attach to the sails? They're used for raising, lowering, shaping, and controlling the sails. It's called running rigging because the lines *run* through pulleys and around winches. They move. If you study the lines closely, you'll see they vary in thickness, and you'll see that some lines are white with different-colored markings and others are solid."

"Are they the same on all boats?"

"Nope. Manufacturers offer different color schemes so a sailor can pick up a line and know what it controls just by its markings and color. There are no standards. You can't pick up a white line with blue markings, for example, and assume it's for the same purpose on all boats. On our boat, I'm familiar with the lines and what they do. Lines for sheets and halyards are solid, and the lines for sail adjustments are white with colored markings. They could be different on this boat, which is why I'm checking them out. See the rigging holding up the mast? Those are called standing rigging. They just *stand* around. They are also called stays because they *stay* in one place. Ha ha, get it? They don't go anywhere. If any one of those cables snaps, it puts pressure on all the others. That's why all the standing rigging needs to be replaced every seven to ten years."

"That's gotta cost a bundle," Quinney said.

"Bring on another thousand, baby. That's where you get the acronym B.O.A.T."

Nelson cocked his head and sat up straight.

"What's wrong?" Quinney asked.

"I've never seen that before." Nelson was looking at two rigging lines that ran from about two-thirds up the mast to the port and starboard sides of the rear quarter. It was his first glimpse of standing rigging that was not cable and could be adjusted.

"Hey, Frank, what's that?" Nelson said, pointing to the mysterious rigging.

Frank looked up and then out to sea without saying a word. Then, without looking at Nelson he said, "Rigging."

"Well, that's helpful. I know it's rigging, but I haven't seen that kind of configuration before."

"It's called a running backstay. Very common on larger boats. I'm guessing you've never been on a boat this size."

"I have been but have never focused on its rigging."

Frank looked up the rigging and back to his work at the helm. After a minute of silence he said, "That's the first thing sailors do when they get on a boat, you know. They study rigging. I'm guessing you didn't do that when you were on larger boats."

"I've just never come across standing rigging that's actually adjustable."

"You haven't been on larger boats much, have you? This running backstay is used to depower the mainsail and stabilize the mast in a strong wind. From the look on your face, I'll bet you don't know much about what I'm saying, do you? Look, I have to go below for a while. Take the helm, would you? You know… the helm—this thingy—the steering wheel."

Nelson bristled but moved to the helm. His conversation with Frank was over. "Well, Quinney, me dear, that certainly was instructive. From his body language and tone, I got the impression he was mocking me. What do you think?"

"Somehow you got on his bad side—that's for sure. That didn't take long," Quinney said.

A few minutes later Blake came topside, sat next to Quinney, and looked around. "Where's Frank? Isn't it still his watch?"

Nelson shrugged. "He said he needed to go below. I assumed it was to use the head. He didn't say."

"Don't let him get away with that," Blake said. "When it's your watch, it's your responsibility to be in control of the boat. If you leave the helm for any reason, you get someone to take your place, but you have to tell them when you're coming back. Did he say anything?"

Nelson shook his head. "I'll talk to him," Blake said.

"Got some time to answer a question? I've been looking at the running backstay. It seems to me that when we come about, it will get in the way of the boom. Am I reading that right?"

"Yep, that's what'll happen if we don't get it out of the way. This rigging configuration requires a crewman at the mast to tie and untie knots to pull the windward backstay out of the way. Because of the way it's configured, this boat cannot easily be solo sailed. Running backstays stabilize the mast. Without them, there could be too much tension on the mast in a strong breeze, and that could lead to disaster. On smaller boats like yours, a running backstay isn't needed. When you see how we get it out of the way, it'll make a lot more sense. Any more questions?"

"Yes, heavy weather sailing… In school, my instructors were emphatic that breaking waves in a following sea pose the greatest danger, which was why practicing heaving to was a critical skill. Do you agree with that?"

"Yes, that seems to be how most tragedies occur. It's OK to sail with a following sea. Most of the time you just surf down the wave or it goes right under you, but when the wave begins to curl, it can break and flood the cockpit. If the water doesn't drain before the boat is hit again, excess water could change all the dynamics of its stability, or it can tip the boat, making it more vulnerable even to small breaking waves. Boat design these days focuses on quick drainage. That's why you see so many open sterns."

"I don't see any drain holes on this boat."

"They're in the bottom of the wheel well."

Nelson cupped his eyes and looked into the well. "Ah, I see them. I also see a squashed cup. Are those drain holes big enough?"

"The boat designers seemed to think so. They're not big enough for my liking. We just have to be careful and watch the following seas for breaking waves. If you ever see us in that situation, close the companionway hatch right away. We need to get that cup out of there."

* * *

Entry from Nelson's personal journal—April 20, 2010

Sultry with light winds. Attempted sextant readings to hone celestial navigation skills, but sextant out of calibration. Was 400 miles off. Had knot lessons. Frank can't keep his eyes off Quinney, and he can't seem to get close enough to her. The seas went dead flat. Blake said he's never seen it this flat in all his passage days. A bad omen?

THE COMMODORE

Nelson and Quinney lay in their cabin on their backs with hands cradling their heads as if they were lying in a field of tall grass on a lazy summer day. They couldn't figure out what Nelson had said or done to trigger Frank's terse response to Nelson's rigging question. Rather than allow it to fester and grow into a stubborn dispute, Quinney suggested they learn more about Frank by getting him to talk about himself. Since Frank had taken a greater liking to Quinney, she would be more successful at drawing him out.

On deck, Frank sat at the helm. Blake sat looking out over the water. Quinney made small talk for a minute, then asked Frank, "How did you get into sailing?"

Frank looked Quinney up and down admiringly and replied, "Oh, I don't know. Why do you ask?"

"We're going to be together for the next week, so I thought it would be good to know something about you."

"So you want to get to know me better, eh? OK. I grew up around water and always sailed. As I got older, the boats got bigger. I love racing. I was good at it because I took it seriously. I excelled at the competition and personal challenge, not for trophies. If you want to be a good sailor and get the most out of your boat… take up racing."

"Is that your job?"

"Racing? No. Like I said, I've always sailed. I did a lot of crewing, and that gave me experience on someone else's dime. I found I could sail without ever having to worry about boat ownership. Being crew doesn't pay much, but it gives you a bunk and provisions. That makes up for the bad pay. Like Blake here, I did some captaining, but there's much more responsibility than I wanted. I still have my captain's license and that's always a good credential. I'm Captain Frank, by the way," he said with a smirk and bobbing head.

"So, this is what you do for a living?"

"This? No. This is filler work. I'm the commodore in a sailing school for rich kids. I set the schedule, the classwork, and manage the instructors. The kids come into my school and can't even tie their shoes. They're all swabs when they come in and competent able seamen when they graduate."

"Is that an all-year thing?"

"Nope, just summers. I get them right after school lets out and cut them loose over Labor Day. Graduation is a big deal. We have races, picnics, and time for the kids and their parents to sail together. The kids can show off, but they also show their parents how responsible they can be and how much their self-confidence has improved."

"You sound very proud of what you do."

"Those kids are my life. A lot of adults I know can't stand kids, but to me, it's a matter of how you treat and trust them. Give them responsibilities and treat them like young adults, and they always step up. Always. With them, everything is an experience—no matter how good or bad—that helps them improve. We have a saying… 'There's no such thing as failure, only steppingstones to success.' We spend a lot of time teaching them how to race. That gives them a sense of competition, they learn fast, and they learn how to be good winners and good losers."

"It sounds like you like being around kids. Are you married?"

"Nope. Tried it a few times. I guess I wasn't meant to be the marryin' kind. I had kids from my first marriage, but she moved away, kids and all. That was the end of that."

"Do you ever get to see them?"

"Oh, they moved a few hundred miles away. I went to see them a few times, but it was obvious the well was poisoned beyond redemption."

"That had to have been hard."

"I went through a resentment stage but got over it. I think it's sad. In an effort to punish me, she tainted *them* for life. I get my parental fix from the sailing school. But enough about me. What about you?"

"What about me?"

"Well, you know. You guys. How long have you been married?"

"We're not married," Quinney said. "Not yet. It's in the plan, but we haven't set a date."

"So, you're not married, eh?"

"Nope, not yet."

"You sure? You act and treat each other as if you've been married a long time."

"Is that good or bad?" Quinney asked.

"You seem to respect and like each other. That's an important trait to have in a relationship. I think that's what keeps marriages going."

"Whoa! You said you weren't the marrying type, yet you know what keeps marriages together. How do you explain *that*?" Quinney said.

Frank shrugged. "I don't know. Sometimes you learn what works by watching others, but you can't seem to get it working for yourself. So how did you guys meet?"

Quinney gave the background, including how Nelson had proposed on a beach in Monterey and lost the ring in the sand. They had dug around for fifteen minutes until they found it.

"How come you're not married yet?" Frank asked.

Nelson and Quinney looked at each other. Nelson gestured to Quinney to respond. "We haven't gotten around to it," she said. "Getting married is a ceremony. Marriage is about commitment and respect. We already have that. When the time comes to marry, we'll know."

"OK, I know *who* you are and how you guys met. I know nothing *about* you. Who is Quinney?" Frank asked, wriggling around the lazarette as if he were privy to deep, dark juicy secrets and was about to get an earful.

Quinney tapped her mouth in thought. "Hmm. Who's Quinney? What does she want you to know about her? Well, I think I'm outgoing, much more so than Nelson, who keeps a very low profile. I'm curious and I'm not afraid to ask questions. At times that makes me look like I'm sticking my nose in other people's business. I believe in justice and karma. What did I miss, Nelson?"

"She didn't mention that she speaks her mind. You'll always know where you stand with her. She's kind, forgiving, and deeply empathetic, but she gets mighty prickly if someone takes advantage of that."

The relaxed conversation about Quinney seemed to lessen the tension between Nelson and Frank.

"So, Nelson, tell me about *your* boat," Frank said. "Blake told me you have one."

As Nelson began describing his forty-foot sloop, Frank began hurling questions—about the kind of rigging it had, whether the foresail was a jib or genoa, whether the boat was fractionally rigged, the engine size, its fuel consumption, how large the fuel and water tanks were, whether he had an automatic identification system, the kind of GPS he had. Nelson gasped for air as he attempted to keep up with Frank's questions.

"What's its displacement?" continued Frank.

"Displacement?"

"Yeah, the boat's displacement. You know, Archimedes' principle—a body at rest in a fluid is acted upon by a force pushing upward called the buoyant force, which is equal to the weight of the fluid that the body displaces. When a boat is placed in the water, it displaces water… Displacement. Get it?"

"Yeah, I know what displacement *is*. I just don't know *what* the displacement tonnage is."

"Good God, Nelson. I can't believe that! Of all the questions I asked about your boat, you answered all of them except the most important one."

"You're saying that displacement is the most important?"

"Wow! You have no idea, do you? Do you know if your boat is even stable?"

"Excuse me?"

"You know, the swabs in my sailing academy learn this on the second day. You're a boat owner and don't know about stability? That doesn't give me much confidence in you. Displacement is a critical component of determining a boat's stability, and stability defines how well your boat rights itself when an external force, such as wind or the sea, ceases acting on it."

"Frank, you asked what the displacement was, not if I understood what it meant. There are a number of factors that determine stability, and displacement is only one of them. It sounds like you're reciting something out of the textbook."

"You'll learn pretty quick about stability if the wind knocks down your boat or a wave pushes it over. Stability determines how long it will take for her to right herself or if she will at all. I know from talking to Blake that you've been through most of the ASA sailing classes and have a drawer full of certificates and you own a fancy sailboat. I would think you'd at least know what stability and displacement are. I think—"

"Frank, I told you I know about displacement and boat stability. You're pontificating. Didn't you hear me? It sounds like we're having two conversations and you're not even listening…"

"I think I'll just call you 'swab' from here on. You don't deserve to own a boat."

Frank gave Nelson a dismissive hand gesture and turned away.

Nelson felt gut punched.

Quinney gave Nelson a sympathetic look. Nelson quietly went below. Moments later Quinney joined him. "That went well," Nelson said. "So much for getting to know one another. I was just beginning to like him."

"Don't let him get to you. He's a bully and you don't do well around his kind. You gotta shake it off. This is too small a boat to let a guy like him jerk you around."

"Did I do something to bring that on? What am I doing? Why have I become a target?"

"Well, he started it. You didn't do anything. You have things he doesn't. I think he's jealous."

"Jealous? Over what?"

"Two things. You own a boat, and you have me. He's jealous. Be a duck. Let the water roll off your back, 'cause he ain't gettin' either one. Look, if you spend your time sparring with Frank, you're gonna lose, and you'll be distracted from your tasks and duties. And then you'll have Blake to contend with, too. Let it go."

Nelson sat on the bunk as he stared through the bulkhead, trying to find answers.

"OK, I can see that you can't let it go," Quinney said. "Let's talk about it. How do you feel about what just happened up there?"

Nelson shook his head. "If someone has it out for me, I'd like to earn it. I've been searching my mind, looking for answers, but I'm drawing a blank. Like you just said, I have to let it go. Easier said than done, though. Frank came out of the woodwork swinging. Poof! All of a sudden he was there. Aggressive people like that don't care about win-win outcomes. He's a jungle fighter. They want to win at all costs, and if guys like me get in their way, we get trampled."

"You're beginning to sound like you're back in work mode. I asked how *you* felt."

Nelson nodded and cracked a half smile. "Well, I feel kicked in the stomach. I'm angry. I'm embarrassed. I feel defeated, but, you know, I bounce back quickly. All it takes is a short nap. People tend to like me, and when they don't, I feel like I've done something wrong. Like, you know, I sent the wrong message."

"What message? The one that said, 'I don't like the way you're being disrespectful?' You mean that message? Don't be upset with yourself because he's being a jerk. You know that if you did something wrong, I would be the first to tell you. And I saw nothing."

They got the "drowsies," their eyes becoming heavy with the gentle rocking of the boat. Quinney drifted off to sleep. Nelson decided the best way to deal with his frustration with Frank was to become engrossed in ship's duties. He was the navigator, and it could take up to an hour to record the ship's position, plot information on the chart, write in the log, and elaborate on his feelings and experiences in his personal journal. He looked up to see Frank coming below. *Is this to continue the bullying? There's no audience, Frank. What point is there without witnesses?* Nelson could feel the tension spreading through his body like a flash. First there were prickles on the back of his neck. He felt like a hot injection was working its way through his bloodstream down through his legs. His peripheral vision became obscured by a cloudy dark ring, and Frank became a partially blurred body. Nelson's heart raced. His focus shifted from his recordkeeping tasks to squaring off with Frank. *What's gotten into me? He's turning me into something I'm not. God! I teach people how to deal with situations like this. Why can't I listen to my own stuff?* He sat tall at the nav-station and glared at Frank. "My turn to wash the morning dishes," Frank said as he pointed to the galley sink.

Nelson exhaled and relaxed. He returned to his writing. Sweat rolled off his head and face and splatted onto his journal. In the tropical heat, the cabin had become a stifling sauna. It was difficult to focus. He looked to the cabin ceiling in search of prose when he noticed Frank taking an inordinate amount of time washing dishes. But he wasn't washing dishes. He swayed as he peered through the narrow space on the hinged side of Quinney's cabin door. Frank had discovered Quinney, and by shifting his body back and forth he could get a full view of her sleeping… without a top.

"Excuse me. What are you looking at?"

Frank, startled, stood stiff and tall as he quickly resumed his tasks. "Um. Nothing. Why?"

Nelson stood next to him and looked through the gap. "Frank, you Peeping Tom, haven't you seen a woman's breasts before?"

"Well, if she wants to show 'em off, I'll be glad to accommodate her."

"You're being rude and disrespectful."

Frank shrugged. "Rude and disrespectful? In what way?"

"I get it. You're the type of guy who tries to pick up girls in the bar by checking the size of their breasts before looking at their faces, right?"

"Your point?"

"You don't see how it's disrespectful to not give people their privacy—especially in close quarters?"

"On a boat, swab, there is no privacy. If you don't want me to see your wife's titties, or whoever she is to you, then she should keep 'em covered. Don't get on me for something that's not my responsibility."

Nelson looked down at the salon sole, attempting to disengage and cool down. He felt the heat spreading throughout his body and his emotional intelligence draining away. He looked into Frank's eyes as he took a step closer. "You know, Frank, I'm not sure what I dislike more about you—your attitude or your arrogance."

"Ask me if I care. Now, if you will excuse me, I need to go up to the cockpit."

Nelson took a deep breath and stepped aside. Frank gave him a smug look, daring Nelson. His superior attitude told him, *I have you beat, pal.*

I came here to learn and to face my fears, Nelson thought. *Now it seems like I'm getting practice in anger management. We gotta make a truce.*

"That guy's getting on my nerves, too," Quinney said as she stepped out of her cabin. "I heard all that. He's in full bully mode, and you've gotta punch him in the nose. Not literally, though. I have the urge to do that myself, and I'm not even a violent person. C'mon, I have an idea. Let's double-team him." She pushed Nelson up the companionway.

"Hey, Frank," Quinney said. "Stand here a moment. Right next to Nelson. Yeah, now stand up as straight as you can—both of you." She stood back and looked at the two. "What do you call Nelson?"

Frank pointed and chuckled. "Him? Why, he's the swab. Where are you taking this?"

Quinney took a step toward Frank. "Does that make you feel bigger—calling him a swab? Does it make you taller, superior, more significant? Well, you're no taller. In fact, you're the small one. I see you as being inferior and insignificant, so why don't you knock it off and quit being a bully? I thought you were doing pretty well in our conversation. I was beginning to like you, but then you had to undo it all."

Frank scoffed and sat down.

Blake stood from behind the wheel. "Quinney, take the helm, please." Blake sat next to Frank and motioned Nelson to sit. "Guys, we've got to take this down a notch. I don't know what it is between you two, but your conduct needs to change. If you want to hate each other, that's fine with me, but the tension between you is making this boat unhappy, and we need a happy boat."

Frank humbly put his hand to his chest. "No tensions here. I'm fine."

"I'm not taking sides," Blake said to him, "but I spent four days with this guy before you came aboard. And I saw an immediate change in him when you stepped onto the boat, so don't tell me you have no tensions. Look, we missed our weather window and we're heading into some rough weather in a few days. This boat will need all three of us when the storms hit. I worry that we're going to be in trouble unless we come together as a team. Can I have your word that neither of you will contribute to making things worse?"

Frank leaned over to Nelson and extended his hand. "I was kidding about calling you a swab. I was just having a little fun."

Nelson hesitated momentarily, then took Frank's handshake. He held on firmly for a long moment and looked Frank in the eye. "Fun? Maybe for you. Knock it off, and we'll be OK."

"All right, then," said Quinney. "Now that we've cleared that up, I know it's stifling hot below, but I need to freshen up and give myself a spa hour. If you'll excuse me, gentlemen."

* * *

In a matter of a few hours, the sea rose to four feet. That doesn't feel like much in the cockpit, but it's enough to make a soul queasy down below. Easier to lose balance and trip over something not stowed away. Nelson watched barefoot Frank head up to the mast and back. He seemed to have suction cups on his feet. He never lost his balance and seemed unaffected by the boat's movements. He seemed fearless—as though he never gave a thought to the sea conditions when a task required him to go forward or lean over the side. Frank knew his way around boats.

Quinney was adventurous and a risk taker, but not to the point of pushing the limits. Under Nelson's tutelage, she respected the rules of boat safety. While there were numerous "first rules of sailing," the real first rule was to protect oneself. While in blue water, a PFD and a safety harness were mandatory. She wore one. Nelson wore one. Neither Blake nor Frank wore one. And Quinney found that bothersome. She had "mother hen" traits with an appetite for protecting all those around her.

Frank took a step to head back to the mast. "Where are you going?" Quinney asked.

"Do I look like I have to account to you?"

"You're not wearing a PFD."

"So?"

"I thought that was a given out here."

"I guess not," Frank said as he continued to head forward.

"Don't you teach safety at that sailing school? I'm sure none of those kids get on a boat without a PFD. I'll bet you hammer safety into their heads, but I'm looking at a commodore who ignores the safety rules you force on others. How do you explain that?"

"You're pushing it, lady. Besides, I had only an hour to get to the plane for BVI and didn't grab it."

Quinney took hers off and offered it to Frank. He snatched it in defiant compliance. "You don't leave much room, do you? I'm wearing this for you."

"Well, Frank, I worry about you."

"That's why God made women… so someone can do the worrying," and Frank went forward wearing Quinney's PFD.

"Frank," Quinney yelled with cupped hands around her mouth. "It doesn't do any good unless you fasten it." She mimicked fastening a seat belt on an airplane.

She watched Frank until he fastened the PFD, then smiled and waved. He didn't smile or wave back.

Blake sat at the helm watching the exchange between the two. "If someone's stupid enough to go forward without a harness in heavy weather, no one should prevent them from dying out there."

When Frank returned to the cockpit, the PFD was not fastened. He scowled at Quinney. "Have you ever thought about minding your own business?" He wore the PFD for the rest of the day, allowing it to dangle open in blatant defiance.

NO SURVIVAL PLAN

Quinney sat with Nelson on his afternoon watch. The sea was steady with consistent four-foot swells. For Nelson, it was time for a visit to the head. Quinney took the helm. Nelson went below where Blake and Frank sat at the salon table. Their faces were somber as they stared at an emergency position-indicating radio beacon, EPIRB, and four personal locator beacons, PLB, on the table. The EPIRB was the size of a milk carton, and the PLBs were about the size of a handheld radio.

"You found them!" Nelson said. "I don't have an EPIRB on my boat. This is the first time I've seen one up close. How do these things work, Frank?"

"These are designed to float and have a transmitter that sends a beacon to a satellite. EPIRBs and PLBs are registered. When activated by water or manually, those who monitor beacons know the boat and contact information. The smaller PLBs do the same thing and are easier to attach to yourself than the larger EPIRB."

"Where did you find them?"

Frank pointed to the stuffed junk drawers and cabinets. "I went on a scavenger hunt. They're mandatory by Coast Guard regulations, so I knew they would be around here somewhere. They should be mounted in the cockpit or on the mast. They don't do much good stuffed in the back of a cabinet."

"Can they transmit underwater?" Nelson asked.

"They're water activated between one and four meters," Frank said. "How far underwater they have to be before they can't transmit, I don't know. These are designed to float, so the owner should have mounted them where they can be reached quickly and can float without obstruction."

"So, if we have an emergency and, for instance, the boat turns over. If we can't communicate our lat/lon coordinates and don't have a working EPIRB, we're screwed?"

"If you don't have a working PLB, you are," Frank said.

"We should leave those out, right?" Nelson said, pointing to the devices.

"Won't do any good," Blake said.

Nelson gave Blake a blank look.

"Batteries are dead. All of them," Frank said.

"How do you know that?"

Frank picked up the EPIRB. "Look here. I'll show you. First, pull out the antenna, push down the 'test' button, and hold it for one second. See this indicator on the side? The red LED is supposed to come on to indicate I initiated a test. Do you see a red flash? No, because there is no flash. The battery is as dead as dead can be. Same with the PLBs. All of them."

"This could be bad," Nelson said.

Blake said, "People put more faith in EPIRBs than they deserve. They think that if they get in trouble, they can just activate the EPIRB, sit back, and wait for the Coast Guard. If you're cruising up and down the West Coast like you do in your boat, you're within radio shouting distance of the Coast Guard and other boats. Out here, we're past the USCG radio range. EPIRBs are just one part of the emergency communication plan. If we had a working EPIRB, it would send the beacon, someone who monitors activity would initiate a search and rescue, and eventually the cavalry would arrive. We could be floating around in the safety raft for two or three days before any rescue effort reached us. Most likely we'd be found by a passing tanker or freighter first. Some debate the value of having an

EPIRB at all, but it's comforting to know a signal is being sent right next to where you are. Ultimately, though, rescue begins with self."

"Is that cord to tether the EPIRB to the boat or life raft?"

"Yeah, but when you consider how fast things go south when losing a boat, there's little or no time to be looking around for an EPIRB," Blake said. "There should be a PLB in the life raft ditch bag."

"Do we know if we even have a ditch bag?" Frank asked.

"Back in BVI, Chaulee pointed to the lazarette and said there's one in there," Nelson replied.

"We should dig it out just to make sure," Blake said. "Nelson, something for you to do tomorrow."

Nelson returned to the cockpit and related the news to Quinney. "Are we in trouble?" she asked.

"No, but remember back in BVI our feelings when we first saw the condition of this boat? It made me wonder if it was ready for the sea. I trust Blake, and if he said she was seaworthy and ready, I'm ready. My confidence in Frank is increasing in spite of my personal issues with him."

* * *

Nelson adjusted his PFD and readied his harness to attach to the lifeline. "Blake, permission to go forward to inspect the sail package. It looks like it shifted. I want to make sure it's still secure."

Blake stretched his neck and looked forward. "Go ahead."

Nelson went forward. His movements anticipated the shifting boat in the changing sea. He felt sure-footed as he kept his balance. He held the rigging and stood tall with the wind in his face. While maneuvering his way around the bow, he no longer resembled a drunk stumbling through an alley. He had found his sea legs. It was time to quit taking seasickness pills.

He inspected the lines that held their hitchhiker sail to the deck. The port lines were taut, while those on the starboard side had slackened. The load had shifted. His checkup effort would not be in vain. He loosened all securing lines except one—the "just in case" line—just in case the package decided to suddenly shift and slide overboard. The sail was like a dead body—heavy and limp. There were no grab straps. The sail was not about to budge with only one person attempting to move it. Nelson was able to get a line under a corner and use leverage by wrapping it around a cleat. With great effort he centered the sail, and it was ready to be secured. He felt Frank's scrutinizing eyes from where he sat back in the cockpit. He seemed to be hoping that Nelson would falter and do something worthy of a spiteful corrective comment. When done, Nelson inspected his work, double-checking to make sure no working lines were blocked. *That sucker ain't going nowhere!*

Nelson leaned against the mast. He felt a difference in himself. He was more confident in how he moved about and how well he could perform an assigned task. He felt as if he were a contributor. He was *not* a swab.

The boat sailed smoothly through the swells. *Momentum* was happy. And, per Blake, if the boat was happy, they shouldn't have any worries. And yet…

Extracted from Nelson's personal journal—April 21, 2010

Our first glimpse of Momentum *told me she was unfit for sea duty. She's a scow. Blake said she's a fine ship. I believed him. Somewhere on this boat there may be a ditch bag. We have no emergency communication plan. There's no survival plan.*

PEE IN MY FOULIES

Blake stood and looked toward the northwest. "Feel that?"

"Yep. Winds are shifting," Frank said.

"Yesterday we had a good easterly. Now it's coming from where we want to go. I think we should start the motor and tack to starboard; otherwise we'll be luffing the sails all night and have to change our heading to east or southeast. The starboard tack is the favored tack. Nelson, go forward and prepare the running backstays. You do remember what to do, right?"

"Yes, sir."

Nelson went to the mast, partially untied the block, and waited for Blake's command. Blake and Frank worked like a well-oiled team without speaking about what needed to be done. He watched the two work together as if they had been a team for years.

"Let loose!" Nelson untied the last of the knot and freed the port running backstay. The boat made a slow turn—the boom swung to starboard. Blake winched in the port backstay. The sail filled with air. Nelson secured the starboard backstay. For the less experienced Nelson, handling the running backstay during a tack was complicated and nerve-racking—especially when his movements had to sync up with Blake's. The absence of comments was good feedback. Blake ordered the sails to be taken down to third reef, which would depower the boat and expose only one-third of the sail to the wind.

"Nelson, you'll stay on this course while on your watch," Blake said. "We didn't keep a port tack because if the wind shifted and strengthened, we'd be forced to sail southwest, and that's not our direction—not the favored tack."

Nelson went below, made a log entry, and to save time at the beginning of his next watch, donned his foulies. It can take up to fifteen minutes to completely outfit for weather. Twice that time when fatigued. While no weather was expected, the cooler climate would leave the deck cold and wet. And what if a squall hit while he was on watch? He was off watch until 0300 hours, which gave him a good six hours of sack time.

* * *

SHIP'S LOG—APRIL 22, 2010—0300 HOURS—22° 46′52″N, 066° 55′62″W

Nelson's alarm rang at 0245 hours, giving him enough time to freshen up, make log entries, and be in the cockpit before the end of Frank's watch. The turnover was simple—nothing to report, all systems working. Frank stopped in the companionway and turned. "Oh, you might want to keep a watch for that squall."

Momentum was on a 3-5-0-degree course, the favored tack set earlier by Blake. It was east of the 3-4-5-degree course Nelson plotted on the chart. Nelson balked. When taking navigation classes, Nelson had learned the discipline of order, preparedness, and sticking to a plan. His instructor, a Naval officer from the aircraft carrier, SS Enterprise, was emphatic. "When the captain sets the course, you stay the course. Period." Nelson kept an eye on the compass like a soaring eagle on a field mouse. The five-degree difference consumed him, but he knew that altering the course would be mutinous. And unpardonable. His mental melee yanked him from left to right. He had an almost uncontrollable urge to squeeze *Momentum* back five degrees to the plotted course, but Blake was captain, and the boat was not the eleven-hundred-foot naval vessel. He took a deep breath and thought it through. *I have no business challenging the captain. He said 3-5-0 so 3-5-0 it must be. Let it go. The heading I set in the chart is a guideline, not a mandate.*

Every ten minutes Nelson stood, stretched, and stepped around the helm. He gazed out into the darkness, looking for tankers, freighters, and beasts that created fearful illusions of impending danger. The wind speed increased, and the boat heeled over as the sails responded. A faint flash of light caught the corner of his eye. He fixed his eyes on the direction from which it had come. Another flash came and lit up the clouds. And then another and another. Tension impaired his reasoning. He thought about trying to outrun the storm and cross in front of it. He gave thought to turning downwind, hoping to evade a collision with it. He could beckon the captain, but the captain probably already knew the situation and was standing back to see if Nelson was a seaman or truly a swab.

Flashes of lightning occurred with greater frequency and intensity. He could see a gray line where the squall and sea met—the storm was nearby. The rumble of thunder became audible. It was closing in on him. He took a deep breath to stop running in mental circles. He fought the craving to panic. Blake had taught him to veer behind a squall where the weather front was weaker or slow the boat down and allow the storm to pass in front of him. Turning behind the squall required tacking—an untenable option without help. Sailing close to the wind to the point of luffing would definitely slow the boat down, but if the boat lingered in the boat's no-sail zone, she would stall and be blown backward out of control. Winds constantly shifted, and that posed a high risk of stalling when sailing so close to the wind.

The squall intensified. Whitecaps formed, hitting the side of the boat with a *thump*, pushing her toward a collision course with the squall. Rain began. A few splats at first. Then more. Nelson needed to slow down before his situation became dire. A heeling boat is a sure sign that enough air remains in the sails to keep the boat from stalling. *Keep the boat heeled. Don't let the boat come up straight! If it does, steer away.* He had to accurately read the wind—anticipating gusts and wind shifts. Rain pounded his vision and flattened the sea. Water poured down his neck. His mouth remained cotton dry. His heart raced. His breathing quickened. His only reference to the squall was wind, rain, lightning. Nelson could not determine whether it would intensify or if it had already peaked.

He played Russian roulette with the wind—constantly sailing close to it while flirting with the no-sail zone that could put his boat "in irons" and stall. His attempt to slow down the boat only fueled his panic. The wind intensified. Jabbing lightning had yet to cross the bow, a sign that Nelson had not slowed sufficiently to sidestep the storm.

Everything I do is wrong. I'm not the first sailor looking down the throat of a storm. What am I missing? Why can't I slow this boat down?

Talking to himself didn't help. It was like he had slashed a blood vessel and no matter what he did, the bleeding continued.

Go ahead… panic. If you do, your decisions will do more harm than if you did nothing at all. What am I missing? What am I missing?… Argh! Stupid me! Spill the air from the sail. Ease the sheet, you idiot! Set it as far out as you can.

He steered away from the wind; the luffing stopped. But the boat picked up speed, which began pushing him faster to the front of the storm. He eased the sheet, spilling most of the wind from the sail. The boat sat almost straight up, and she slowed. Lightning stabbed the water, and the sound of thunder was more pronounced. The storm moved across his bow.

Phew!

With that problem out of the way, Nelson felt he could handle anything else related to squalls. Twenty minutes passed, the rain let up, and whitecaps returned. The clouds broke, revealing the sparkling heavens. Nelson saw movement belowdecks. It was the silhouette of Blake backlit by his flashlight. *He stayed below. He could have come up and taken over or told me what to do, but he stayed down there. I must have done something right.*

With the clothing inside his foulies as wet as if he hadn't worn them at all, Nelson couldn't be more uncomfortable. Water had collected in his boots. It sloshed and squished when he moved around. Rainwater on the mast, sails, and rigging continued to drip down on him, but it was welcome. The squall had passed. And Nelson had done it alone.

* * *

Entry from Nelson's personal journal—April 22, 2010

Survived first solo squall at night. Blake moving about below. I think he was watching to make sure I didn't do something stupid. Had to pee badly but could not leave the cockpit, and getting at privates hard with layers and layers of clothing, my foulies, my PFD. Had a terrible urge to panic but talked myself out of it second by second. Would have lost respect from Blake. So relieved when I saw lightning flashes passing in front of the boat. Am I still afraid? I think I peed in my foulies. I must have. The urge passed. Oh, God.

WEATHER WINDOW LOST

SHIP'S LOG—APRIL 23, 2010—1345 HOURS—025° 52′69″N, 068° 00′77″W

A sailboat must sail "off the wind," to the left or right of it. When the wind comes from the left of the boat, it's a port tack. From the right, it's a starboard tack. The "favored tack" is one that creates the shortest distance to the destination. For the past few days, the favored tack had pushed *Momentum* one hundred miles east of Nelson's charted course, and farther away from it each minute. Nelson, who had learned navigation in tight places, fidgeted. "Nelson, settle down," Blake said sternly. "Why do you get so edgy when we don't stay exactly on course?"

"In my coastal cruising sailing class we had to stay on course for the entire one hundred miles to pass. We were constantly adjusting for current and wind."

"That was a training exercise. This isn't. In blue water you sail to the wind, not to compass," Blake said. "When sailing close to shore you sail to compass. We're hundreds of miles away from a coastline. We want to get the most we can out of this wind, so sailing to wind is more important. And since you're our navigator, can you tell me how many miles we've come?"

"By my calculations, *Momentum* has sailed four hundred forty-three nautical miles since we began." Nelson was pleased with his math.

"Did you just say four hundred forty-three nautical miles?" Blake asked.

"Yes, that's right. Is there something wrong?"

"Is something wrong? I'll say. When we planned this crossing, we estimated *Momentum* would sail around a hundred and sixty miles each twenty-four hours. That works out to a speed over ground at seven to eight knots, which this vessel is easily capable of doing. Go below and check your numbers, and be quick about it. I want to know how many more days it will take to get to port at the average speed we've been going. Get on it."

Nelson knew his numbers had to be accurate to withstand Blake's scrutiny. Quinney joined Nelson at the nav-station. "It's important that you get this right, yes?"

Nelson sighed deeply. "Yeah. Very."

"I don't know anything about what you're about to do, but I'll check your math when you're done, OK?" Quinney squeezed Nelson's shoulder for reassurance.

"I know you don't understand what I'm doing, but I'm going to talk it through as we go. It'll slow me down and help make sure I don't make a mistake. I gotta keep it simple. I'm using one hundred twenty-five nautical miles traveled per day. That's been our average so far. I got that by dividing nautical miles over land by how long we've been out—four days. We have nine-hundred-plus miles to go. We'll reach port in seven and a half days. Blake wants a number more like four to five. He's gonna blow a gasket when he hears these numbers. Let's go over this again."

Quinney watched closely as Nelson scribbled and talked. "Something's wrong," he said. "Now I get nine more days to port. What am I doing wrong?"

Quinney looked over the numbers. "Take a deep breath. Slow down. Your math looks good, but wait… Where'd *this* number come from?"

"Miles left."

"Here you show one thousand, six hundred and thirty, and on

this one you show one thousand, four hundred and sixteen. What do these numbers mean?"

"That's total passage miles. Ah! I see my error. This is nautical miles and that's land miles. You can get the same answer using either, but you can't use both nautical and land miles in the same calculation. Let's run it again."

*   *   *

Blake lifted one eyebrow and impatiently motioned with his hands for Nelson to give him the numbers. Nelson had no pleasing news—he stood tall and cleared his throat. "We'll make port in another seven and a half days. Two days more than you originally planned."

Blake looked at him without expression. "Show me," he said calmly.

"Uh, show you what?"

"Your calculations. What do you think we're talking about?"

Nelson went over his math. Blake challenged the numbers, asking if he hadn't crossed nautical with land miles or misrepresented the boat's speed over land. Nelson handed Blake his notes and stood back. Blake held the paper in one hand and pointed to the figures with the other. He pursed his lips and nodded as he noodled the numbers.

"You know, this doesn't account for adding time for hoving-to or trying to outrun squalls."

Nelson looked at Blake apologetically. "I know," he said softly while looking down.

"We left four days late." Blake shook the paper at Nelson and raised his voice. "And with this we will have missed our weather window by six days. Six days! That's almost a week! We may as well have no weather window at all. No telling what we're gonna run into."

Blake's arms fell to his sides. He said nothing as he looked around and then back at the numbers. "This isn't your fault. I need to get ahold of the meteorologist to find out where that front is and where it's heading." Impatience returned to his voice. "In all my days on the Atlantic, this is the worst wind for sailing I've ever known. The absolute worst. And I have never sailed outside the weather window. This is downright dangerous! We have no idea what we're getting into."

Blake looked astern and out to sea. He continued his tirade-to-self with low-volume mumbling—cursing the condition of the boat, the lack of Chaulee's sense of urgency with having it ready, their inability to repair the autopilot, a normally predictable strong easterly wind turned unreliable and fickle, and growing concerns about depleting their fuel supply.

Blake took a deep breath and sighed. "It is what it is. This isn't an urgent matter today, so I have some time to think on it."

"We can always head over to the Stream and catch the current," Frank said.

"What? The Stream is six hundred miles away. It'll take four days just to reach it, and all we'll get from it is a northbound push of a few knots."

"Well, we don't have to sail straight for it. We can head northwest and catch it higher up."

"Listen to me, Frank! We're not going over to the Stream. Especially not with a storm heading down from Canada." Blake checked his watch. "It's 1530 hours. I need to call the meteorologist. Nelson, take the helm until I finish my call. I'll take watch until 1900 hours. Then Frank, you take it to 2300 hours, and Nelson, you're up next until 0300."

* * *

Blake's call ended and he returned to the helm. Nelson went below. Quinney stayed on deck and slid over the lazarette to get closer to Blake.

A breeze snapped at the sail. *Momentum* responded. She sailed on a port tack that quickly pulled her bow toward Nelson's plotted course. She heeled over twenty degrees and sped up to seven knots.

"Do you think it will last?" Quinney asked.

Blake grunted. "There's no telling what it will do. If it continues, we'll shut down the engine. It could be Mother Nature just tossing us a bone."

"What did the meteorologist say?"

Blake hesitated and momentarily looked away from Quinney. "You know, there's something I've been meaning to ask you, but we've never really had an opportunity to talk. You put some interesting responses in your sailing application, and I never learned what prompted you to sign up. What was it?"

"You really want to know?"

"Yeah, I think you have an interesting story to tell. I'd like to hear it."

"This was something I'd wanted to do all my life. I thought it would be exciting to be crew on a boat. Not a cruise ship but something smaller, more like *Momentum*. Nothing spelled adventure for me more than that. I got busy with my life and that idea went to the back burner. My father came down with cancer when I was in my early twenties. It changed him. He was constantly in pain, which made daily life almost unbearable. His cancer was inoperable. My parents spent their entire lives working and raising a family. Neither had ever left the United States, so they started traveling, making new memories to salvage what time he had left. After he died, Mom kept traveling. And it was the best lesson in life my parents could've taught me: Don't wait… Live life to its fullest *now*. I made a mental bucket list of everything I wanted to do. I started scuba diving and sky diving, and went camping up and down Baja, Mexico. Crewing on a boat was on the list, but the opportunity didn't come until this passage. So here I am."

Blake sat listening and nodding. "There's a lot to you. You have no watch duty. What do you do during the day?"

"I don't know if any of you have noticed how clean it looks below. I would appreciate a little gratitude from time to time. I don't think you guys know how to make a good meal. Without me, I think you all would be eating moldy bagels the entire way. I don't mind cooking. I just don't want to do it all the time. People like Frank, who don't have a high regard for women, probably think that a woman's job is to clean and cook. And he'd take advantage of that if I let him. I know it's easy for a person to become grungy pretty fast on a boat. I spend time trying to look my best. It takes a lot of effort to do that. I take care of personal hygiene, washing my hair, keeping my fingernails looking like they belong to a lady. You know, things like that. It might all be a losing battle, but at least I try. You never told me what the meteorologist said."

"Huh? Oh, that." Blake shrugged. "It was just a conversation about weather. Nothing more."

Quinney excused herself and headed down the companionway. *Twice he avoided my question about what the meteorologist said. What's he hiding?*

The wind remained consistent, and the seas grew to four feet. *Momentum* was, once again, happy.

*   *   *

There was no moon, not even a sliver. The night was chilly, dark, damp. Frank's turnover at 2300 hours to Nelson was terse, with nothing to report. Any oddity would be Nelson's to discover. The cloudless sky gave the sense of enormity that seemed to diminish the claustrophobic feeling of smallness. In his attempts to gain Blake's respect and step beyond being a swab to Frank, Nelson knew he could not share his lingering fear of night sailing with anyone except Quinney.

Nelson's watch was nearly over. Blake came to the cockpit at 0250 hours. He looked around the horizon, up the mast, and then at Nelson. "Anything?" he asked.

"We're flying at a little more than seven knots. We're on a 3-4-5 heading. Battery indicators are OK. I sailed without autopilot for about thirty minutes."

"Humph. Why'd you do that?"

"I get a good feel for how the boat responds to the water and the wind."

"Keep that up and you might become a sailor after all. I'll take over from here."

Nelson went below, updated the ship's log, and opened his journal. He wiggled his pen as he searched for something to write.

Entry from Nelson's personal journal—April 24, 2010

It's three o'clock in the morning. Very quiet. Boat rocking but no queasiness. I have a disquieting sense of aloneness. Why am I uneasy about it? This hasn't been the adventure I thought it would be. Something feels different. What? Blake called the meteorologist but didn't share what was said. What's he hiding? Blake is not being Blake. Makes me nervous. Frank sits and watches. He shows no feeling for anything. He's a shark looking for opportunity. Temps dropping as we get into northern latitudes. Sack time. Nelson... out.

MAL DE MER

Sailing magazines and brochures lure dreamers to boat ownership with photos of lovers strolling on secluded beaches or sipping wine while watching the sunset. Handsome silver-haired men looking sailor-like in bright white shirts with rolled-up sleeves helm their sailboats in a brisk wind. Attentive women look fashionable and fit and sit nearby sipping iced tea. It's a lie. All of it.

On any passage, all mariners, regardless of gender and age, eventually begin to smell like dead fish and wet chickens. Their clothing is tired, torn, chafed, holey, bleached, stained. Tall seas test the constitution and the stomach of even the saltiest of old salts. There is no sleeping—only dozing in short bursts and always with a vigilant ear to a changing sea or shifting wind. The body becomes sensitive to any changes in boat behavior, how it moves, flows, resists. Sometimes foulies do a better job of gathering water than repelling it. While on watch, there's no leaving the helm for the comfort of a damp, cold bunk. There is no happiness on a sailboat. Only the boat can be happy.

An offshore sailing expedition can unravel a mariner. Days can come and go and soon blend into weeks. Days can become a blur, and one can lose track of time and all things. Sailboats are confining. Space is tight. Privacy is nonexistent. There are no secrets. Personalities tend to collide and grind on one's patience. Sailors eat, sleep, spend four-hour shifts at the helm, and perform routine chores, and they do it around the clock, day after day. They are perpetually tired, perpetually wet, perpetually cold. Remaining alert becomes a trial. They sail in the cold, in the rain, and get blasted by razor-sharp water blown sideways by stiff breezes.

Then there's mal de mer—seasickness—the worst kind of curse. It occurs when there is a conflict in the inner ear where the human balance mechanism resides. Resolve the conflict and seasickness vanishes. Seasick remedies exist in all forms. A remedy, however, is something that corrects an evil. Ginger, medicines, and apples are common preventive measures but less effective as remedies. Most describe seasickness as nausea, vomiting, gagging, retching, and sweating. In reality, it's worse—much worse.

Seasickness turns the body inside out. Victims pray for a death that fails to come. It's a syndrome that can send the body into a hard-to-reverse downward spiral. A churned-up stomach does not want to be fed—food or water, even though those are effective combatants. Dehydration, common with seasickness, is the true enemy of reason and mental clarity. A mariner riding out sea swells in the cockpit can be fooled into thinking he has conquered his susceptibility to seasickness until he goes into the confines of the galley to make a sandwich or to visit the head.

Why do sailors go to sea? What drives them to put themselves through Mother Nature's most grueling and death-defying trials that leave them spent and thoroughly humbled, only to return home, look out to sea, and say, "Let's do that again?"

A mariner's prize is an addictive independence. Sailing feeds an insatiable sense of adventure, builds confidence and self-reliance, and bonds man with his inner self. An inexplicable exhilaration comes with using God-given resources to plot a course and arrive safely at an intended destination, or being allowed to live, or to punch through one's most horrifying of personal fears.

* * *

Nelson sat at the helm, battling the urge to purge. He swayed from left to right with each motion of the boat—decidedly not in control of his body. His eyes glazed over as if recovering from a hearty party the night before. He was expressionless. All he wanted was to complete his watch and find a place on the boat where he could be left alone to moan or, better yet, die quietly.

Quinney awoke, stretched, and stepped out of her cabin to welcome a new day with new adventure and opportunity. She seemed immune to the malady. She stepped into the salon just in time to witness Blake, in the forward head, puking whatever was left in his stomach, and he continued puking after there was nothing left to puke.

Frank sat in the salon with his elbows on the table, holding his head. He momentarily looked up to Quinney and then resumed his blank stare at the table. For once, lecherous Frank had no interest in her.

Quinney joined Nelson at the helm. Their moods did not blend well. She was chipper, chatty, and pleasant. He wanted her to go away so he could silently resume his prayer for death.

"You look terrible. Are you OK?"

"No-o-o."

"Are you seasick?"

"Yes-s-s."

"Did you throw up?"

"No-o-o."

"Do you want to throw up?"

"Yes-s-s."

"Can I get you something?"

"Yes-s-s, something to harm myself and end this misery."

"Have you had this long? Seasickness, I mean."

"Yes-s-s."

"Since you've been on watch?"

"Yes-s-s."

"Are you taking seasickness pills?"

"I am now-w-w."

"Are they helping?"

Nelson looked at Quinney with a scowl. His eyes growled. He murmured something about Quinney's question being dumb.

"I take it you're not in a talkative mood. I'll just sit over here and enjoy this beautiful day."

"Wait," moaned Nelson. "How is it that we're all dying or wishing we were dead and you're bubbly and bouncing around?"

"I'm the smart one. I never quit taking the seasickness pills."

* * *

Momentum continued her journey with brisk northwesterly winds. She sailed in the groove while rolling and pitching with the sea swells. Every now and then the sail snapped in the wind and there was the sound of water splashing as a whitecap broke near the boat. Even with the calming effect of fresh air and the sea, seasickness prevailed.

* * *

Nelson's shift was close to ending. Blake stepped out to the cockpit. He was almost as talkative as Nelson, who stood to relinquish the helm as Blake slid behind the wheel. "Anything?" Blake asked.

"Nope."

That was the turnover.

"I did see two sunrises this morning and two green flashes," Nelson added.

To Blake, Nelson had gone over the edge. Seasickness had taken him to the dark side. "Oh?" Blake said.

"Yeah, I watched the sunrise and saw the green flash. Then the boat went into a trough and the sun vanished behind a wave. When we came high, the sun came up again with another green flash."

"Interesting."

Nelson went below. He found a dried bagel rolling around the galley floor. He snapped it in half and took a bite. Quinney's voice was in his head. *Eat.* It was the first introduction of food into his body in twenty-four hours. The dry bagel was tasteless. There was no spit left to moisten it and no energy to try. The boat bounced around too much for anyone to prepare food, and no one knew whose turn it was to cook. After two hundred chomps and coaxing his throat, the bagel bite slowly worked its way down. His stomach was not pleased. The "kicked-in" feeling returned, but his stomach did not act like it was going to reject the morsel. He decided he was full and didn't need to eat any more. He placed the uneaten part of the bagel in the rim of a hat hanging on the cabin door, where it remained for a few days.

Without removing any clothing, including his foulies, Nelson crawled into the bunk. The heeling of the boat quickly rolled him downhill. He drifted off to sleep—half of his body in the bunk and half against the wall of the cabin with Quinney stuck beneath him.

* * *

The wave size increased to six feet by midafternoon. The crew's seasickness had gone beyond projectile vomiting. It came in the form of extreme fatigue, dehydration, and lost appetite. They knew eating and drinking water was salvation, but when food revolts the body, it becomes difficult to reverse the effects brought by seasickness. Lying flat with one's eyes closed was the best way to combat it. Even with its debilitation, the crew had to muster the will and strength to carry on with the ship's duties and hope emergencies didn't add to their problems.

* * *

Quinney became irritated with a banging noise coming from the head. *Bang! Crash! Bang! Crash!* She commanded Nelson to investigate. The medicine cabinet in the head was not closed securely.

Nelson returned to his bunk. *Bang! Crash! Bang!* Nelson closed it again. *Bang! Crash!* The problem was not to be resolved by playing with the weak latch on the medicine cabinet. Nelson gave up—it was only a mirror. Quinney pictured airborne glass and persisted, but Nelson didn't care and gave her a blank look. He became deaf to annoying noises. Boats being battered around in tall seas have omnipresent noises—stop one and another takes over. *Bang! Crash! Bang! Crash!* Quinney's voice grew stern. Nelson was having an out-of-body experience but responded, "Talk away, lady. I can't move anymore, and I don't care."

Quinney's frustration soared. "That noise is glass banging on glass. Am I the only one on this boat who finds something wrong with flying glass?"

"Probably," mumbled Nelson.

"I guess I'll just have to fix it myself."

"Yes-s-s. I suppose so."

Frank staggered past the cabin's doorway. Quinney nabbed him. He fixed the problem with string—a temporary repair. The banging in the head stopped, but then they could hear other noises.

* * *

Almost everything becomes more challenging on boats during high seas. In a heeled over boat, bulkheads are not vertical, and soles are not horizontal. Walking, eating, charting, cooking, cleaning… all can be challenging and energy draining for the sailor trying to maintain a balance. All things on flat tables attempt to dramatically slide toward gravity. Rubber grips on dishware offer no protection. Unlatched drawers or cabinets can spray their contents to all corners of a cabin or galley in seconds. Peeing, however, presents its own special challenges.

Women sometimes lament that, unlike men, they cannot conveniently stand while peeing. Women have the advantage in terms of both stability and aim. The head (toilet) is in a compartment roughly the size of a telephone booth. When *Momentum* heeled over hard, Quinney was able to pee without losing her balance by sitting on the head with her feet propped against the angled bulkhead. The men faced a greater challenge by the very nature of standing. They had to have stability, free hands to take care of business, and an accurate aim that became exponentially difficult when layered in clothing and foulies.

Nelson had an engineering mind and figured it out. He put his solution to the test. He wedged each foot on the leeward (downhill) corners of the head. His forehead provided a third pressure point as it pressed against the mirror on the windward (uphill) side. His hands were free to conduct business. Nelson felt confident that no matter which way the boat pitched or yawed, he would not miss the target. He then spent ten minutes navigating through numerous layers of clothing and foulies to get to his plumbing. Theoretically, his maneuver was workable, but he overlooked the laws of gravity. Nelson felt vertical, which would be normal given the orientation over everything in his space, but the boat was heeled over at a fifteen-degree angle. Nelson was perplexed to see pee take a sharp turn between his legs while the bowl was directly beneath him. This was one of the many reasons why sailing and happiness are not synonymous.

* * *

Quinney sat with Nelson on his watch. The sun had set, and clouds hovered over the horizon. The end-of-the-day light was quickly turning to darkness. Nelson spotted a "blip" on the automatic identification system. A nearby ship passed behind him. With binoculars, he could see the freighter and could confirm by the AIS its name, the type of ship, its heading, and its final destination. A few minutes later he looked at it again. Another five minutes and another look.

"What the...," Nelson said with the binoculars fixed on the freighter. "It's on fire!"

Quinney looked and confirmed that red flames were coming through clouds of smoke.

Flames had fully engulfed the freighter. The sight was almost beautiful with its red colors and contrasting clouds. "We gotta tell Blake!" Nelson said. "We gotta turn around and help. Quick! Go wake the captain!"

Quinney went below and found Frank sitting at the salon table. "Come quick! There's a freighter on fire!" She raced back to the helm.

Frank came partway up the companionway and stretched his neck to see the burning freighter. "Nice moonrise."

Nelson looked back at the conflagration. The freighter continued its southerly route, and the moonrise, which out on the open sea can look like a glorious sunset, peered out from puffy clouds on the horizon.

"It looked like a fire," Nelson said, with humble pie dripping down his head.

"I think you still have some delirium from being seasick," Frank said as he retreated back into the salon.

* * *

Night watches continued to plague Nelson with marauding squalls, burning freighters, imaginary breaching whales, and containers bobbing inches above the water directly in front of the boat. With the haunting darkness came spectacular beauty with the wonder of the bigness in the endless heaven. The Milky Way looked more like a cloud than trillions of stars.

Nelson enjoyed Quinney's companionship, especially when his watches began before nightfall. There was comfort in facing the unknown while in the company of his companion.

Momentum glided on the waves, rocking from port to starboard. When she rolled into the oncoming sea, she pushed water out of the way with a distinctive *swoosh* that told Nelson the boat was performing well, and they were riding in the "groove." With exposure to night watches came diminished fear and increased confidence that nothing bad would happen in six-foot waves. They were too small to pose a threat, but not too small to kill a man who turned his back on them if only for a moment.

Nelson and Quinney sat pressed together as the night chilled and dew formed on boat surfaces. They looked from horizon to horizon, afraid they would miss something spectacular.

Nelson looked west over Quinney's shoulder as a dim light appeared on the horizon. He glanced down at the AIS, looking for a "blip" to reveal the nearby ship. Nothing there. The light increased. Something was approaching at an incredible speed. Nelson shook Quinney's shoulder and pointed. "It's heading right toward us." A collision was eminent. Evasive measures flashed through Nelson's head. *Turn away! Come about! Yell to alert Blake and Frank to brace for a collision!*

"It's a large sailboat," Nelson said. "Look how tall the mast is. It's flying spinnakers. Wait! I see two. How is that possible? Why would a boat fly a spinnaker at night and with seas this high? That accounts for its speed. Can't they see us? My God, we're going to collide!"

They embraced each other as the approaching sailboat bore down on them. The closer it came, the tighter they held one another. "It's going to run over our bow," Nelson said. "Hold on to something! Here it comes!"

Suddenly, the sailboat stopped its forward plunge. The light on the top of its mast broke off, but it did not fall. It traveled horizontally across the sky. The outline of the sailboat and spinnakers hung in the air and faded like magic dust. They watched the moving light vanish as it moved farther south.

They sat back and breathed deeply. "I know what that was," Nelson said. "Wait here a moment." He dashed below, made a log entry, and returned to the helm. "You know what's out there? Seven hundred miles that way is Florida. Cape Kennedy. We just watched a space launching. What I thought were spinnakers was the vapor trail from the rockets. And that light we saw heading south was a satellite. They launched a satellite, and we witnessed it. Is that exciting or what?"

"It wasn't a phantom ship sent to destroy us?" Quinney asked. "Well, that's enough excitement for me for one night. I think I'll kiss you good night and go to bed."

Nelson sat at the helm. The six-foot swells were no longer intimidating. The boat was happy. The darkness did not appear impenetrable, and that made it less fearful. He thought about the burning freighter and the giant high-speed killer night ship. While seasickness continued to hold him captive, he found the events of the evening enough to scrape the edges off his debilitation.

ADELIA

Nelson and Quinney sat at the helm, gazing out at the changeless seascape. An hour passed without a word. The moment was being etched into their forever memories.

Nelson's watch had ended. He gave the helm to Blake along with a "nothing to report" turnover. The dry air gave the world a crisp look. The sky was deep blue. The water was clear and indigo—a rich blue-purple. Color psychologists, those who study how different colors affect human mood and behavior, define indigo as the color of wisdom and intuition—representing and reflecting an inner awareness of spirituality. They claim that those who feel a connection to indigo tend to be faithful, idealistic, intuitive. Planet Ocean is as near as man comes to another world. Perhaps this and the color indigo explain why so many people are drawn to and mesmerized by the sea.

The wind was cool and steady. Whitecaps punctuated the waves, accentuating the contrast with the water. Nelson looked astern and could see waving ribbons of light extending into the far depths of the Atlantic. The sun was directly overhead, leaving the scenery the same in all directions. He felt gratified for the opportunity to experience its frightful serenity—the illusion of tranquility and safety, the comforting arms of Mother Nature, whose moods can change instantly. He sat in the cockpit, six hundred miles from land, realizing that his feeling of being intimidated by the sea was waning while his respect for it was deepening. He had known when he stepped on *Momentum* and sailed offshore that he might never see land again. Years before, an old fisherman on an island off Cape Cod had told him that thinking any differently comes from the mind of a fool. Such a person, he said, was unprepared—physically, mentally, spiritually – and was fair game for the sea to take him at her whim. Being far out at sea and without proper care, the victim of any major medical condition can only be made comfortable and wait for death. In heavy weather sailing, a sailor must obey Mother Nature, deal with it, or die. Boats break from electrical or mechanical failure, broken masts, shredded sails, rudders that float away, leaking below the waterline, and being too close to a breaching whale. The cavalry will not be coming.

The singularity of the sea brings a calming yet terrifying reality.

Ten days had passed since Blake had sat in front of Quinney, looked deep into her eyes, and said, "We're going out of sight of land for what will seem like an eternity. Can you do that? If you can't, you need to get off this boat now. Out there, there will be no turning back for you or anyone who panics about the lack of land."

She had replied, "They asked me the same question on my sailing application, and I thought, *Of course we're going out of sight of land.* I've never been frightened by the thought. Not then. Not now. Should I be?"

Nelson was less afraid than he had been, and feeling like he was getting what he had come for was satisfying. Yet he also felt alone and disconnected, as though he were nothing but a speck of sand in a vast desert. The enormity of the encompassing emptiness filled him with a sense of insignificance and powerlessness.

To the south he spotted the tip of a distant sailboat. "We have company," he said as he picked up the binoculars. Through the wave action he could identify a single-masted sloop with full sail heading in their direction. Quinney stood and shaded her eyes. Nelson handed her the binoculars. She smiled broadly and began hopping around in delight. She was like a child waiting for her father to return from work and seeing him appear in the distance. She pointed. "Look! It's coming our way! Can you see it?" Nelson watched her quizzically, hunting for justification for her glee over a far-off sail-boat. It was as if it were coming to her rescue. Quinney was neither handing out clues nor hiding her excitement. She seemed elated to have company in the big blue expanse of water.

Quinney handed the binoculars to Blake. "I'm surprised they're sailing with no reefing in these conditions," Nelson said. "I'm guessing they're no more than ten miles away."

Frank quipped disdainfully, "Is that a silly, wild guess?"

"Sort of," Nelson replied. "I figured any sailboat out here would have a sixty-foot mast. Our eyes are about ten feet above the water. Between the two, you get seventy feet, and the distance charts would indicate that the sailboat out there is about ten miles from us."

Frank looked at Blake. "He's right, you know," Blake said.

"OK, swab, where'd you get that?"

"Mr. Swab here aced the ASA navigation course," said Nelson.

"Well, how did you know the distance? Did you memorize the tables or something?"

"In scuba, there's an easy correlation about how long a person can stay at depth. I tried to find something like it in the distance charts. I didn't have enough time, so I memorized the formula."

"And what is that formula?" Frank asked.

Nelson looked at them with a partial smile. "You don't think I know, do you? OK. You take the square root of the height times 1.225. If you know the square root of numbers, you can get close by upping the result by twenty percent. Watch this… Let's say you're standing ten feet above sea level and you're looking at a lighthouse that is ninety feet tall. That's one hundred feet total. The square root of one hundred is ten. Up that by twenty percent, or two, and you have twelve. Twelve miles. Ta-da. Kinda rough, but it gets you in the ballpark."

Blake grinned and Frank looked dumbfounded. Quinney, sitting nearby, waved her hands. "What can I say? He's good with numbers."

Frank shook his head, scorning Nelson's explanation. "They taught you that in nav-class?"

"No, like I said, there wasn't enough time. I did that on my own."

"So, tell me… how far away is that sailboat now?"

Nelson looked back at the approaching sailboat. He extended his arm in its direction, then stuck his thumb up to use it as a measure against the boat's mast. He closed one eye, squinted, and said slowly, "Oh… I'd say 9.2 miles." He laughed and paused. "Just kidding. The distance formula works, but if your eyeball and mast height estimates are inaccurate, the number will be off. It's mostly a guess."

"Mostly a guess? Ha, that gives me a lot of confidence," Frank said.

"Columbus used deduced reckoning. His crew lost confidence in his calculations, but ole Chris' educated guessing got them to the New World, didn't it?"

"Wasn't he aiming for India?" said Frank.

"So he was off a little," Nelson retorted.

"Well, you might be good with numbers, but you still don't know your boat's displacement. In my mind, that keeps you in the swab category," Frank said dismissively, looking toward the approaching sailboat.

A cold silence oozed over the boat.

"Does it surprise you that I know something more than swabbing… things like distance formulas or even navigation itself?" Nelson asked.

"Yeah, it does, actually."

"That's because you labeled me as a swab, and you've blinded yourself so you can't see anything else. I guess you're not going to give me credit for anything, are you?"

Frank kept his eyes out to sea and said nothing. Quinney looked at Nelson. She slowly shook her head—code for "don't go there—it's no use."

"I think I'll hail them on the radio," Nelson said as he headed for the companionway.

Quinney followed him down. "You're letting him get to you. We have a long way to go," she sang in a soft voice.

"He's getting on my nerves. He's like a stick poking an open wound. He reminds me of a bully at a camp I went to when I was ten. That guy went around bullying everyone in our cabin. He was relentless. I made friends with a boy who, like me, was deathly afraid of lightning, and whenever a storm came, he cowered in the corner of his bunk. When the bully discovered it, he was all over my friend."

"What did you do?"

"I went berserk. I made a running tackle, pulled him away from my friend, and threw him to the floor. I jumped on him—screaming with tears running down my face. I kept pounding his head on the cabin floor. Luckily, the floor was wood planking; otherwise I could have really hurt him. All the other boys in the cabin surrounded us, cheering. A counselor heard the yelling and knew it was a fight. He intervened. We both were sent to the office. They sent the bully home."

"So you want to bash Frank's head on the deck?"

"The thought kinda came to mind."

"Tell me, Mr. Bully Basher, why did we sign up for this passage?"

"So I could face my fears of heavy weather and sailing at night and become a respected able seaman. Was that a test question?"

"And how's bashing Frank's head going to get you there?"

They both chuckled.

"You need to focus on why we're here. Focus, Nelson, focus."

Nelson made an entry in the ship's log, noted their location on the chart, and wrote in his personal journal.

SHIP'S LOG—APRIL 25, 2010—1128 HOURS—028° 57'75"N, 071° 08'00"W

"Sailing sloop, sailing sloop, sailing sloop. This is the sailing vessel *Momentum*. We are north by northwest of you. Can you see us? Over."

Frank came down from the cockpit. "They're not going to respond. There's no reason to. Besides, his radio is probably turned off."

Nelson repeated the hail.

Moments later came a crackling over the radio and an excited response: "*Momentum, Momentum, Momentum!* We are sailing vessel *Adelia*. Yes! We can see you. Good to hear from you! How are you doing? Over."

"Doing well, *Adelia*. We're heading to Chesapeake Bay from US Virgins. Been out six days. There are four of us on board. Over."

"We're a thirty-six-foot steel-hulled sloop. My son and I are heading to Bermuda from the British Virgins to pick up my other son. From there the three of us are heading north to pick up the Stream and ride it over toward the UK and then sail down through the Straits of Gibraltar on to Italy. You say you're heading up to Chesapeake Bay? Over."

"Affirmative, *Adelia*."

"*Momentum*, we heard there's a powerful weather front coming down from Canada and they're expecting it to pass north of Hatteras—directly where you're heading. Are you aware of that? Over."

"Affirmative, *Adelia*. We heard that from our meteorologist as well. We ran into some mechanical problems and missed our weather window by four days. The captain said we still have a number of options, including running up to Bermuda and holing up there until the front passes. Who knows, we might meet up with you if we have to run."

"*Momentum*, that would be nice. Yes, it's always nice to put a face with the voice. I know a pub where we can grab a few. I take it you're not the skipper?"

"No, *Adelia*, I'm the navigator and the swab. My name is Nelson."

The voice of *Adelia* laughed. "Hello, Nelson. I'm Christian, and I know what you mean about being the navigator and swab. It's good to hear a voice, Nelson. It makes this empty expanse less hostile. You're the first vessel we've seen since leaving the Virgins. It's nice to know we're not alone."

Nelson coughed through a lump in his throat. "I hear you, Christian. It can get lonely out here. I can't tell you how good it feels to be talking to you."

"Likewise, Nelson. Let's remain in contact every ten minutes until we're out of range. I'd like to know how far my radio can transmit. Right now, I can barely see your mast."

Quinney stood behind Nelson, gripping his shoulder while leaning into the speaker to ensure she heard every word. Every few minutes she raced to the deck to see if *Adelia* could still be seen. Somewhere while running back and forth, her elation evaporated. The farther away *Adelia* sailed, the quieter and more disengaged Quinney became.

Adelia went out of sight, taking her voice with it. Quinney returned below and joined Nelson at the radio. Her eyes welled up as she attempted to hide her feelings. Her face wore a look of sadness as if she had lost a loved one to death. Nelson looked over his shoulder. "Are you OK?"

Quinney's lips pursed and quivered as she choked out, "She's gone from us. We're... we're alone again." Quinney's soul seemed to go silent. The Atlantic Ocean covers forty-one million square miles. Quinney took up a mere two square feet of it. Even though she was with someone she loved, she looked sad, empty, disconnected. Her eyes scanned the cabin, as if searching for words to describe her feelings, but none came.

"Look at this, Quinney," said Nelson. "While talking to *Adelia*, we traded chart coordinates. See this little hash mark on the bottom of the chart? That's about five nautical miles. Right now they're about fifteen miles from us." He adjusted his calipers. "See the distance between these two points? That's how far away they are. It puts perspective to how small we are out here."

"Wow. When they were right behind us, it amazed me that they could be so close yet so far," Quinney said, sounding as though she were in a dreamlike state.

"Well, that sure was a waste of time," Frank said.

Nelson gave him a blank look. "Excuse me. What?"

"What did you learn except he's heading to Bermuda with his son and has a thirty-six-foot steel-hulled boat?"

"Not having any contact with another vessel since we left, the conditions, and the weather front Blake keeps telling us is heading our way, it's nice to hear another voice. That's all."

"Still, it's a waste of time. I bet he knows what the displacement of *his* boat is."

"Frank, you need to give that a rest," Nelson said. "It's getting old and boring. If you want to pick on me, find something else. Your bully stick isn't sharp anymore."

Nelson's stomach was not faring well in the rocking boat. He needed to return to the cockpit or lie down and close his eyes. He didn't have the same level of confidence in the changing sea as Blake. Trusting Blake's experience would be the wiser thing to do. He was the captain and had the helm. *Momentum* was in his hands. But just in case things got dicey, Nelson needed to be prepared. He lay down beside Quinney—fully dressed in his foulies.

"*Adelia, Adelia, Adelia.* This is *Momentum.* Over," came Frank's voice on the radio. He waited a minute and repeated the call. *Adelia* had gone beyond its radio range. Nelson lay quietly and shook his head. "Didn't he just tell me that was a waste of time?"

Then he turned to Quinney. A tear rolled out of the corner of her eye. "Quinney, you were so excited and then you became quiet. What's going on?"

"When I looked out there, I couldn't tell direction. It all looked the same. I realized that we're alone, very alone. I thought we might see other boats and ships all along the way, like we see them in the channel out to Catalina."

"Quinney, when we go to Catalina, we pass through one of the busiest shipping lanes in the world. Of course there's a lot of ships. You thought we'd be surrounded by freighters and tankers?"

"I did, but until I saw that sailboat, I thought I was OK being hundreds of miles away from land. Then I realized how alone we are. It made me feel small and insignificant. If we run into trouble, we can't rely on anyone but ourselves. Seeing the *Adelia* gave me great comfort, knowing we aren't really alone. Somehow I thought we could come together and meet them in person rather than on the radio. Silly thought. I know better. The closer they came, the more excited I was. It gave me a sense that we weren't so far away from land. But then when I saw them pass behind us, I realized they would be getting smaller and smaller each minute and then they would disappear, and we would be alone again. As long as I could see them, it made me feel not so alone. I'm glad you talked to them. It made them real, and it felt like they were near. I can't believe how looking at all this beauty out here can make me feel so alone and small. I guess all these feelings crept up on me."

Quinney sighed deeply and looked at Nelson. "I'm OK. I don't get Blake, though. He's the captain, and yet he lets Frank ride you. Why doesn't he step in?"

"The captain can't settle every dispute that comes up on a boat," Nelson said. "Frank is pushing me to see how far he can go. I was hoping he would get out whatever was stuck in his craw by now. There's not much room on this boat, and making the situation worse won't help anything, but you already said that, didn't you?"

"What if he doesn't stop? Got a plan?"

"I'm gonna have to stand up to him. You know, punch the bully in the nose and hope he doesn't come back with a bat. I'm more concerned about Blake. I wish he would talk more. Now there's a perfectly good example of a man of few words. Very hard to read. I have no idea where I stand with him. I worry that Frank may be bending his ear and convincing him I really am a swab. Sometimes I wonder if he even knows I exist. But we have time yet. We're not even halfway into this passage."

"Is this turning out the way you hoped? You know, this trip?" Quinney asked.

"Well, in my view, this boat is a scow. I have no confidence in her seaworthiness. That's disappointing. I'm getting the experience I was hoping for. I hadn't considered that twenty-five percent of the crew would be total jerks. You know I'm easy to get along with, but Frank isn't interested in that. How about you? Is this trip meeting *your* expectations?"

"I gave you my feelings about being alone. Blake keeps saying that we're not gonna have good weather all the way, that we're gonna run into storms. We heard about the big storm coming from Canada, and then the man on the *Adelia* mentioned it. Are we heading into something terrible?"

"Blake's a good seaman. He won't do anything that deliberately puts us in danger."

Momentum rocked, rolled, and sailed forward. *Adelia* had passed and was well to the north and over the horizon. She had become a silent voice on a barren sea.

Talk between Quinney and Nelson softened, and they both dozed off in a sea of openness, aloneness, and stark beauty.

Like all mariners, they were gripped by the way of the sea.

QUINNEY

"What are you doing up here?" Nelson asked. "I thought you were going to stay below."

"I changed my mind."

Quinney sat quietly and gazed around. Usually when she came to the cockpit, she made eye contact with everyone and greeted them. But this time she seemed withdrawn, content to be alone with herself.

It was April 25. Late afternoon tends to settle the seas and changes the sharp colors of the day to soft pastels. The passing of *Adelia* left lingering thoughts in Quinney's head. She wasn't ready to let it all go. They were ending their sixth day at sea, and much had happened since they had pushed off the night of April 19. Quinney's thoughts went within. *It seems so long ago, but it's been less than a week.* She closed her eyes and could feel the wind, taste the salty air, and feel the afternoon sun on her face. She drifted off in thought and smiled while recalling how all this had begun.

* * *

"I want to go with you," Quinney said. "I want to be on the boat with you. Can I go?"

"You've got my vote," said Nelson. "But it's not up to me. Let's talk with the company that runs the delivery business."

A sailing application came via email. Quinney quickly filled in the blanks.

- Sailing Experience: 74 days "at sea," which meant she was on water.
- Approximate Hours Logged: 590.
- Location of Experiences: San Diego Harbor, Pacific Ocean, Catalina Islands, British Virgin Islands.
- Seamanship Skills: steering, mooring ball pickup, keeping cockpit orderly, sandwich making, responding well to polite orders.
- Crew Position Desired: galley slave.
- Qualifications for Desired Position: Italian ancestry with excellent culinary skills, fastidious organizer, self-starter, takes initiative, enjoys being with people, fast learner, not shy.
- Goals for Being on Board: adventure, bucket list, shared experience, improve sailing skills.

Quinney reviewed the application and hit the Send button. She acted giddy with anticipation. She opened her closet to search for "sailing clothes." She tried on dozens of beach hats. She waited for a reply. A day went by. Then two. Self-doubt crept in. She saw the opportunity of a lifetime slipping through her fingers like sand.

Then came an email from the boat delivery company. "Please describe how you would feel when you look in all directions and there is no evidence of land."

"They're trying to disqualify me, aren't they?" Quinney told Nelson, expecting that whatever answer she provided would be summarily rejected. She was confused by the question, unable to relate desire and skills with losing sight of land.

"They're playing with me. I don't have time for this."

"What's the worst thing that can happen?" Nelson asked.

Quinney pounded out her response: "Don't understand the question. Please explain."

"We simply want to know if you have any concerns about losing sight of land for a week," came the reply to her reply.

"I don't get the question. Why would I have a problem losing sight of land?" Transmit.

"We welcome you, Quinney, as a crew member," came an immediate reply.

Quinney jumped around like a happy puppy dog. "I need a *completely* new wardrobe!!"

"We have a fifty-pound baggage limit on the plane, and much of what we bring will be needed sailing gear. Don't go overboard," quipped Nelson with a wink.

* * *

On the first day they were out at sea, Blake had summoned everyone to the salon table to review the rules for boat safety and etiquette, night watch schedules, the rotation for cooking and cleaning, and what to expect with weather as they sailed into the cooler northern latitudes. He concluded with the disquieting warning about the possibility of encountering a large weather front from the Great Lakes and the steps they would take to monitor and avoid it.

"Any questions?" Blake asked.

Quinney sat tall and cleared her throat. "You mentioned nothing about my role as ship's cook. On my sailing resume, I was joking about being a galley slave because I wanted to be accepted even though I have limited sailing skills. Blake, you talked about the rotation for cooking and cleaning. I want to carry my weight, and I'll step in to cook even when it's not my turn if all three of you have to be in the cockpit or you're sacked out cold when it's your turn in the galley. I don't want you to think I'm stepping in to take over. I'm a clean freak and hate messes. You'll see a lot of me with rubber gloves getting this boat in livable condition. If you leave things for me to pick up, I'll get testy with you."

"We've been forewarned," Blake said.

Quinney spent her first few days cleaning away sticky, caked-on dirt and grease that she asserted hadn't been cleaned since the boat was new. She made soups, sandwiches, and egg dishes. Blake must have liked her cooking. He always had seconds and thirds until nothing was left but an empty pot.

She spent her idle time tending to personal hygiene. When Blake spoke in general about water conservation, she knew he was addressing her. Spit baths and saltwater hair washing made hygiene challenging. Quinney did her best to look her best, and the crew appreciated her. Her sailing wardrobe never failed to draw complimentary comments. When Frank came too close to her "no pass" line, she glared and gave a convincing "stink eye" that would have scared off a bear.

But the quality of her personal care deteriorated when rough seas tossed Quinney from bulkhead to bulkhead. The onset of seasickness debilitated the crew, which ended regular eating schedules. Menus went from savory egg dishes to dried bagels. Even though Quinney dodged seasickness, the rough conditions sapped her energy.

Quinney's abundance of empathy gave her passage into the hearts of everyone. She sensed things, and she was "there" to tend to her crewmates, no matter how they showed their not-so-nice personalities during times of stress or when their proximity to one another became unbearable. She sat in the cockpit and silently watched the others, figuring them out and trying to be emotionally useful when the need arose.

Mother Nature provided spectacular light shows with distant thunder squalls, chameleon seas that mimicked the vast colors of sunsets, meteor showers that performed like a shower should, and mind-boggling wonderment when gazing at the billions upon billions of stars from horizon to horizon. When someone called, "You guys need to see this," Quinney dashed to the cockpit. She sat quietly, transfixed, her mind captured and taken away. Whatever stress or fatigue clung to her face relinquished its grip and dissolved the lines created by years of struggles and hardship. In those moments, talking to her was folly—she heard nothing but angelic songs in her head.

Ship life was strenuous at best. Passages offer no physical comfort. Alertness is essential. Sailing a boat the size of *Momentum* required a cohesive team—a crew who respected one another's skills, and whose abilities dovetail with and complement each other. Fatigue, exposure, and the constant bombardment of tension promised to fray nerves, which, as Blake constantly reminded them, impacts a boat's happiness. Quinney became the ambassador of peaceful coexistence and an advocate of forgiveness. Frank was a hopeless jerk, yet Quinney interpreted his behavior as a hurting person screaming for help and understanding. She gave it to him. Nelson was a self-doubter. Quinney became exasperated with it, but instead of chastising him, she found the patience to help open the spigot and drain out the deadly toxins of doubt to buy him time to regroup and recover. Through her, the overly serious Blake let his guard down and allowed himself to be known.

When Quinney was challenged about her sailing skills, she retorted, "Oh, I never said I could sail a boat, but I can sure steer one."

ASLEEP AT THE WHEEL

Momentum spent the day gliding through a dead flat sea. At sunset, a respectable sailing breeze picked up, allowing her to move on wind power. Blake adjusted the sails and turned the boat over to Nelson. "If you lose the wind, leave the sails alone and run the engine," he said.

An overcast sky robbed Nelson of the wonders of the heavens. It promised an uneventful four-hour watch. Quinney stayed with him until droopy eyes lured her to their cabin.

Harsh words came from the salon. Blake was on Frank for something. It was uncharacteristic of Blake. Normally, he was soft-spoken and polite, and chose his words carefully. His outburst was short-lived and indiscernible. Nelson knew Frank was a good sailor, but he also had an uncanny ability to quickly piss people off. In all likelihood, Frank had the tongue-lashing coming. He was the villain in the stories Nelson told himself. Frank retreated to the cockpit and Blake turned in. With the absence of privacy and space, it was easy for conversations that were meant to be private to spill into the ears of others. Because of this, among the many rules of boat etiquette was "be deaf to what is not meant for your ears." But the temptation was too great for Nelson. "What was that all about?" he asked.

Frank, busy cleaning his teeth with a toothpick, looked out into the blackness and put a foot on the companionway to return below. He turned and said softly, "The captain's edgy. Tread lightly."

* * *

SHIP'S LOG—APRIL 26, 2010—0234 HOURS—30° 31′31″N, 072° 22′11″W

The wind shifted slightly to the northwest and began to luff the sails until Nelson turned away from the wind. It seemed like a replay of several nights earlier when he had had his skirmishes with the squall. He seemed mentally programmed to stick to a compass setting more than sail to the wind. When the wind shifted slightly to the west, Nelson turned the boat toward the plotted course. As the wind shifted, the sails luffed. He steered away and the luffing stopped. Back and forth he went, trying to second-guess the wind and anticipate a shift. He looked down at the engine gauges, scratching his head as he attempted to figure out why they were mounted close to the deck and were almost impossible to see unless squatting to one's knees. He stooped over for a better look.

Suddenly, Blake was on the deck in his skivvies. He winched in the mainsheet and jib sheet. Luffing stopped. "Steer away from the wind!" he snapped. Nelson complied.

"You were sleeping, weren't you?"

"No."

"Yes, you were. You were asleep at the wheel, and you let the sails luff."

"I was bent over looking at the gauges."

"What's to see on those gauges?"

"I didn't get close enough."

"There's nothing to see. Everything you need is right in your face on the console. You were sleeping at the wheel."

"Blake, I wasn't."

"You know how I feel about that. I told you when you first came aboard."

Blake went below and returned fully dressed. "I'm taking over your watch. You're relieved."

"But Blake, I was not asleep at the wheel."

"I said, you're dismissed."

Nelson trembled. Not from fear of Blake but from the thought that he had failed him and would not be given the opportunity to "present his case." Without a word, he went below.

"Is your watch over already?" asked Quinney sleepily.

"Wake up, Quinney. Something has happened."

Quinney sat up and leaned against the bulkhead, rubbing her face as Nelson related his experience. "Nelson, you're shaking."

"I've been trying to prove myself to Blake and was doing pretty well. It seems like it all got flushed because I looked down at the gauges and Blake thought I was sleeping. This trip is not turning into what I was hoping. Frank's opinion of me is in the toilet, and now Blake wants to toss me overboard. I didn't sign up for this."

"Forget Frank. He doesn't matter. Blake does."

"To me, Frank does matter even though he shouldn't."

"Let's go back to what happened. You weren't sleeping, or were you?"

"No. I was a little drowsy and looking around for things to keep me alert. I did the stand-up thing and looked around every ten minutes. I was doing well, sailing as close to the wind as I could, but you know how it shifts, so the sails would luff every now and then. When I looked down at the gauge, I guess the sail luffed too long and that brought Blake abruptly on deck. That explains why he came in his skivvies."

"What are you going to do?"

Nelson shook his head. "I don't know. I don't know if there's anything I can say that will change his mind. He reminded me of that story he told about the guy who fell asleep and all he wanted to do was throw him overboard. Blake would like to throw me overboard. This is bad. If ever I felt like a failure, this is it."

"Well, now is not the time to try to solve this problem. I would suggest you try to let it go for tonight, get some rest, and take another look at it with a clear mind. I'm sure Blake's upset, too. Tomorrow would be a much better time to talk with him. You have to get him to listen with an open mind, and then tell your side. Persuading others is what you did for a living. You have the skills and the personality, and you know how to influence others. Wait until the morning, OK?"

Quinney kissed him and lay back down to sleep. Nelson lay on his back, pondering and worrying. Thoughts bounced in his head. He felt humiliated, incompetent, demoralized. Recovery with Blake was hopeless. Redemption was beyond reach. Being dismissed from the helm felt like being cast aside like rubbish. Whatever goals he had come to achieve were shattered. Nelson's sense of failure was a black blob inside him that oozed to the far corners of his body. Maybe he should save Blake the trouble and just jump off the boat without his PFD when alone at the helm—if he would ever be allowed at the helm at all. Maybe he should go forward in a frothing sea and pitching boat without his harness. He spent the remaining part of his watch staring into the darkness of his cabin—punishing himself, fretting, and wallowing in the desolation of aloneness.

SHIP'S LOG—APRIL 26, 2010—0630 HOURS—NO COORDINATES RECORDED

Nelson awoke with a fresh sense of optimism. He was confident he could sway Blake. Truth was on his side. He updated the ship's log, made entries in his personal journal, poured a cup of coffee, and headed to the cockpit. Frank was at the helm. Nelson looked around for Blake.

"He's not up here, if that's why you're looking around," Frank said. "He's asleep. He'll be up soon. I hear you got yourself in a little trouble last night. What happened—did the boat snitch on you? I warned you that he was edgy, and you should tread lightly. Didn't listen to me, did you?"

"What did he tell you?" Nelson asked.

"Enough to know you're on the outs with him."

"Well, that doesn't tell me anything. How's that supposed to help me make amends with him?"

"Who said I was trying to help?"

"You think this is funny, don't you?"

"Gotta have some entertainment on an otherwise boring trip. It's gonna be interesting seeing how you wiggle out of this one, swab. So what *are* you going to say to him?"

Nelson cradled his coffee cup and stared out at sea. Quinney's counseling the night before echoed in his ear. *Frank does not matter.* "Conditions are changing. The swells are growing, and the wavelengths are longer. Looks like we might be in for some heavy weather," Nelson said with conviction.

He looked over to Frank, who looked back with a smirk.

* * *

Blake came to the cockpit. Nelson nodded and Blake gave him a cursory glance. Blake switched positions with Frank and sat at the helm. Nelson's heart pounded. He knew he was about to make the most important speech of his retired life. He breathed deeply as he watched Frank go down the companionway. Doubts filled Nelson's head, but they would not serve him well if he was going to recapture any lost ground with Blake.

"Can we talk about last night?"

"Sure. You can say whatever you want, but you were sleeping at the wheel, and that is the worst offense a sailor can commit on a boat. If you want to make a try, go ahead. I'm all ears."

"Are you the least bit interested in my perspective?"

"It should be interesting, but let's cut to the chase. The boat luffed long enough to alert me. Luffing happens. I get it. But if you had been awake and attentive, you would have corrected it right away. A long luff is the boat saying whoever's at the helm isn't paying attention. So, if not paying attention, what's the helmsman doing?"

"Well, it's easy for me to say I wasn't asleep, and I know that won't get me anywhere. Let's talk about luffing. The wind shifted and I kept steering away, and that put the boat east of the plotted course. I…"

"How many times have I told you not to sail to compass? Out

here you sail to wind. Why do you insist on sailing to the compass? Let's start by you telling me that."

"I learned to sail by compass. I was taught that when a sailor can stay on a compass heading, he has control of his vessel. I did a lot of predawn sailing around the Channel Islands off California. Out there, you can't see anything except the distant lights of the mainland, and all they did was ruin night vision. Around the Channel Islands, drifting off a compass heading could mean a hard grounding. When we did our coastal cruising class down to Mexico, we had to show that we could keep the boat on the compass heading and overcome the effects of current and leeway. Even out in the ocean at night we had to steer to compass. Down in Mexico, night is as black as here, and we had to navigate around the Coronado Islands, which are extensions of the Channel Islands, only in Mexican waters. I learned to sail and steer by compass. It was pounded into me. More time out here will help me know when to sail to compass or to wind. Last night the wind shifted constantly, and I kept sailing off and steering her close again."

"Blah, blah, blah. I understand all that, but the sails luffed longer than they should have. That's what brought me up, not that you were sailing on or off the course."

"I was checking the engine gauges down by my feet. We discussed this last night. I know they don't give us anything we can't get at the console except engine RPM. Ever since I came aboard, I've been wondering what those gauges do and why they're located where they can't be seen, and last night I wanted to see. That's when you came to the cockpit. I was just trying to look at the gauges."

"From my point of view, you were asleep. You sat up pretty quick when I showed up on deck, and that tells me you didn't want me to think you were sleeping, so you must have been."

"If I'd truly been sleeping, I would not have heard you coming up and you would have caught me dead to rights. I can see how being bent over like that would look like I was sleeping, but look down at those gauges. It's almost impossible to see them unless you put your glasses on and duck down and get close. Time yourself. I think you'll find the amount of time it takes will be as long as you heard the sails luffing last night."

"I'm sure you spent the night thinking about what you were going to say, but the way I see it, you were asleep at the wheel. I've lost confidence in you. I no longer trust you at the helm at night. Frank and I will make the night watches. If we were closer to a port, I'd take an extra day just to get you off the boat."

"Your mind is made up, then?"

"It was made up last night."

"This conversation is over. So I'll do all my other duties except night watches, right? And I'll do more watches during the day, right?"

"And you can be on watch just before dawn and until an hour after sunset."

With Blake's affirmations on Nelson's assignments, Nelson retreated to the salon to share the misguided conversation with Quinney. After Nelson cleared the companionway, Blake pulled out his reading glasses and attempted to see the boat gauges. He stooped lower and lower until his nose was almost parallel to them. He sat up and looked over to the companionway and then back to the gauges. He raised and lowered his eyebrows as one might do when making a discovery. He nodded while looking around. It appeared as if Nelson had been more convincing than he thought.

* * *

Nelson noticed the door to their cabin was open. Quinney must be up and about. He turned the corner to find Frank standing over Quinney, who was still asleep and without a top. He stood, peering down at her, his hands limp at his side. He didn't seem to hear Nelson entering the cabin. Nelson's hair felt like it was on fire. His body felt flushed. He stiffened. He felt pressure in his eyes. His ability to remain rational had been drained by his conversation with Blake, and now he was standing next to the man who enraged him to the point of near insanity.

"What are you doing in here?" Nelson demanded loudly.

Quinney was jolted awake by a tone in Nelson's voice she had never heard before. When she saw Frank standing over her, she sat up suddenly, grabbed her shirt and covered herself, crossing her arms over her chest as she felt the violation.

"I said, what are you doing in here!"

Blake leapt into the cabin, brought in by the rapidly escalating fracas. His eyes darted around, and his body stiffened. He looked at Quinney, then at Frank, and then at Nelson. "What's going on here?"

Nelson's eyes were burning holes in Frank, who appeared unflurried and unengaged.

"What's going on here?" Blake repeated, louder this time.

Nelson's jaw became square as he gritted his teeth and clenched his fists. Frank looked unfazed and blasé. Nelson saw a sense of arrogance in him that pushed him closer to the edge of rage.

"Nelson," demanded Blake, "Stand down. Stand down now!"

Nelson's eyes were myopically focused on Frank.

"Nelson, it's OK. I'm OK," Quinney said as she pulled the shirt over her head.

"No, it's not OK," said Nelson with an angry growl.

"I don't know what the fuss is all about," Frank said. "He knows there is nothing private on a boat. We've already had this conversation."

Blake stepped between the two, facing Nelson.

Nelson leaned around him and pointed at Frank. "Would you willingly barge into the head knowing someone was already in there? I don't think so. You'd respect their privacy, right?"

"Well, yeah."

"And you say there's no privacy on a boat? Then why is it OK to walk in here and gawk at Quinney while she's sleeping? You know it's wrong. I will *not* tolerate anyone who disrespects her. This cabin is off limits to you. Get it? Off limits. If you need something in here, you ask. Period. Do you follow what I'm saying?"

"Yeah, you made your point."

"Jeez, your such an arrogant ass," said Nelson while shaking his head in disbelief.

"Settle down, Nelson," said Blake with a disarming voice.

Nelson took a deep breath and exhaled. "If I ever catch you in here again or even see you looking at her lewdly, you'll see a really ugly side of me that will truly frighten you. You call me a swab, but you don't know what I was before you branded me a swab. And you don't want to find out."

Quinney extended her arm to reach Nelson. "Please, Nelson."

"Please? He just disrespected you in the most offensive way."

"If I had my shirt on none of this would have happened."

"The hell. None of this would have happened if Frank here had any decency and respect for privacy – especially in tight quarters like a boat."

"Maybe if we could open the hatches it wouldn't be so stifling hot down here," said Quinney.

"Boat rules. No hatches or portholes open while the boat is moving," said Blake.

"Look, everyone," said Quinney. "This makes for a lot of angry and bad feelings that will interfere with working together if we face an emergency. Nelson, I'm as upset with this as you, and I'll bet Frank is not going to cross that line again. His pompousness is maddening, but I'm sure he heard you. Frank, I can forgive you, but don't think for a minute I'm gonna take my eyes off you. You behave and we'll be all right. Now, let's sit back, let this all marinate, and get back to being crew members. OK?"

Blake looked at Frank and Nelson. "The lady asked a question."

Nelson looked down and nodded. Frank looked like he was ready to dismiss the entire melee as overplayed theatrics.

"And how about you, Frank?" said Blake.

Frank casually shrugged. "Yeah, I'm OK with it."

Blake put his captain's hat back on. "Nelson. Take the helm. You. You keep your shirt on from now on whether you're in the cabin with the door closed or open. And you, come with me." Frank followed Blake to the anchor locker in the bow.

Nelson looked to Quinney. His rage faded. He dropped his head, ashamed of his incapacity for self-control. He looked up, and his saddened eyes met Quinney's. She nodded and gave him an empathetic hug. Nelson headed up to take the helm.

He was surprised at the change in the sea conditions. The wind had shifted again and was coming from the southwest—behind them. When he stood tall, his view was eight to ten feet above water level, given his height and how far the deck was above the waterline. When *Momentum* was in a trough, some waves blocked his view of other waves. That's how Nelson measured average wave height.

Momentum was happy. Her sails, while at the second reef, filled with air, pushing her smoothly through the water. The trim of the sail reflected Blake's skill. "I wish Blake would believe me," Nelson whispered.

Raised voices came from below. They were audible, yet Nelson couldn't make out the words except when Blake ended with "This is my boat, get it?" Nelson was glad to hear it, for it might draw Blake's ire and attention away from him. It was the second time Nelson had heard harsh words between Blake and Frank.

Quinney joined Nelson at the helm. She wrapped her arms around him and held on tightly without saying a word. She looked him in the eye and gently patted his cheek. She looked out at the growing sea. "Wow, this *has* changed. Are we going to be OK?"

"We have Blake. As long as he's aboard, we'll be OK."

Quinney pointed. "Is this a following sea?"

"Yep. That it is."

"It's not so bad. Why is a following sea dangerous?"

"It's not *why* but *when*. Anytime we run from the wind—like we did that time in BVI where we were wing-to-wing, we had a following sea. You know, Jimmy Buffett kind of sailing. When you're running from the wind and the waves get big, that's still not a problem. It's when the waves act like breakers on a beach that it gets serious, dangerous, or even deadly. That's what's called a breaking following sea. See those whitecaps over there? They're not acting like a breaker on a beach. When they pass the boat, they ride under it. If a wave breaks over the stern and dumps its water on the deck, that's when you have to be concerned. If the water can't drain before another wave breaks on the stern, water in the cockpit can make the stern sit lower in the water and more vulnerable. If water in the cockpit can flow into the salon, all kinds of problems unfold. We have to minimize the amount of water that gets into the cockpit and drain it quickly. I don't mean to scare you, but a breaking following sea is the one thing that worries me the most out here."

"How do we get the water out of the cockpit?"

"On this boat, there are drain holes in the bottom of the steering well. I don't think they're large enough to drain the cockpit quickly. In our boat, the stern is open."

"You've talked several times about a sailboat race that ended in disaster. What was it?"

"That was the Fastnet Race in 1979. Remember the gal whose cottage we rented in Eleuthera? Remember the night we were over for cocktails, and I sat talking with her husband for an hour? He was in that race. I was lucky to get a firsthand account of what happened. Of the three hundred boats in that race, twenty-four or twenty-five were sunk or abandoned, and fifteen sailors died. A number of studies looked at what was common among those boats that survived and those that didn't. Guess what? Many of the boats in the center of the storm survived by hoving-to and riding it out. After that, there was a lot of emphasis on knowing how and when to heave to. That's why we practice it a lot when we're out sailing outside the harbor."

"What's the difference between heaving to and hove-to?"

"They're the same. Blake says hove-to, so I say hove-to. I think it's just the past tense of heave to. But what do I know?"

"What happens when the boat is hove-to?"

"Remember how on our boat when we turn, I yell 'Helm's alee' just as we come about?" Nelson used his hands to demonstrate. "We steer the boat through the wind, allow the wind to push the jib leeward, readjust the jib sheet, and off we go. Easy. When we heave to, we do the same thing except we don't loosen the jib sheet. That counteracts the force of the mainsail. The jib pulls the bow leeward while the mainsail pushes it to windward. The trick is to keep the boat at an angle to the wind so it won't sail off, and that's done by turning the wheel hard over to windward and lashing it in place. The boat stops moving, but it will drift downwind, and water flowing over the rudder creates something called a slick, which creates a becalmed area on the windward side. The magic of heaving to in a storm is that the waves will go around the boat instead of directly at it. There's much more to this, but that's basically how it's done. Does that make any sense?"

"It's way more than I wanted to know. It sounds complicated. Why are we talking about this?"

"You asked me about it, that's why. I practiced it alone on our boat many times until it became easy, but it's more challenging in heavy seas, and on this boat, those running backstays make it nearly impossible to do it alone. When the sea is up and the waves get dangerous, the timing of when to begin the turn is crucial…"

Quinney put her hands up. "OK, I'm on sensory overload. No more heaving-to lessons." She snuggled up to Nelson to ward off the cooling air. "Let's just sit and watch the waves." A few minutes passed. "Nelson, I was just thinking. If Frank knew about what you did in Central America after you came back from Vietnam, do you think he would still be the bully he is?"

"Maybe. Maybe not. It was a crazy, mixed-up time. It's better if that part of my history faded away."

"I'm sorry. I shouldn't have brought that up." They sat quietly, just being with one another.

"I'm getting weary, Nelson. I need to head below, but I hate to just leave you alone."

"I'll be fine. My watch is nearly over. I'll be down soon."

* * *

Nelson sat at the helm. Soon Blake or Frank would come and relieve him. He thought about the conversation he might have with either of them. *Will Frank scorn me, and will Blake pay any attention to me at all?*

Entry from Nelson's personal journal—April 26, 2010

Conditions are changing. Began watch with four to five-foot waves, but they grew to ten feet in a few hours. I spend a lot of time sitting and watching, thinking about how this adventure went south with Frank's arrogance and Blake's refusal to listen to my perspectives. No convincing him but will keep trying. I was NOT asleep at the wheel!

MUTINY

Frank came to the cockpit and looked around at the changing conditions. "What's your heading?"

"3-4-5 degrees," Nelson said.

"You know Blake is concerned about those storm fronts," Frank said. "I've been trying to convince him to go around them, to head over to the Stream now instead of waiting until we get hammered on this heading. He refuses to budge."

"Well, I overheard you two arguing about something. Is that what it was about?"

"Yeah, some of it. Here's my thinking. If we stay on the current course, we'll run head on into the weather fronts coming our way. Blake thinks they might peter out or turn. I say why take the chance when we can avoid them altogether. We could head west, pick up the Stream, ride them north, and come in behind them."

"We know the weather fronts are heading this way, but we don't know how strong they really are," Nelson said.

"You can never be sure about the strength of a storm. I've seen some big ones head right at me and suddenly die or veer away."

"You said Blake won't go along with sailing around them? Why not?"

"I don't know. Maybe it's because he's the captain and thinks he has to know more than everyone else. But here's my thinking. You're the helmsman, and that means you're in charge. You have the authority to make the decision to alter the heading."

"I've never heard anything like that before. I've seen a lot of movies and read a lot of books about the sea, and none of them showed the helmsmen altering the course because he thought it was better. That would have been mutinous."

"Look, I teach this stuff. I should know. But when you think about it, it makes sense. This boat is old. It hasn't been well maintained, and I don't think she's seaworthy enough to survive one weather front, let alone two. What do you say? It's up to you. It's a smart decision, and it will protect the boat."

"If Blake didn't like the idea when you presented it, why would he like it any better if I did?"

"Blake didn't give me the chance to explain my reasoning. At least you did."

"You call me a swab. You step all over Quinney's privacy. Most of the time you talk down to me. Now you're talking to me as an equal. Why the switch?"

"If I were in your shoes, I wouldn't trust me either, but let's deal with that later. What matters is the boat, not us. If this boat goes down in a storm, you and I are brothers in death, but if we work together, we can avoid unnecessary risk. I think you'll agree I have much more passage experience than you do, right?"

"I don't know. I suppose. So?"

"So I know about storms. Blake has every reason to be concerned. I know he hasn't had a weather update lately, but he knows we're on a collision course with the low fronts heading toward us. That's why he keeps telling you we're in for some rough weather. It can get wild crossing the Stream even without a storm."

"So you're saying to just alter the course to 2-7-0 and that will get us out of harm's way?" Nelson asked.

"No, it will *keep* us out of harm's way."

"I need to think on this a little."

"Don't spend too much time on it. I'm gonna get a jacket and I'll be right back."

Nelson was alone to ponder. *There's no emergency here. This is not my decision. Never was. Never could be. What's he up to? He's trying to get me to do something that's insubordinate or mutinous. If the helmsman can make the call, why can't Frank just wait and do it on his watch? Why is he suddenly my pal? I know I'm dehydrated and seasick and not thinking very well, but this is insane! I'll bet Frank already knows there's no turning Blake, so why get me to do it? No, this is a setup. If one of my grandkids were steering and changed the heading without permission, he would never be allowed on my boat again. Ever. Frank's trying to make me look bad. He must think I'm stupid. I'm an idiot for giving it a moment's thought.*

Nelson changed the view on the GPS, enabling him to determine distance to the Stream and get an aerial view of Cape Hatteras and the Outer Banks.

"What are you going to do?" Frank asked when he returned.

"We're going to talk about the wisdom of heading over to the Stream, that's what we're going to do."

"Fine. Let's talk wisdom."

"The east side of the Stream is about three hundred nautical miles from here. Under ideal conditions, that would add two or two and a half days to this trip. We left BVI four days later than planned. I can see why Blake hesitated. Look at the chart here on the console. If we were to head on a northwesterly course instead of due west, we'd shave sixty miles off the distance."

Frank shrugged. "Fine, so head northwest."

"It's called 'the graveyard of the Atlantic' where there's something like three thousand shipwrecks around Cape Hatteras and the Outer Banks."

"I'd rather take my chances with those conditions than the ones we'd get into if we ran into a storm front from the north," Frank said.

"And be guaranteed we run into a shoal? Frank, part of the reason that area has so many shipwrecks is the strong leeward winds that pushed those ships into the shoals. And, like you said, you never know what a storm's gonna do. You said this one could veer away. In an effort to get out of the way of a storm, it could veer into us. With a lee shore, that could be disastrous."

"I think you did too much thinking while I was below."

"Or not enough. Tell you what, Frank. Because you told me changing direction is my call, I'd like to know more about why Blake nixed your idea. I'm not going to take your word for it, even though you might be right. Blake is the captain, and he has the final say. You take the helm while I go lay out the proposed new heading. If he agrees, then I'll alter the course. But I'm not sure I have any more pull with him than you do. If he likes it, I'll make sure you get the credit."

"Well, I know he's sleeping now, so I wouldn't want to wake him up. You stay here at the helm. When he wakes up, he might be more receptive, and I'll go ahead and try to get him to listen to our idea."

"Our idea? Frank, this isn't *our* idea. It's one hundred percent *your* idea, and you can take full credit for it. Meanwhile, I'm staying the course."

"Have you noticed how agitated he's become? He's been on both of us for insignificant things, and..."

"Wait—he's on me because he's convinced I was asleep at the wheel and a few days before you came aboard, he told me nothing infuriated him more than that. So to him, that's significant."

"My point is this… Blake has been acting different lately. The stress of this passage must be getting to him."

"He's made this trip a dozen times. He knows these waters well."

"I've seen this kind of behavior before. I'm beginning to think he's unfit to command. We should keep an eye out."

Nelson looked at Frank in disbelief. "And do what?"

"Well, you know, take over command if the situation calls for it."

"Wow! That's drastic, isn't it?"

"Drastic situations call for drastic solutions."

"I don't think things have become drastic," Nelson said. "Now we're talking mutiny. You can count me out."

"OK. I just wanted to keep you in the loop." Frank slapped his knees, stood, and went below.

Heading to the Stream from here is nuts! If a storm's gonna hit us, I'd think Blake would contact his meteorologist first and then make a course change. And since he hasn't, he must believe we're on the best course. I'm not going against the captain. I think I'd better call him Captain Blake from now on just so Frank will know where I stand. When Frank relieves me, I've gotta tell Quinney. She won't believe this.

REINVENTION

Boats can sail in almost any direction except directly into the wind. They can "beat to windward"—sailing as close as possible toward it—unless Mother Nature is in a particularly ferocious mood, sending punishing waves that can harm a boat's structure. It can test the grit of the crew while rewarding them with an exhilarating adrenaline rush. Sailing downwind on a broad reach, however, puts the wind at the boat's back. This kind of sailing is docile, without drama, and can bore the thrill seeker. Its tameness can lure a sailor to sleep. It can also be the deadliest for a boat—especially when an angry sea dumps breaking waves into the cockpit.

Momentum sailed to the northwest on a broad reach. Her bow pitched up and down. She yawed—swerving slightly sideways as she slid down the waves. Nelson sat at the helm feeling the autopilot working—continually making small corrections to keep *Momentum* on course. A working autopilot is like having additional crew members and extra hands to steer. The advantages of an autopilot are many, which become abundantly clear if it fails.

Just listening to the sound of the water passing under *Momentum*, Nelson grew nervous because of the strain on the autopilot. Autopilot systems consist of "eyes," "brains," "controls," and "arms." The latter is what turns the rudder. The "steering arm" assembly is a black box containing precision gears, a protruding drive actuator, and a powerful electric motor. For thousands upon thousands of miles, the "steering arm" had turned the boat to the left and right, left and right, left and right—never resting while engaged. It was unclear if, back in BVI, the "fixed" unit reinstalled in *Momentum* had been repaired or replaced with something new or rebuilt. Nor was it clear which part of the assembly had failed. Good questions asked at the wrong time. Since an unwritten law says that when all mechanical things break, they must do so at the most inopportune time, Nelson decided to give the autopilot a rest and switched steering to manual without first seeking permission—a bold move for him.

Everyone knows that boats are steered by the rudder. A helmsman turns the wheel, and the rudder responds. The rudder provides the "feel" of the boat. Sailors talk of "sailing in the groove" when the boat is performing well. They make a connection to the boat when steering. Water pushing on the sides of the rudder can be felt at the wheel. Every boat has its own characteristics, and sailors have to learn the feel of a boat just as drivers do with a new car. What happens between the wheel and rudder is magical. And somehow the magic of the boat's "feel" remains intact as the energy passes from the rudder through the cables, pulleys, and chains of the steering mechanism into the hands of the helmsman. Magic, pure magic.

For the first time since leaving port, Nelson sat at the helm in manual steering mode. When he grasped the wheel, it was as if volts of electricity shot through his body. His connection was instantaneous. *Momentum* was no longer derelict, a scow, or a dilapidated tub. She may have been untidy and uncared for, but her personality and soul were well intact.

Nelson felt the water pressure on the rudder, resisting his commands. He gripped the wheel firmly and reacted to what he felt through the wheel. *Momentum* fought back like a spirited dog on a leash. At first, *Momentum* zigzagged as Nelson oversteered and overcorrected. He experimented with his touch on the wheel. He felt when the water pressure was greatest and when it began to wane.

When the sea released its grip on the rudder, Nelson eased up on the wheel. He began to anticipate how *Momentum* would behave and altered the steering before it actually needed it. Each time she rolled to the left or right, Nelson felt the force of water as *Momentum* plowed it aside, making distinct sounds of waves curling off the boat and splashing back to sea. Within thirty minutes he could read the waves—predicting what they would do. He was sailing on a run, a broad reach, and he was as exhilarated as if beating to wind.

He was no longer sailing on the sea. He was sailing *with* the sea. *Momentum*, the sea, and Nelson became one. When he turned the wheel to the left or right, his entire body turned with it. He eased his grasp on the wheel and *Momentum* became more responsive. She was now freed from the mechanics of the autopilot. They worked together and the boat behaved differently. Sideway waves rolled away instead of slapping her hull. Gliding down waves was gentle. Instead of reacting to the sea, Nelson thought the sea was responding to him. *Momentum* sailed in the groove. And Nelson put her there.

Thirty minutes became an hour. Nelson whispered to *Momentum*, his mistress in the sea. She came to life, no longer fiber-reinforced plastic, cables, wiring, instrumentation, and a mast. She had a soul and revealed herself to Nelson. He smiled and said softly, "We'll take care of each other."

He thought of the effects Frank had on him with his scorn, his sarcasm, his bullying. He stepped outside his body and studied himself from another perspective. He saw a broken man lying on the deck like a plastic blow-up toy without air, stripped of his dignity, left with nothing. Bullies can do that to a person. Frank had cracked his self-image, and as long as Nelson allowed it, nothing would change.

While Nelson took command of *Momentum*, he also needed to take command of his personal ship. When Nelson was a boy, his father chastised him for his sensitivity, warning him that whining would bring him nothing but scorn and no one would take him seriously. As he reexamined his reaction to Frank, he realized that he was, indeed, whining. Nelson's new experience with *Momentum* flushed out the toxins that came with defeat. Ending Frank's reign of control was easy—he had to stand up to him. He chuckled as he recalled a scene in the movie *Back to the Future*, where Marty's cowardly father finds the courage to rescue the love of his life from the evil Biff by bashing him on the chin. He knocks the bully out of Biff and infuses himself with distinction. Nelson needed to become like Marty's father: Make a mental fist. Find Frank's chin. Break the bully syndrome.

Nelson's connection with *Momentum* was an inoculation of empowerment that comes when one reclaims his self-respect and takes back his lost dignity. He was no longer a beaten-down bystander on a boat. He was a participant and contributor to a sailing event. He belonged on *Momentum*. And all it took was turning off the autopilot.

Nelson decided the best way to manage Frank was to demonstrate that he had more intelligence than a swab, laugh at his insults, challenge his unacceptable bad conduct, and confuse him with kindness. The more he thought about it, the more he liked his strategy. Not falling for Frank's plan to change direction and head to the Stream played into his tactic to show more intelligence than a swab.

Blake was another matter. Perhaps Blake wanted to expel an incompetent, but it would not be that day. Nelson's self–pep talk nourished his confidence and made him stand taller and look like he was in charge. He was. He was the helmsman.

Blake would require persuasion. Nelson may have been a swab to fuel Frank's contempt, but Blake may have considered him a swab, too, because he was acting like one—standing around waiting for instructions.

It was important to Nelson to earn Blake's respect. In less than a week the passage would be complete, and they would go their separate ways. Having Blake's respect mattered. Nelson had been born during World War II and had grown up on a small New England farm. The small-town culture made it safe for children—everyone had eyes on everyone else's little ones. Chores were not a choice.

Everyone in the home contributed to its tidiness and cleanliness—inside and out. Children were not given allowances—they had to earn money for the movies, ice cream, or that toy at the five-and-dime. All kids were expected to hold themselves accountable and pull their weight. The coveted prize for good behavior was personal freedom. Effort counted as much as the result. Earning respect was nonnegotiable.

Nelson had never been permitted to wallow in self-pity, and being at the wrong end of Blake's perception was no excuse to begin at this stage in his life. Nelson never waited around for anyone to tell him what to do, and it would not serve him well to begin now. If he didn't know what to do, asking would be doing something, and that was better than nothing.

If only Blake knew about my upbringing, he would know that I'd never be asleep at the wheel, Nelson thought. *He needs to know more about me than what I know about sailing. I need to reassert myself and do it quickly.*

Like an injection, energy gushed through Nelson. His body language changed. So did his posture. Unstoppable creativity trampled his overcrowded sense of defeat. The self-doubt that had fueled his hesitation and eroded his confidence faded. His career in business was successful because of the Nelson they had yet to discover. *Sell them the Nelson you know and are.*

THE DEATH WISH

The swooshing of whitecaps became more prominent, and the waves grew another foot. When in the trough, Nelson could still see waves on the horizon, which told him they were still less than eleven feet—below the level that Blake had said was dangerous for *Momentum* when they'd talked about it a few days earlier. He watched for waves to curl and break, but none did. He didn't know if breaking waves would develop slowly or suddenly become deadly. Without experience in knowing what to watch for, he had no idea when to call for help. As captain, Blake was already ultra-sensitive to *Momentum* and well aware of the conditions, even from down below. Nelson decided to watch and learn, and when it began to get hairy, Blake would appear on deck and take over. Until then, Nelson would prepare *Momentum* for heaving to.

He placed the boat in autopilot and flattened out the mainsail and jib by sheeting them in. He removed the working lines from the canvas bags in the cockpit and recoiled them to ensure there would be no tangles with neighboring lines. He stuffed deck cushions into the lazarettes. The sails were already set at the second reef. If they had to heave to, the boat was ready. When the prep work was done, Nelson disengaged the autopilot and went back to manual steering.

A few hours later Blake and Frank came on deck. They studied the sea conditions and gazed up at the sails. "Why did you tighten the sails?" Blake asked.

"I was preparing the boat to heave to. *Momentum* is old and tired. I don't know how old the standing rigging is and didn't want to test it if the boom made an uncontrolled swing."

Blake looked around and nodded. "We came up to do just that and lower the sails from double to triple reef. Why are you sailing without autopilot?"

"I wanted to have a better feel for how the boat is responding to the wave action."

Blake took the helm and Frank worked the sails. Nelson returned to his swab status and watched, ready to leap in as needed. As Frank eased out the mainsheet to spill air, the boom swung over the water. Frank wrapped the halyard line around a winch, opened the clutch, and slowly lowered the mainsail to third reef. As it dropped, lazy jacks—a network of lines that cradles the mainsail on top of the boom while it is being lowered—neatly stacked the sail like accordion bellows. A gust of wind caught the bottom of the folded sail and ballooned part of it out. A flapping sail could tear and be rendered useless. The longer it was permitted to luff, the greater the risk of tearing. Sheeting in would put a greater force of wind on the ballooning sail.

"I can reach and tie the reef lines faster. Don't sheet in," Frank yelled. He stood on the gunwale and leaned his legs against the lifelines. He stretched his body over the water, reaching for the boom to tie the reef lines and secure the sail. His center of gravity was over the water, and he would not be able to get himself back into the boat without help.

Nelson's world went into slow motion. He imagined Frank falling overboard. *Momentum* would travel one or two miles before she could be turned. He pictured *Momentum* roaming around in a growing sea and strengthening wind, attempting to retrieve a man who could not be found.

"Frank, not safe," Nelson shouted. "Let's head to wind and sheet in."

"No! I'm fine. I have it."

"I don't like this. Not safe! We can head into the wind and spill the air, and then we can sheet in without risking a tear. It's much safer, Frank," Nelson said.

"Leave it! I know what I'm doing. You're the swab. Remember?"

"Blake! What's wrong with heading to wind?" Nelson yelled.

"We have a man half over the side and a luffing sail that could tear," Blake said. "Turning will add another element of risk. We've got to give Frank a chance to finish."

Nelson looked to the stern for the exact location of the life ring. He found the man overboard button on the control console. If Frank fell overboard, Nelson would push the MOB button to lock in GPS coordinates of the ship's position at the time of the fall.

A wave hit Frank, knocking him off balance, but he was able to hold on like a monkey on a vine. Tying reef lines normally requires two hands, but Frank attempted the task with one while using the other to hold on to the boom. One end of the reef line got away from him again and again. Each time he reached for it, he had to stretch farther beyond the safety lines. "This is not going to end well," Nelson blurted out. "We need to get him in."

"I said I'm fine," Frank snapped. "Quit mothering me!"

Nelson quickly fastened his safety harness around the grab bar on the console. He stepped closer to Frank with one foot on the cockpit sole and the other on the lazarette. He gripped the grab bar around the console with one hand and grabbed Frank's pants and belt with the other.

Blake stood by the winch holding the mainsheet. He had his hands on the crank to bring in the sail at the moment Frank had secured the luffing sail. Frank was taking more time than it would have in normal conditions, and the reef lines kept getting away from him. The urgency for action was increasing by the second. Blake looked up to the masthead wind indicator to see the wind direction. "Nelson, we're turning into the wind. Do you have a firm grip on him? The boom could swing, and he could be knocked off."

"I have him by the belt, but he's too far over. We could still lose him."

Frank continued struggling with the reef lines, ignoring his predicament. Nelson checked his own footing and tightened his grip on him. *Momentum* rolled from side to side, almost dipping the boom into the water. An instant later, water splashed onto the deck and Frank's feet slipped out from under him. His body stretched between the safety lines and the boom. Nelson, mothering Nelson, was his last connection to life. Without help, Frank would drop into the water and Nelson's crazy images of him being lost at sea would come true. Frank clung helplessly to the boom while Nelson maintained his grip. Blake lunged and grabbed Frank's belt. If Frank lost his hold on the boom, he would go down and could take Blake with him. Nelson was the only one tethered to *Momentum*.

"It's getting harder to hold him! Come into the wind!" Nelson yelled.

Blake let go of Frank and steered into the wind while rapidly cranking the winch to sheet in. The boom came over the boat, bringing Frank with it. Frank finished tying the reef lines and adjusted his pants as if nothing had happened. He leaned close to Nelson. "I wouldn't have slipped if you had left me alone. If I had gone in, it would have been on you."

His mouth agape in disbelief, Nelson watched him head to the companionway. "Frank, I gotta tell you… that was the most reckless thing I have ever seen in all my sailing days. Even I, the swab, know that was dumb. Do you have a death wish?"

Frank looked at Nelson disdainfully. "Does saying that make you feel more like a man?" he said as he went below.

Blake and Nelson looked at each other. Nelson pursed his lips and slowly shook his head.

"You just saved that man's life," Blake said. "That's all he gave you?"

"He told me his death would have been on me," Nelson said.

Blake shrugged. "I don't get it."

"Do you think the seas are going to get worse?" Nelson asked.

"Hard to tell. The sea has a mind of its own. We just have to keep an eye on it and respond. We're secure on third reef. I have the helm. You go below and get some rest. And try to put this behind you."

WE MUST HOVE-TO NOW!

"We must hove-to now!"

Nelson scrambled out of his bunk—groggy and half awake. He had been asleep for less than thirty minutes. Blake had never yelled from the helm. The sea wasn't slamming the boat from the side, which would have abruptly awakened him. Blake's voice meant something urgent was happening that commanded immediate action.

Nelson stood in the companionway, clenching the grabrail, and looked up to the cockpit to find Blake contending with an angry sea. He looked like a character in a nail-biting thriller movie. His legs were wedged on each side of the cockpit to keep himself balanced on the bucking boat. The boat heeled over hard. Rain pelted Blake. His long hair obstructed his vision, but there was no time to push it away. The waves had grown to twenty feet and were following the boat like a pack of wolves. One broke over the stern and flooded the cockpit. *Momentum* faltered and dipped under the weight of water. When it drained, she lunged forward down a wave. Another wave broke and flooded her again. Moments later yet another wave refilled the cockpit before the last wave had time to drain.

Nelson saw firsthand what the textbooks said about the dangers of breaking waves. They were menacing and unpredictable. Sometimes a wave would come beside the boat and, instead of breaking forward, spill its water sideways into the cockpit. The waves acted and sounded differently from whitecaps. Whitecaps swooshed, and breaking waves dumped. Whitecaps stayed on top of the wave, while breaking waves lunged forward. Because waves traveled faster than the boat, *Momentum* could find herself on the wave's crest, the trough, the front side, or the backside. She sped up surfing down a wave and slowed when going up its backside. Her stern was lower in the water when climbing a wave, and that made her vulnerable to one coming from behind. The larger the seas, the greater the risks. The sea/boat dynamics constantly shifted. In one moment the boat could evade a large breaking wave, and in another she sat helpless and could do nothing more than take the beating.

SPLASH! Water filled the cockpit.

"Where's Frank?" Blake yelled to be heard over the noise of the storm waves.

Nelson ducked his head back into the cabin and saw Frank standing beside his bunk, holding up his pants to find the front. "Frank! Let's move it!"

Nelson stuck his head back into his cabin and yelled, "Quinney! Wake up! Seas are up. We're heaving to. Stay in the cabin!" He grabbed his PFD from a hook in the companionway and joined Blake. "What can I do?"

"We need Frank on deck. Where is he?"

Nelson ducked and looked a second time for Frank, who was sitting on his bunk, putting on his shoes. "Frank!" He turned to Blake. "He's coming."

SPLASH! Another breaking wave flooded the cockpit.

Blake fought the wheel to keep the boat from turning broadside to the waves while struggling to keep his own balance.

Gusts slammed against the sails, attempting to push *Momentum* away from the wind. Waves came from behind and then from the side, sending white billows of sharp spray up and over the deck.

Wind howled in the rigging like a haunting beast. Breaking waves were omnipresent, thundering like giant waves on a beach.

Threatening waves sent out a deep belch as they broke. Most fearsome were the ones that broke close to or immediately behind the boat. The infuriated sea caused chaos in the salon, sending crashing sounds from anything not tied down. The noise resembled rocks and glass tumbling in a tin can or dishes falling from a shelf. Junk drawers, crammed so full that they were unable to be latched, flung their contents throughout the cabin.

Frank stepped into the cockpit. He looked around, expressionless, as he assessed the situation. There was no sense of urgency when he said, "Let's bring her around."

Blake gave the helm to Frank. He left the cockpit and worked his way to the mast to untie the running backstays. Spray continued to shoot from windward, and breaking waves grew taller and came more frequently. Blake held on to the mast with one hand and attempted to untie the line securing the running backstay.

SPLASH! The cockpit filled up to the companionway step. Nelson jumped to close the companionway hatch to prevent water from spilling from the cockpit into the cabin.

CRASH! A wave slammed into *Momentum*'s side. She lurched away, almost knocking everyone off balance. Crashing continued down below.

Blake inched his way back to the cockpit. Sharp spray and a severely rocking boat challenged his balance. The running backstay remained attached to the mast.

"What's wrong?" Nelson yelled.

"I don't know what kind of knot you tied," Blake shouted angrily. "You go figure it out—and be quick about it!" He resumed command of the helm. Frank readied the mainsail sheets in preparation for coming about.

Nelson fastened his harness strap to the safety lines and kept a low body profile while fighting his way through spray and a jerking boat. He wrapped his secondary harness strap around the mast. When a wave rocked the boat windward, Nelson felt an overpowering tug toward the sea, but he was secure and confident in his tether.

CRASH! Another wave hit the side, and *Momentum* jerked. Nelson's harness kept him tethered as the force of the wave attempted to pull him from the mast. *Momentum* snapped upright, smashing Nelson's face into working lines and the mast. Being fastened to the mast gave him two hands to loosen the knots on the running backstays. When sea spray sent its next assault, the sound it made on his foulies was like hail on a tin shed. With the knots loose Nelson cupped his hand and turned toward the helm. "Ready!" he yelled, waiting for Blake's command to loosen the last of the securing knot.

SPLASH!

"Nelson!" Blake shouted. "Prepare to come about!"

Nelson waved and waited.

Blake studied the waves. Timing was critical. He had to initiate the turn the moment a wave broke on the windward side. He had to complete the turn and place the boat into the angular hove-to position before another breaking wave hit. The turn had to be precise and without hesitation. *Momentum* was most vulnerable during the turn. The three had to work as a team. No more clarifications. No more questions. Just do. If anyone faltered, they would be fodder for a broadside breaking wave.

"Everybody ready?" Blake shouted.

"Ready!"

SPLASH!

Blake waited as the water drained from the cockpit. He watched the wave action and waited until the exact moment. "Wait!... Wait!... Wait!... Now! Nelson, let loose!" Blake turned the wheel hard to windward, and the boat responded. Frank stood ready with the mainsheet, and as soon as the boom swung toward leeward, he scrambled to trim the sheets.

Halfway through the turn, a wave broke. *Momentum* was in its path.

"Nelson! Hold tight!" Frank yelled. "Wave! Wave!"

A twenty-foot wave charged *Momentum*'s beam. Moments before it broke, the wave clobbered *Momentum*. Water crashed against her side and attempted to roll her over. Water yanked forcefully on Nelson, but he remained secure with his harness. Another wave hit the stern and pushed it forward, turning the bow toward and through the wave as Blake had originally intended. The bow came around, the boom swung, and the jib remained in place with the sheet secured on the windward side. *Momentum* stopped at an angle to the oncoming waves.

Blake made steering adjustments. Frank watched the sails and the boat—ready for fine-tuning. Nelson tightened the leeward running backstay and waited at the mast until Blake and Frank were satisfied with their adjustments. As exhausting as it was, Blake had made it look easy.

Momentum lay at a sixty-degree angle to the wind. She sat straight up as she drifted leeward at the wind's mercy. Cushioning *Momentum* from the angry sea was a becalmed area that looked like an oil slick. Water churned up from under the boat. Waves continued to break, but they went around *Momentum* as if avoiding a collision with her. Blake lashed the wheel hard over to keep the boat in the angled position.

Momentum was hove-to.

The magic described in the storm tactics textbooks was exactly as Nelson was seeing. He looked on, breathing hard, in awe. It was as if she were floating peacefully, enshrouded in a protective bubble and unreachable by a tenacious tempest thirsty for destruction. The howling wind through the rigging eased up. The razor-sharp spray was gone. Mayhem in the salon had ended. *Momentum* was happy. It was as if someone had turned off the storm switch.

Blake, Nelson, and Frank sat side by side in the cockpit, panting, leaning forward with their elbows on their knees. Nelson attempted to recover from an overdose of adrenaline. As much as he had practiced the heaving-to maneuver, nothing had come close to what he had just experienced.

"Is this enough adventure for you?" Blake said as he looked toward Nelson.

"One thing's for sure… I'll never use the word *easy* to describe heaving to again," Nelson replied. "Would you look at that mess down there," he said, looking down into the cabin. "I'd better go see how Quinney fared."

Nelson stood at the bottom of the companionway, looking around the salon in disbelief. What he saw was the most compelling argument in favor of being unbending in the discipline of latching cupboards and drawers. *Well, that's one way to clean out the drawers,* he thought with the crack of a smile.

Groaning came from their cabin. Quinney. The cabin door resisted. Nelson was unsure if it was Quinney, books, or clothing blocking the way. He pushed gently but firmly while calling Quinney's name but heard no response. The door moved enough for Nelson to be able to look through the gap between the door and the jamb. Quinney lay on the bunk, grasping her arms in pain.

"Quinney!"

She moaned.

Blake appeared by Nelson's side. "What's going on?"

"Quinney's hurt. The door's blocked."

Nelson pushed, and the cabin door plowed back books and clothing.

Quinney lay in a fetal position.

"What hurts?" Nelson asked.

Quinney whispered slowly, "I think I cracked a rib."

"Can you move?"

"It hurts too much."

"How did it happen?" Blake said.

Her breathing labored, Quinney tried telling her story. Most of it was jumbled or inaudible, but the gist was that she had been attempting to climb the companionway steps when the boat was suddenly jolted from one side to the other. She'd lost her balance and been slammed against the edges of the companionway steps. She then struggled to return to the cabin.

"Did you feel or hear any ribs breaking?" Blake asked.

"No, that's why I think it's cracked. It hurts when I breathe."

"We need to bind her up," Blake said. "I'll look around for a first-aid kit."

"Look for a roll of duct tape, too," Nelson said.

Blake returned, holding out a roll of duct tape. "You got this? I want to see how things are going on deck."

Nelson turned his attention to Quinney. She refused to move and fought the pain when she breathed. "C'mon, Quinney. We've got to get you sitting up. I'm going to bind you up with duct tape. It'll make everything less painful. I promise."

Quinney moaned and yelped and cried as Nelson helped her sit up. He removed layers of clothing. Each twist brought a protesting scream. He found one of his clean T-shirts and gently pulled it over her head. He wrapped the duct tape around and around, repeatedly asking if it was too tight. When done, he stood back. "Well, me dear, you look like the Tin Man."

Quinney chuckled pitifully and held her chest. "Don't make me laugh! I hope this works. I'm eternally grateful you didn't put the duct tape on my skin."

"Ouch! That hurts just thinking about it," Nelson said.

"Where's the raging sea? Did it calm down? I don't feel anything, and it's so quiet."

"It's still there. That's the magic of heaving to. I wish you could see it, but I'm sure Blake will confine you to quarters until you're feeling better."

They talked a while longer, and Quinney's eyes got heavy. Nelson lay her down carefully. He picked up the books, clothing, and everything else strewn about the floor and restored the cabin to how it had looked before the thrashing. He returned to Quinney's side and stroked her shoulder. Quinney began sobbing. "I was so scared. I thought we were all going to die."

"We're OK now." He held her hand and gently curled her fingers as he wrapped his hands around them. "Don't worry, kid. Nothing bad is going to happen to you while I'm still alive. Get some rest."

Nelson grabbed his pocket camera and returned to the cockpit. He snapped pictures of the cockpit and surrounding sea. The sun was getting lower in the western sky and created a postcard view of blue water, foamy whitecaps, and turquoise breaking waves. "No one back home is gonna believe this when I tell them what happened."

"You're going to be very disappointed in the pictures," Blake said. "Waves in pictures always look smaller than they really are. They've settled down. They're down to about twelve to fifteen feet, but when you see the pictures, they'll look like three-footers and your friends will say, 'What's the big deal?'"

Frank excused himself and went below.

"So, Nelson, tell me," Blake said. "How did you feel when you were out there strapped to the mast and Mother Nature was throwing some of her worst work at you?"

Nelson searched for a response. "I'd have to think about that one. It all happened so fast. I didn't have any time for feelings. I was just trying to hear you."

"Were you afraid?"

"Afraid? Strangely enough… no. There was plenty to be afraid of out there, but now that I think about it… no, I wasn't afraid at all."

"Sailors die out there. Didn't that cross your mind?"

"I was strapped to the mast. The only way I was going to die was if something really ugly happened to the boat. Anyone doing what we do out here—hundreds of miles from anywhere—has to have had a talk with themselves about being ready for death."

"Are you?" said Blake.

"Ready for death? It's easy to say yes to that, but looking death in the eye is the real test of one's fear of dying. Luckily, I'm spiritual. This world is too interconnected for all this to be an accident. If I get tossed overboard, my life expectancy can be measured in minutes. No sense in panicking, because it's not gonna buy me any more time. Why should I squander my last few minutes being afraid? I have made my peace with death, but not with life."

Blake gave Nelson a blank look. "Where'd that come from?"

"With death, there are no negotiations," Nelson explained. "It comes when it comes. Period. When I talk about making peace with life, I'm referring to the quality of life. I get into a lot of debates with people about this, but I think the world has natural harmony until you add man to the mix. There are just too many deceitful, greedy, ruthless people out there, and they mess it up for the majority of civilization who just want to get along. How about you? Are you a believer?"

"Yeah, I believe. Have you ever had a near-death experience?"

"I've had close-to-death experiences a few times," Nelson said. "Once in an earthquake and another while scuba diving."

"Were you afraid then?"

"Yes, at first, but when death was inevitable, I got very peaceful. You—do you have fear?"

"Like you, I think all sailors have that talk with themselves. And the more you believe, the less you cling to life as you're about to lose it. How about squalls at night? Does the thought of them still frighten you?"

"Hmm. I think if I could see the back end of a squall, I might be less fearful."

Blake laughed. "That's not the scary end, Nelson. It's the front. You don't need to see the whole thing, but you have to know where the front of the storm is. That's where you'll find the wind, the churned-up seas, and the pelting spray."

"The other night in that squall, I had more fear about not knowing what to do than fear of the squall itself. I was afraid I'd put the boat in danger."

"I was watching you. You did OK. You wanted to tack, didn't you?"

"Yeah, but I was afraid to yell for help and have you come up and say we didn't need to tack. Now I know that out here, sailing to compass is not my friend. I can see how sailing to wind makes me a better sailor."

"Well, you handled the situation, and you didn't put the boat in danger. You did your job as the helmsman."

"Why are you asking me about my fears?"

"I've been watching you. It definitely looks like you've overcome them."

Nelson looked up as he searched for a response. "Yeah, I guess you could say I have, but there are storms out there much worse than what we just came through—the ones so large and deadly, you know you're not getting out alive. Each situation is a different test, and each experience makes me a more competent sailor. You haven't answered my question about why you're asking."

"I was just wondering if what I see matches how you feel. You told me early on, before we left BVI, that you wanted to face and conquer your fears. And it seems you have."

They sat in silence. There was no more to say about that topic. The two of them weren't so different, Nelson realized, and from that point forward, conversations between them would be longer than five words.

"We don't need to stay up here while she's hove-to," Blake said. "The boat is happy. You can go below if you want. I'll check the conditions every hour, and when it's safe to move, we will. I'm going below."

"It's OK to leave the cockpit unattended?"

"Normally, there should always be someone on watch, but we're not near any shipping lanes. So far all we've seen is one sailboat heading to Bermuda and the burning freighter. We'll be fine."

"Hmm. You heard about the burning freighter, huh?"

Blake started his climb down the companionway. "Blake," Nelson said. "I wasn't asleep at the wheel."

Blake gave Nelson a half smile and went below.

Nelson sat, watching what he considered the second-best part of the day. The sun was going down. It cast a soft light on the boat, the waves, everything. The wind let up and the whitecaps were settling down. The boat was happy. She had just gone through a harrowing event that had tested both her and the crew. He pondered Blake's questions about fear and was gratified by his responses. Blake, for the first time on the passage, showed an interest in Nelson beyond the task at hand. He seemed more interested in the person within. It wasn't a test. There was no pass/fail. Blake's questions gave Nelson permission to see where he stood on his personal "fear-o-meter," and to his surprise, the "numbers" were good.

In the cockpit, lines were strewn throughout. The untidiness of it annoyed him. Nelson coiled and stowed lines and then looked around his world, assessing where he was and what he was experiencing. For being grateful, his list was long—Quinney was safe, his fear had significantly diminished, his connection with the sea was growing, and he had good health to endure the rigors of blue-water sailing.

Then, in keeping with his pattern of meaningful prayer, his mind wandered as always. *In any given moment around the globe, tens of thousands of commercial vessels are en route from one port to another. On the Atlantic, a thick stream of cargo and tanker vessels is flowing to the United States to and from the Mediterranean and the English Channel. Why haven't we seen more of them?*

Sitting on watch for hours on end with no one to talk to or anything to change the scenery can become monotonous. A mariner has an abundance of time to ponder the "what-if" scenarios of the world, reflect on self, and ask deep "why" questions. With plenty of time to talk with the inner self, it's understandable why blue-water sailing can create a person of few words.

Nelson pondered the volume of global traffic, wondering how it could be possible that the freighter they'd thought was ablaze was the first and, up to this point, only one they had seen. When he considered that a six-foot person can see only three miles before objects become hidden beyond the curvature of the earth, his provocative question about where they all were became moot. Granted, the higher up a person stands—on a ship's bridge, on a cliff, in a lighthouse—the farther he can see. He concluded that encountering any vessel from his vantage point would be more of an accident than a certainty unless they were on a collision course.

Nelson leaned back, resting on the stanchions. His imagination began driving his mental bus at high speed. "What-if" thoughts popped into his head. *What if I were in a life raft without an EPIRB transmitter… How close would a vessel have to pass to see me? I say less than three miles if the vessel were looking for me. What if I were in a life raft and there were typical seas of three to four feet? Could I be seen at all? Less than a mile and the vessel would have to have someone on the lookout with binoculars. What if I fell overboard in high seas and all I had on was this PFD? If others watched me fall overboard and they could turn the boat quickly, they might be able to rescue me. If I fell overboard while alone on deck without a harness, never. What are the chances of being spotted by a tanker or cargo ship if I were floating around in a life raft? Slim to none.*

The more Nelson thought, the larger the ocean became and the smaller he felt in it. It was good exercise. Man needs constant humbling.

HOVING—TO... AGAIN?

Momentum bobbled tranquilly in her hove-to cocoon. Breaking waves surrounded her but dared not breach the protective slick. She looked like a scene from immediately after a hurricane—abandoned, alone, and betrayed by Mother Nature.

Compared with twenty-foot seas and following breaking waves, the hove-to position was like sitting in the windless, waveless, rainless horse latitudes. It gave *Momentum* time to breathe and the crew time to rejuvenate their spent muscles.

Frank sat at the salon table sorting through the cache of projectile stuff. Without a hint of which drawer or cabinet an object called "home," he could organize and sort any way he liked. Concern about how the boat owner would react didn't matter. He began clustering duplicates and like items. With all the duplication, he considered it evident that the owner had bought replacements instead of hunting for what could not be easily found. Examining the booty of stuff on the table was another distraction to help them relax.

Blake picked up whatever had been scattered to the floor and corners of the cabin. Nelson went on a scavenger hunt for navigation tools, charts, pencils, and logs. He cleaned standing water out of shelves before replacing books and magazines. The passageway to the engine compartment was blocked by trash, duffel bags, and loose clothing. Luckily for Frank, his task took the greatest amount of time. Nelson's tasks were straightforward. The passageway cleanup went to the next available person—the swab.

Blake made numerous trips to the cockpit. After *Momentum* had been hove-to for two hours, he returned from the cockpit and studied Frank's progress on his mission. "How much longer do you need to finish sorting all that stuff?"

"I can be done in a few minutes if you need me for something," Frank said.

"You don't need to stop. The seas are down. It's safe to continue. I just don't want the boat to heel over and dump all your work on the floor."

"Don't wait for me. I'm good here."

SHIP'S LOG—APRIL 26, 2010—1307 HOURS—31° 05′06″N, 072° 46′50″W

Nelson followed Blake to the cockpit. "Winch in the jib sheet," Blake said. "I don't want it flapping when we release the windward side." Nelson complied. Blake unlashed the wheel and turned it to center. *Momentum* began turning away from the wind. "Let loose the windward jib sheet!" commanded Blake. The jib flew leeward and snapped to attention. Nelson cleaned up the lines while Blake trimmed the sails. *Momentum* was underway.

Quinney appeared in her cabin doorway. She moved slowly and clutched her chest with one hand and the doorway with the other. Her hair looked as if she had just lost a street brawl. Frank looked up from the salon table. "Well! Look who's up! How are you doin'? Feeling better?"

"Uncomfortable and sore. The tape helps. I need a little food. We all need some. You should eat while you can. Tell Nelson he needs to eat." Quinney shuffled back into her cabin.

Frank prepared dinner—bagels with sliced cheese and meat. He brought a half sandwich to Quinney and two to the cockpit. He handed one to Nelson and said, "Quinney got up to tell me to tell you to eat. Here. Eat."

"Quinney's up?" Nelson asked.

"Not anymore. I gave her a sandwich. She's in the cabin. Says she's feeling a little better."

Nelson attempted to eat Frank's "cooking." The bagel was dry and tasteless. He had little spit, and water tasted like a millpond filled with tadpole eggs. His appetite was satisfied with two bites. Same with Frank and Blake. The meal was over. Nelson went below to check on Quinney and found her asleep. Nelson got a whiff of an odor emanating from the cabin that smelled as if a dead fish had been stashed in one of the cabinets for days. But the aroma came from the inside of his foulies. No one had showered in days. Nelson, who had been living in his foulies, could not stand himself. He caked on deodorant. He still smelled like a dead fish. His situation had gone beyond the help of deodorant.

Growing up in New England, the word for rainy weather outerwear was *slickers*. When he used the East Coast term in the West, he was corrected. Out West, *slickers* were *foulies*, short for "foul weather gear." Nelson joked that *foulies* referred to the way sailors smelled after days at sea. After smelling himself, it was no longer a joke.

Several hours had passed. Nelson returned to the cockpit just in time to see a blood-red sunset. Blazing red spread across the sky. The water became red. It morphed into orange and then yellow and then gray blue as the sun set. From the east came the moon—night's friend. Nelson broke the silence on deck. "Isn't it amazing how only a few hours ago we were battling twenty-foot seas, breaking waves, and battering rain. And now we get this."

"Conditions can change fast," Blake said. "Nelson, I want you back on night watch. Get some rest. If it gets rough again, Frank or I will be on watch with you. Be back here at 2200 hours."

Nelson went below. He thought about removing his foulies to air himself out but decided it would be unfair to Quinney and he wouldn't be prepared if called to the cockpit in an emergency. He set the clock and drifted off, surrounded by the smell of dead fish.

* * *

SHIP'S LOG—APRIL 26, 2010—2145 HOURS—32° 18'9"N, 073° 42'0"W

Nelson's alarm went off. Time to prepare for his 2200 hours watch. He slid out of the bunk, washed his face, and made an entry in the ship's log. He was ahead of watch schedule by fifteen minutes. He sat at the nav-station and began to doze.

"We need to hove-to!" came Blake's bellowing voice.

Again?

Nelson shook Frank awake and stood by him until he sat up and began to dress. Nelson picked up his PFD as he went to the cockpit. The seas were up, and breaking waves were night prowlers—a person knew they were there, but they were invisible until upon them. *Momentum* rocked and yawed as Blake kept control against the attacking waves pounding at her side.

Nelson stood looking at this new enemy. He felt like he was in a horror movie, creeping down a dark, narrow, musty hallway with hidden doors and lurking ghouls waiting to leap upon him. Earlier he had told Blake that he hadn't felt any fear during the heaving-to maneuver, but in the dark—the dark night on the sea that was already his enemy—his mouth became cotton dry. Nelson had heard stories about the boogeymen that prey upon the minds of night sailors. Toss in dehydration and fatigue, and the boogeymen swirl in a person's head like cigarette smoke. Nelson had scoffed at what he'd heard about such monsters, but now, anxiety began to overtake him. The more he dwelled on them, the more ineffective he would be as an able seaman. He had a job to do when they hove-to, and he had to stop believing in what was unbelievable.

Frank came to the cockpit and immediately grabbed hold of the mainsheet. Nelson knew he had to act with similar conviction—his recovering credibility was at stake. He attached his harness to the safety lines, worked his way to the mast, and lashed himself to it. He turned on his flashlight and held it tight in his teeth as he untied the knots on the running backstays. Then he waited for Blake's command.

Blake did not explain himself, but his actions indicated that the urgency to heave to was not like earlier. Nelson felt the waves slamming into the boat, but they were not as harsh or strong. He heard the occasional crashing of something being hurled around the cabin below him, but not a full dumping of an entire shelf of dishes. He could see the whitecaps and heard the sounds of spilling water from the breaking waves. They were not furious. His fear subsided when the boogeymen left his head.

"Nelson! Ready?" came Blake's voice.

"Ready!"

"Wait for my command! We're tacking to port." Nelson knew he had to loosen the port running backstay first. He knew his knot and no longer needed the flashlight to see it. He put it away and waited.

Blake watched the breaking waves on the port side. When one broke, he yelled, "Helm's alee! Nelson! Let loose!" and turned the wheel hard over. "Nelson! Watch that jib comin' at ya!"

Moments later *Momentum* was hove-to with a fraction of the excitement from earlier. Blake watched and made minor adjustments to the sail to achieve the desired boat angle to the oncoming sea. He looked out to the sea and up the mast. "Well, that's all we can do now. We're gonna stay hove-to all night, even if the seas settle. We all could use the rest. We may as well turn in."

Nelson's personal journal—April 26, 2010

Continued high seas and thirty-knot NW winds. Boat moving seven–eight knots hourly. Hove-to boat in twenty-foot seas with breaking waves. Unable to contain/control seasickness. Living on sips of water and bites of aging bagel. No pee to pee. I stink. I think my clothing is sticking to me under my foulies. No longer a regular passage but a lesson in storm tactics. What am I doing way out here? This has become a very hard experience. Sailing again at 1300. Hove-to second time at 2200 hours. Magically settled seas coming directly at us. Boat taking a beating. Water pouring down windward side of hull in Blake's quarters. Quinney broke/cracked ribs. Storms all around and beautiful.

WHAT THE *HELL* ARE YOU DOING THERE?

A deep rumbling rolled through the hove-to *Momentum* and awakened Nelson. He looked at his watch—0140 hours. They had been hove-to for three hours. Quinney lay next to him—sleeping quietly. Nelson gently rubbed her shoulder and whispered her name. Her response was incomprehensible, but a response was all he was hoping for. He sighed and leaned his back against the bulkhead. *Where am I and what am I doing here? Has this adventure become insanity?*

The rumbling continued. Nelson's eyes opened wide as if it would help locate the sound's origin. Another rumble. Thunder. Nelson scrambled to the cockpit. There was a light show to be seen! They were surrounded by storms—not squalls, but storms that reached high into the sky. They resembled the summer storms he had experienced growing up on the farm.

Nelson sat, watching the lightning show. Most of what he saw happened high inside the clouds—flashing without thunder that gave the billowing clouds depth and character. Occasionally a bolt hit the water. Nelson counted the seconds—one one hundred, two one hundred, three one hundred, four one hundred, five one hundred—and then came the rolling thunder that told him the lightning had hit one mile away.

Nelson's mind wandered back six decades to a time when lightning topped his list of fears. His ear was trained to hear the slightest decibel of an approaching nocturnal summer thunderstorm. It triggered terror—more than the snakes that hid under his bed. He would dash to the window and listen for confirmation, then grab his pillow and race to Mary's room, where he could see light spilling from under the closed door. Mary, a renter, was always there for him when he needed protection. She would put him in her bed, close his eyes with her gentle fingers, and continue to write letters to her "folks back home." When Nelson awoke to the greeting of a crowing rooster in the early dawn, he was magically back in his own bed.

As a young schoolboy, his fear clung to him. He feared that when he became an adult, the village would scorn him and even his own children would point and laugh. In grade school, an early afternoon thunderstorm excited the other children while Nelson sat, frozen with terror. He sat near the tall windows in the school room, certain a lightning bolt would crash through and strike him dead. But his teacher, like Mary, stood by him saying nothing and made safe his world. When it came time for a class project, his teacher looked over what he proposed to study, set it aside, and gently said, "I have a better project just for you." Nelson reported on lightning—its causes, its dangers, and how to protect oneself. He learned that since sound travels one mile every five seconds, a person could easily detect how far off the lightning bolt hit. Most importantly, he learned that lightning did not have a mind of its own that chased little boys, stabbing at them, sending them screaming into the comforting breasts of Mother.

Frank came up to the cockpit and brought Nelson back from his reverie. "Looks like we're in for it," he said as he looked at the lightning show. A bolt hit the water, and thunder followed a few seconds later.

"We're right in the middle of it, and the boat is the highest object around," Frank said. "We're sitting ducks for a hit. We'd better prepare the boat. We're lucky to be hove-to. We can completely shut down the systems. A hit to the mast will fry all the electronics, and then we're screwed." Frank went below. A few minutes later the boat went dark except for the required running lights.

"That was quick," Nelson said. "Now what? Do we just sit here and wait it out?"

"I shut off the breakers. We need to be away from all metal. We're sitting right next to the stanchions. If the boat gets zapped, so could we. We should be lying flat on the sole."

They lay with their arms crisscrossed over their chests, enabling them to fit side by side in the narrow cockpit. They lay quietly, rocking in a hove-to boat while large waves continued to veer away from *Momentum*. Five minutes passed. Then ten.

Lightning flashed all around. Strikes hit the water less than a mile away. Some thunder was close enough to vibrate the boat, and some sounded like a distant throat clearing. The high seas showed signs of settling. The slick, created by being hove-to, gave *Momentum* protection from breaking waves, yet she still rolled with the swells. Lying on the sole, both Frank and Nelson could feel the gentle rise and fall of the boat.

"I've always loved lightning storms," Frank said, breaking a long silence.

"Really? I didn't think you loved anything."

"Touché. I had that coming."

The silence resumed.

"I guess we're not gonna talk much," Frank said.

"Why should we? All you've done is play me for a fool or put me down."

"When have I done that?"

"What? You want examples? How about thinking I would buy into your bit about being the captain because I was steering the boat?"

"I was just testing you."

"Yeah, and if I had taken the bait, my actions would have been mutinous."

"You're being dramatic."

"And *you're* being dismissive. If you're trying to get a conversation going here, you'd better try a different approach."

"Dismissive? I have no idea what you just said. Care to translate?"

"When you brush aside my feelings or what I'm trying to say, it's like you're saying they don't count. That's being dismissive. Is that what you mean?"

"No, but…"

"What's up? You're not acting like your usual brash self. Where'd you stash your arrogance? I don't hear it. I sense contrition. I get the feeling you're trying to get past our short but bad history, and you're feeling a little awkward about it, right?"

"I suppose you could say that."

"Then you should say so."

"You're making this difficult. OK, Nelson, things haven't been good between us, and I think we should get beyond it. How did you pick up on this?"

"Up till now, the Frank I know would never have said you love something. You teach kids how to sail. I teach professionals how to disagree and still respect one another. I'm trained to pick up signals from what people say or don't say, and how they say them."

"I didn't know that. Actually, I know nothing about you at all."

"That's because you chose to belittle me instead of learning about me. Your behavior around Quinney is disgraceful. You take pleasure in playing these one-upmanship games. It's hard to feel respected around someone who always acts superior. I've decided that the best way to deal with you is to ignore you and accept the fact that you're just a practicing jerk."

"I've never been called *that* before. OK, I'll bite. What's a practicing jerk?"

"Someone who gets up every day and commits to being a jerk to those around him. Earlier in the trip you spoke about the kids in your sailing school like they were family to you, that you cared for them. They mattered to you. I told Quinney that you had a good heart after all. But then you went and spoiled it all. I think you're addicted to being a jerk, or you're using it as a protective mechanism to keep people from knowing something about you—a way of hiding. Anyway, I quit letting you get to me. So if you think it's working… forget it. You're ineffective. And part of my problem with you has been the way you treat Quinney. She's much kinder than I'll ever be. She continually gives you the benefit of the doubt, yet you still disrespect her. If you want to start over with us, as in you and me, quit with your zingers and put-downs."

Nelson waited for Frank to respond. The short silence that followed seemed like hours.

"OK, I'll tell you something," Frank finally said. He sighed and lay quietly for a few minutes. Nelson figured something important was about to come from him. "I'm leaving myself open here. And defenseless."

Nelson sat quietly, saying nothing.

"I've been sailing most of my life. I teach it and I'm good at it because I love it. Unfortunately, the pay sucks. I own a small tract house in Arnold, Maryland. Growing up, I worked around boatyards, doing whatever grunt work I could get, but I was around boats, and it didn't matter that they were all on the hard and all I saw of them were hulls and keels. Like you, I earned all the sailing certificates, but I went further to get instructor certificates that brought weekend work at the marinas. I worked as crew on commercial boats in Baltimore and eventually received my captain's license. All I got from that was a job piloting a ferry service. Boring. Then I applied for an instructor position at the summer sailing school for kids. I outlasted all the other instructors, and now I run the whole program. When the summer session ends, I hire out as crew on deliveries like this or one-on-one instruction to new boat owners. My dream was to own a sailboat rated for blue-water sailing and spend my winters slumming around the Caribbean. But you have to have an income to support a land base, the boat, marina costs, and maintenance, and I'm sure I don't have to tell you about those costs."

"Yes. I know. I'm retired and on a fixed income. I have a mortgage for the house *and* a boat. I put the boat in charter to defray costs. I worry that one day my sweetheart will get old and tired looking and get kicked out of the fleet, and there goes that income and my household budget will be running in the red."

"What's the name of your boat?"

"*Ms. Sera.*"

"Hmm. Nice. How'd she come by that name?"

"I tell people a romantic and poetic story about how I named her, but she's named after my cat. I don't want to get off topic. Frank, why are you opening up to me?"

"Why do you own a boat when it's much cheaper to charter?"

"Without getting into all the details, owning my own sailboat brings me a sense of freedom and flexibility to do what matters most to me. But let's get back to my question to you," Nelson said.

"You almost answered it for me," Frank said. "Chartering allows you to sail without the expense of ownership, but owning a boat gives you freedom. I know you get the difference, so you can understand why I wanted to own a blue-water sailboat."

"I'm getting the picture, but I don't understand the connection to this conversation," Nelson said.

"We both have the sailing passion... You own a boat... I don't."

Nelson sat up and leaned against the lazarette. He looked out to the sea, trying to interpret what Frank had just said. "A week or so ago you told me I didn't deserve to own a boat because I didn't know its displacement. Do you resent my owning a boat? Is that it?"

"Anyone who owns a boat should know its displacement. You can't know about the boat's stability without knowing its displacement."

"You *are* resentful, aren't you, Frank? OK, sit up. This is important."

Frank pulled himself up. "Forget the lightning storm," Nelson said. "It's dissipated. Let's talk."

Frank slowly embarked on an autobiography detailing his

personal life—an only child orphaned as a teenager when his parents died in a car crash, jumping from one job to the next, numerous failed marriages, children who were no longer speaking to him, a near disastrous problem with drinking, and the sailing school he claimed saved his life. Nelson hid his tears as Frank peeled back his story. In Frank, he heard part of his own story. His anger toward Frank vanished. He was tempted to give him a hug but thought it would be taking his empathy too far. An hour passed before Frank ran out of things to say.

Nelson thought, *God, we all have the same hardships. We all struggle. We're all so much alike. Why do we spend so much time fighting one another?*

"How do you feel right now?" Nelson asked.

"Drained. Exhausted, but better, actually. I've had this stuff pent up for years."

"I'm glad you opened up, but why are you telling all this to me?"

Frank shrugged. "You're safe. A week from now we'll never see each other again. I can trust you with my story. And you listened with interest."

"How long have you lived in that house in Maryland?"

"About twenty-seven years."

"In three years it'll be clear, right?"

"Yep, three years and she's all mine. What a celebration I plan to have!"

"Frank, refinance your house and go buy that boat. So you die and leave a big debt. Your children may have cut you out of their lives, but they're still kin. And you can bet that when you die, they'll come out of the woodwork to claim their share of your estate. Make them work for it. And… they get a boat with it."

"I'll have to give that some thought. There's a lot of risk in the financial commitment."

"You're sitting on a boat that wouldn't pass a safety inspection, hundreds of miles from land, and worried about risk? When you get home, pencil it out and I think you'll see you might be closer to it than you think."

"You know, Nelson, I began to change my mind about you when you were talking to the sailboat to Bermuda."

"The *Adelia*? Why?"

"The captain asked if you were the skipper. You said you were the navigator and swab. I have to admit, I knew you were sensitive about being called a swab, which was why I poked it at you, yet there you were, laughing about it with the captain of the *Adelia*. It took the fun out of calling you a swab. You could have let me fall overboard when I was trying to tie the reef lines. You had good reason to let me go, but you pulled me in. You've certainly earned my respect." Frank extended his hand.

Nelson shook it firmly, but mentally he kept a "wait and see" attitude.

"While we're in a 'tell all' mood, you've had all those ASA classes, but you acted like you never saw a sail before. Mind telling me what's going on? What's *your* story?"

"Sitting on night watches has given me plenty of time to think about things like that. Without getting into the details, my father wanted… demanded… his children to be perfect, especially my brother and me. My brother had all the brains and a clear path. Mine? My brain wandered in every direction except the one he wanted for me. I must have been very frustrating to him. He constantly criticized me for missing the big picture. 'Look past your nose, boy,' was one of his favorite digs. Everything I did was flawed. Nothing I did was good enough. His interrogations made me feel stupid. Around him, my self-esteem didn't stand a chance. That was my upbringing. Climbing out of that hole has been a lifelong job. I acted like a swab because I didn't believe I could be anything more. And as long as we're being straight with one another, you jabbing at me only sent me back to my boyhood memories of my father. You stayed in my head until I kicked you out a few days ago. I signed up for this passage to overcome my fears and I found that when I wasn't thinking about fear I could do anything that was asked of me. What I just told you was the short answer," said Nelson with a chuckle.

"Did you and your dad ever become friends?"

"Yes, the best. I buried him about forty years ago and the more time goes by the more I respect and appreciate him and what he was trying to do for me."

"Well, you've certainly given me some things to think about. Thanks for your honesty."

They sat in silence. The storm had passed as did the danger of a lightning strike.

Frank jumped to his feet. "Let's light up the electronics and get some rest," he said as he headed for the companionway.

Nelson sat alone in the dark, watching them drift leeward as the seas calmed down. It was safe to resume sailing, and Blake would soon be in the cockpit to get them back underway. Nelson thought he'd remain on watch and wait for Blake, but Blake did not stir. *Momentum* was hove-to. She was resting. They all needed to be hove-to.

* * *

SHIP'S LOG—APRIL 27, 2010—0620 HOURS—32° 32′11″N, 073° 45′4″E

Momentum was moving again. Mother Nature was showing off her wide range of fickleness. In less than twenty-four hours, *Momentum* had drifted in a hove-to position twice for a total of eight hours. Any excitement with heaving to was gone. The crew was on its third day of rough weather and somehow able to function with the effects of seasickness and dehydration. The puking stages of seasickness had passed, yet focusing on tasks remained a challenge. Nelson thought back about his nighttime conversation with Frank and wondered how the two had managed to remain engaged in an intelligent discussion about personally sensitive issues. The wind and currents pulled *Momentum* in a northwesterly direction, about twenty miles west of the plotted course. Of benefit was its effect of shattering Nelson's compulsive urge to adhere to his navigational plans. Somewhere in the storms, the wind, the strong waves, and heaving to, Nelson found the freedom to sail to wind.

Their sailing day was uneventful. Until…

SHIP'S LOG—APRIL 28, 2010—0330 HOURS—34° 08'60"N, 073° 45'9"E

Frank and Nelson were awakened by Blake's alarm: "We must hove-to now!" They scurried to deck, assumed their positions, and brought *Momentum* into the hove-to position with Blake's only command, "Let loose!"

Momentum drifted leeward into the dark, protected by the "slick." Seasickness and dehydration shaped a lax attitude about standing watch on a hove-to position. Blake inspected the boat, to ensure the wheel was properly lashed to windward, and without a word the three went below and back to their bunks. Nelson lay in his bunk, thinking about the constant barrage from Mother Nature and how he had to constantly get up when the situation called for it. There was no sleeping through an event because he was exhausted. Moments before falling off to sleep, a final thought floated through his head: *It's amazing how the human body can take such a beating and continue to function.*

Hours passed. Nelson awoke with a start. He was awakened by stillness. There was no sound of waves slapping the hull. No rocking. No creaking. He sat up, his ears searching for something other than a pervasive silence. Blake's cabin door was open and his bunk empty. Frank's bunk was also empty. It was as if he had awakened and found himself in an abandoned ship. It was disquieting. Nelson thought he might still be in a dream where he was alone on the boat. He remained dehydrated, seasick yet vomit-less, undernourished, and sleep deprived. He was certain he was hallucinating until he heard faint voices from the cockpit.

The breeze was light. They were surrounded by slow rolling seas, no surface chop, and no whitecaps. Mother Nature was truly fickle. She had settled down. For the moment.

"What's the plan, captain?" Nelson asked.

"I'm gonna call the meteorologist at 1000 hours and find out the latest on the Canadian front, and we'll make a new sail plan after that," Blake said.

Nelson quietly returned to his cabin and shook Quinney gently. She opened her eyes, smiled, and sat up.

"Look at you," Nelson said. "You must be improving. You sat up without help. How are you feeling?"

Quinney looked around. Her hair was a bird's nest. She appeared confused, unsure where she was. Nelson handed her a bottle of water and instructed her to drink it all. She looked at her duct tape body wrap. "How did this get on me? When? Who?"

"You don't remember? Wow! You're seriously dehydrated. You slammed into the companionway steps, and we think you cracked a rib."

"Oh, yeah. Now I remember."

"What else do you remember about it?"

"I just remember being tossed all over the place in our cabin. I could hear crashing on the side of the boat. I couldn't see anything. All I could do was imagine, and the more I imagined, the bigger the waves became. It was like they had life and were trying to get at me. I had to get to the cockpit—to see what was going on. Then the boat jolted to one side and slammed me into the companionway."

"Well, except for your hair, you're looking better. You need food. I'll get you something to eat and wash you up."

"I think *you* should be the one washing up. There's a terrible odor, like death, when you come near. Do *I* smell like that or is it just you?"

- "We all do. If the seas stay calm for a while, we can do something about it."
- "Whenever you've been under a lot of stress, you smell different," Quinney said. "That's how you smell now."
- "Well, a lot has happened."
- "I'd like some fresh air. Can I get out of here?"

- "That's the captain's call. I'll ask," Nelson said.
- Quinney sat, brushing her hair in anticipation of being allowed out.
- "Salon only," Nelson reported when he returned. "Captain doesn't want you on deck yet. Baby steps, you know."

* * *

Blake bounced down the companionway steps. "We'll be in sat-phone range in a few minutes. Are the position coordinates up to date?"

"Not since 0620 hours. Give me a few minutes," Nelson said.

SHIP'S LOG—APRIL 28, 2010—1000 HOURS—34° 08'20"N, 073° 48'8"E

Blake looked at the numbers. "Are you sure about these? We're way northeast from where we should be."

"Yes sir, we are," Nelson said. "Since we've been hove-to, we've drifted northeast by sixty-five miles. What am I missing?"

"We've been hove-to for about seven hours. Two nautical miles an hour is considered a fast drift, which means in that time we should have drifted only fourteen or fifteen miles. See why I'm questioning sixty-five?"

Nelson's eyebrows went up. "I'll go back and double-check."

"*Momentum*, what are your coordinates?" Peter the meteorologist asked.

"Stand by, Peter. We're double-checking them now," Blake said. Nelson gave Blake a thumbs-up on the coordinates. "Peter, I have confirmed numbers."

"*Momentum*, please repeat those coordinates."

Blake did so, and there was a long pause. "Peter, did you get those coordinates?" Blake asked.

"Affirmative. Blake, what the *hell* are you doing there?" Peter asked, his voice full of concern.

Silence filled the cabin like smoke. No one moved. Blake spoke. "We've been hove-to three times. We're dehydrated, we've had little or no sleep, we're seasick to the point that we're unable to keep food down, and we have an injured crew member."

"You're hove-to now?

"Affirmative, Peter," Blake replied. "We'll decide on our options after this call."

"What's the condition of the injured crew member?"

"Improved. We believe it's a cracked rib. She is bound up and seems to be doing well. The injury was not life-threatening, and we did not contact the Coast Guard."

"Blake, you are in the direct path of a very dangerous weather front. Are you aware of that?"

Quinney put her hands over her mouth. Nelson stared at the sat-phone. Frank leaned over Nelson's shoulder. Blake sat expressionless. "Peter, you said a dangerous weather front is coming. I thought there were two fronts. Please confirm."

Peter continued. "Last time we spoke, I told you about two strong northwesterly weather fronts. They have now merged and have become one immensely powerful storm. The storm front has widened. You thought you would be at the southern edge of the front, but you are now in the center of its path. You can expect gale-force winds and seas thirty feet on the most frequent waves, much higher on the significant ones. Your boat can't handle waves that large. If you stay where you are, you'll take a direct hit, and I don't need to remind you how lethal that can be. You need to get out of there. I see two options. You can run to Bermuda or run southwest and flank it. Do not, I repeat, do not attempt to flank it on the north. The front extends up through New England. If you make a northwest run to beat it to Chesapeake Bay, you'll hit the waters of the Stream just as the storm front reaches it. The waves will be tall with a very short wavelength."

"Boat eaters," murmured Frank.

Blake listened with a stone face and said, "When will the front be overhead?"

"Two days to where you are now. The front will be weaker on the southern end—that's why sailing southwest could be one of your best options."

"What is the wave field?" Blake asked.

"Right now wave heights are predicted to run twelve to fifteen feet for the next ten hours. Do you want the wave-length predictions?"

"Hold on, Peter. You said we can expect twelve-to-fifteen-foot wave heights, but right now, they're only three or four."

"Trust me, Blake. They're coming."

"What is your forecast if we head southwest to the Stream?"

"If you stay where you are in your current position, the wave field will increase to fifteen to twenty feet. Dangerous for a boat your size. They'll be smaller and more manageable if you head southwest.

"Do you know of any other boats in this area?" asked Blake.

"No, you're my only client sitting in harm's way."

"Well, Peter, thanks for the update," Blake said. "Looks like our best option is to run. All we need to do is decide to go to Bermuda or southwest and under it. We have some planning to do."

"I hate to ask, but have you checked your emergency equipment?" Peter asked.

"EPIRB batteries are dead, and we haven't located the life raft yet. We have no handheld radios. Wait on that one, Peter. Correction: One of the crew members said he brought one."

"Blake, we've known each other a long time. I'm not trying to tell you how to skipper your boat, but what you're telling me is not reassuring. Have you considered calling your coordinates in to the Coast Guard?"

"Will consider that advice," Blake said.

"Did you file a sail plan?" asked Peter.

"Yes, it's standard practice before we cast off, but we've been blown way off the plan. Listen, Peter, we have a lot to do. I'd like to give my wife a call, and a crew member is concerned about being

AWOL at work. I need to do that before we lose our satellite link. I'll contact you in the next day or two."

"Fair winds, good friend," Peter said.

"Quinney," Blake said, "find your boss's number. I won't be long with my wife, and we don't have much time before losing the link."

Blake made his call. Whenever he sailed, his wife monitored the weather and his position. Like Peter, she was concerned. Blake spent time convincing her they were in no danger and all was well. When he ended the call, he turned to see Nelson and Quinney looking at him in disbelief. The lie to his wife had been deliberate. He looked at each one of them and shrugged. "What can I say? She's a worrywart, and she'd worry even more if she knew how serious our situation was."

Quinney anxiously awaited access to the satellite phone. Her company lacked empathy with employees unable to return to work when promised. She worried that the conversation would result in a "return to work by tomorrow" ultimatum when it would be impossible for her to comply. Blake handed her the phone. She took a deep breath and called her boss, the manager of a grocery store. There was not an organized system for handling incoming calls— the probability of actually connecting with her boss was low. To the accounting clerk who answered the phone, Quinney reinforced her urgency. "I'm calling from two hundred miles offshore on a sailboat in a storm. I'm using a satellite phone that's about to go out of range. I need to speak with Mike right away." Her firm tone worked. She spoke to Mike. Her job was secure.

"Nelson," Blake said authoritatively. "Bring your chart here. I'm responsible for the decisions, but I want you all to weigh in on our options. Let's talk about them."

They spread the chart out on the table. "Nelson. Quinney. I don't know your understanding of Atlantic currents, so I apologize if this sounds like you've never heard it before. This is the Gulf Stream. It starts down here at the Straits of Florida between Florida and Cuba. It runs north up the East Coast to Hatteras, and then it sprays out into the Atlantic like an out-of-control fire hose. Here, the Stream comes within fifteen miles of Hatteras. There, it's sixty miles wide and travels at about four knots—pretty swift for an ocean current. Then, down from the north runs a slower-moving current, the Labrador Current. They collide between Chesapeake Bay and Hatteras. There's a twenty-degree temperature difference between the two currents. The blending of currents creates its own weather—wind, high seas, fog, rain.

"Now, here comes that front. It's coming from the northwest and will blow against the Stream. That creates steep waves with short wavelengths. I call them square waves. Very dangerous. As the front moves southeasterly, the wind will shift. Some waves will come from the northeast, some from the north, and some from the south. When you hear the expression *sloppy sea*, it means the waves will be coming at us from all directions. Once in the Stream with storm winds from the north, the waves would crash into the boat no matter which direction it's headed. That's why knowing the length of the wave becomes important. The waves, even smaller ones, can quickly break a boat apart—regardless of size. It's a deadly place to be, and there's nothing we can do once we're in it. We avoid it at all costs. It's like being in a boxing match where your superior opponent delivers blow after blow from all different directions at a rapid pace. Before you can recover, here comes another one. You can't roll with the punches, and in a sloppy sea, we'll get thrown around from one punching wave into the next until *Momentum* can't take it anymore."

Blake continued, "Peter was also talking about thirty-foot waves. Some waves can be twice that size, and the trough in front of a breaking wave is much deeper than the trough behind the swell. Let's not make the mistake of thinking that we can easily get through this unharmed. No matter which option we choose, it's gonna get hairy."

"Which option do you think we should take?" Nelson asked.

"We can go four ways, and two of them would be suicidal. Two viable options are running to Bermuda or slowing down and sailing southwest under the storm. If we run and hole up in Bermuda, it would take five days to get there. That's the safest option, but we could get stuck out there for weeks waiting for a weather window."

"OK, which of the two would you recommend?" Nelson asked.

"Running to Bermuda is the best option to get out of harm's way. The downside is it will add ten or more days to our trip out and back. If more fronts form behind that one, who knows how long we could be stuck out there. I've seen sailors wait there for weeks for a weather window. If we decide to head to Bermuda, we have to commit to the entire distance even if the weather turns in our favor. We don't have enough fuel or provisions to go partway and decide to turn around."

"You said heading west to the Stream and riding it up was not a good option," Nelson said. "Why not?"

"If we head directly to the Stream, we might get there ahead of the storm instead of behind it. I would head southwest to give the front time to pass Hatteras and we'll miss those square waves," Blake said.

"Talk more about square waves," said Nelson.

"That's what I call them," Blake said. "When the northerly current of the Stream collides with intense winds from the north, the waves get steep and the wavelengths get shorter. They're very hard on boats."

"Boat eaters," Frank said again.

"Exactly," confirmed Blake.

"Do you think this boat can hold out?" Quinney asked.

"She's a well-built boat. She can handle the kind of rough seas I think we'll run into if we head southwest to the Stream. Heading north is a different situation. No boat is safe against square waves."

"I have a question," Nelson said. "Peter mentioned calling our position in to the Coast Guard. Is that something we should do?"

"We're beyond the Coast Guard rescue range. It won't do much good except to fool ourselves into thinking they could quickly come to our rescue. We're hundreds of miles from the coast with all that ugly weather between us and land. If we flounder or are adrift, we're on our own unless a boat or ship happens to pass. We're also out of Coast Guard radio range. We all saw how fast *Adelia* went below the horizon, and that took less than twenty miles. Other questions?"

Quinney spoke up. "If square waves are so deadly and to be avoided, how do we know if they're there without being in them?"

"Good question, Quinney," Blake said. "First, they're only at the Stream. We'll know when we get to the Stream. From a distance, square waves look different. If you look out there now, the waves look like mountains with peaks or hills. When they become square waves, they have a silhouette of parading circus elephants. They take on a boxy shape—steep on both sides and flat on top. We'll make sure we time it so we won't be getting near or into the Stream at night." Quinney nodded.

"No more questions? Let's take a vote."

"I thought we should have gone west to the Stream three days ago," Frank said.

"Three days ago?" Blake said. "That would have added three or four days to the trip, and we know much more about the weather conditions now. Because of the currents, the waters around Hatteras are uncharted. As the currents change, the shoals change. As the front passes, the wind would be coming out of the east, and we'd be on a lee shore. That's how the waters over there have claimed so many ships over the years. I would never have allowed it. What's your vote?"

"Go southwest and around," Frank said.

"Quinney?"

Quinney squinted, pinched her lips, and looked at Nelson. "I vote Southwest."

Nelson put his arm around her and pulled her close. "Southwest for me."

"OK, then. The southwesterly route it is. Nelson, plot a course and tomorrow we'll call Peter again. When it's safe to head toward the Stream, we'll change course. If not, we'll stay on the southwesterly course until it is."

"Let's get underway," Blake said as Nelson plotted a new course. "Sorry, Quinney, but you're gonna have to sit this one out down here."

Nelson and Quinney sat at the salon table. Quinney's eyes welled up with tears. She put her hands on her face. "I'm scared, Nelson. I'm so scared, I could panic and run right off this boat. Aren't you scared?"

"Not as much as I am frustrated."

"Why more frustrated than scared?" Quinney asked.

"I was scared when we hove-to in the dark. But I'm frustrated because we have dead EPIRBs, and that should have been checked even before we arrived on the boat. Blake doesn't even know if we have a life raft. He's the captain, for God's sake. Frank has a captain's license, and I didn't see him checking for emergency equipment either. Both Blake and Frank should be ambassadors of safety, yet neither of them wears a PFD. I'm keeping a low profile because I might be as guilty as they are. Being a sailor with all my certifications, I should have known to look for emergency equipment. If I had asked about them, we wouldn't be sitting ducks out here. Blake told Peter they filed a float plan as part of standard procedure. I don't remember being asked about emergency contacts or medical conditions. I don't think they even know your last name."

"What should be in it? You know, a float plan."

"A float plan is what folks back home use if you don't arrive at port when you say you will and you haven't contacted them saying you're gonna be late. There's information about the boat, the planned course, estimated arrival date, crew names, addresses, and emergency contacts. I should have insisted on seeing it. I should have insisted on seeing EPIRBs and a life raft. Chaulee said there was a ditch bag in the lazarette, and I never checked it out. Some able seaman I turned out to be."

"Don't go beating yourself up for that," Quinney said. "You signed up to learn, and they knew it. Just because you show up on a boat, that doesn't make *you* responsible for float plans or safety equipment."

"Quinney, on a boat, we have to take responsibility for our safety. There are some vast differences between coast cruising and blue-water sailing, which this is. Safety is safety no matter what or where you sail. I am accountable to self. Frank took it upon himself to study the rigging without being told."

"Nelson, he's a seasoned sailor," said Quinney.

"On our boat, I check all this out before we go out. I should know."

"Have you ever prepared a float plan?"

"Yeah, we've made two trips to Catalina. I made float plans for both of them."

"I never knew that. Huh. Nelson, if something happens to the boat and we go in the water, do you think you'd be afraid? Do you think we'd die?"

Nelson searched his mind. "I don't know, baby, I don't know. I told Blake that I think a sailor should never set foot on a blue-water sailing vessel without acknowledging that he or she may never see land again, but that doesn't mean he's dealt with his fears. What would terrify me, though, would be floating around alone and not knowing where *you* are. We could be a wave apart yet a world away. I don't know. I just don't know."

There was a long pause as Nelson looked down at the salon table and Quinney glanced around the entire cabin.

"Nelson, what do you think it would be like going in the water?" Quinney pursued. "Have you had any experiences like this where you were in the water and there was nothing around you?"

"When I saved a scuba diver on a trip to Honduras, the seas were about three feet. I couldn't see the boat unless we were on top of a wave. When I could see it, it looked three times farther away than it actually was and I was sure they couldn't see us. I felt very alone out there, but when I was convinced that the woman I rescued had died, I was overcome with a sense of peace. She was gone and her struggle was over."

"Did you feel as alone as when we lost contact with the *Adelia*?"

"Yes, I felt alone but that was different. In Honduras I could see the cays, but there was still a sense of being alone. Going in the water out here would bring about a heavy-duty kind of aloneness."

"Does that frighten you?"

"Aloneness seems to bring finality, and if a person's not ready for that, I suppose it could be quite scary," Nelson said.

"What's it like if the boat turns over and we have to abandon ship, as they say?"

"I can only imagine. I would feel confused and disoriented—definitely. I'm sure a billion thoughts would race through my head. No room to think about fear. I would wonder if we were trapped in a large, sinking bubble. Isolated. Yeah, isolated. If it happened in the dark, that would be worse. Sailboats are engineered so that if they get blown over, they'll right themselves. That doesn't mean they always will. Sometimes they hang upside down and you think you're doomed, but then it turns back over. You can thank a heavy keel for that. You could get knocked out by something heavy or killed from a flying sharp something. That's why it's important to be a stickler about everything always being stowed when not in use. If you're on deck, you could be thrown into the water. You'd have to be careful of becoming snagged in lines and anything else that was loose and floating around. A cable or rigging could cut off a limb. And we can't forget that if this happened, it would be because of rough conditions and it would be easy to lose each other. That's why you always have to be ready for it. Not a pretty picture, eh?"

"Do you think we would drown?"

"Drowning and exposure would be our worst enemy. For me, I think drowning would come first. If we go in, we will have little chance of surviving without our PFDs. Our clothing is going to weigh us down, and if we try to take it off, we'll die from exhaustion or exposure. Look at all this stuff we're wearing. Frank is wearing a shirt and shorts only. At least he wouldn't be burdened by weight like us. That's why we need to find the life raft. It's key to survival."

They sat quietly at the table. The sound of winches pulling in sheets and trimming the sails echoed through the boat. *Momentum* was rolling with the sea.

"I need to go to the cockpit," Nelson said. "I want to know every-thing that's going on. If we get into survival mode, we're responsible for ourselves. Are you going to be OK down here?"

"I'm fine. Go sail this boat. Keep us safe, sailor man."

FIND THE DITCH BAG!

"Nelson! Find the ditch bag!" came Blake's orders with an edge in his voice.

Twelve days earlier in BVI, Chaulee had casually waved his hand across the cockpit. "There's a ditch bag." Blake had looked in the direction Chaulee pointed and said nothing. With the many problems he had caused, Chaulee had become Blake's albatross that prevented *Momentum* from shoving off. If Blake had engaged him, it would have prolonged the agony. Although Chaulee was warm and personable, Blake had once commented to Nelson that he never felt Chaulee contributed anything useful.

Nelson stood and looked around the cockpit. "This may sound very stupid, but I gotta ask. I thought a ditch bag and life raft were different, but now I'm not so sure."

"In the islands," Blake said, "they're considered the same, depending upon who you talk to. The life raft is a tight package containing the life raft itself and life support tools such as lines, repair kits, a manual pump, a knife, a medical kit, and—in some cases—food rations. The ditch bag contains personal items such as identification, papers, cell phones, money, credit cards."

"That makes more sense to me now," Nelson said. "I always thought a ditch bag was for personal stuff. When Chaulee said there was a ditch bag, I wondered why he would say that and why I should care. So, since I've never seen a life raft package, what am I looking for?"

"You're looking for a soft valise about two feet wide, eighteen inches tall, and ten inches wide," Blake said.

Nelson pointed to one of the four lazarettes. "I'll just start there and work my way around. Frank, would you mind moving?"

Nelson pressed the latch. It popped open like a jack-in-the-box. The junk drawer phenomenon from the salon had spread into the lazarette. Spare lines were flung in like spaghetti rather than being furled and tied. Orange life vests were crammed into the corners. Tarps, towels, and cleaning supplies were tossed about. Some supplies had leaked, leaving a janitorial odor. Blake, Frank, and Quinney sat around and out of the way, but looked on intently. They leaned forward whenever a new layer had been peeled away. At first, finding the life raft became a treasure hunt. The more Nelson dug, the closer he came to hitting the bottom of the lazarette, but he had yet to hit pay dirt. Faces and expressions told the story of discouragement moving to despair. Silence took over the boat. No one moved except Nelson. He picked up a life vest buried deep in the lazarette and stopped. He looked around at his boatmates as the words in their minds poured through their eyes.

"Nothing in this one," came the obvious news. "Let's move on to the next one."

"Let's get this all back in the lazarette before opening the next one," Blake said.

"If it's OK with you," Nelson said, "I'd like to just leave it all out so I can sort through it before putting it away. Maybe even make some order of it."

Blake nodded as Frank and Quinney found another place to sit.

The contents of the second lazarette were no more encouraging than the first. Unfurled lines. Rags. Mops. Cleaning supplies. Buckets. More orange life vests. As Nelson uncovered the white bottom of the second lazarette, the mood became more depressed. Blake's movements became jerky. Quinney covered her mouth with her hands as if she had just witnessed a disaster. Frank sat, stone-faced, on the gunwale with his arms draped over the lifelines. Blake rubbed his face, sat up straight, and looked out to sea.

"Two down. Two to go," Nelson said as he stood and began lifting the lid of the next lazarette.

"Hold on there, Nelson," Blake said. "We're not going to find it up here."

"How do you know that?" Nelson asked.

"Look how deep those lazarettes are. Maybe two feet? The life raft package stands eighteen inches. You'd find it right away if it were in there. So if you feel compelled to look in the other lazarettes, you're just making work for yourself by digging all the way to the bottom."

"OK, I won't dig as deep, but I'm still gonna look. Imagine what we'd think if we were sitting at the highest point of the sinking boat saying we were doomed, and our lifesaving life raft was still in the one lazarette we didn't open."

Something about Nelson's description added levity and took the edge off the growing tension. It boosted everyone's spirits, giving a glimmer of hope that the life raft was in one of the remaining two lazarettes.

Lazarettes three and four: More mops. More cleaning supplies. More boat brushes and telescoping poles. More orange life vests. More strewn-about lines. Nelson stood and shook his head. All hope for finding the life raft in one of the lazarettes was lost. His frustration grew. His heart began to race. Quinney gave him a gentle look that asked him to hold himself together.

Nelson picked up one of the mops and waved it in the air. "How many mops does a boat need? We have three up here and I'll bet there's a few dozen more hiding down below. A safe boat needs mops, but not batteries for the EPIRBs. I don't get it. Maybe the owner thought we could build a raft from the mops if we couldn't find the life raft. Maybe the owner brought the life raft on board and took it off when he couldn't find another junk drawer to stuff it in. How can any boat owner be so… so…"

"Nelson," came Quinney's gentle voice.

"God! This is maddening!" Nelson picked up the mop and hurled it overboard like a javelin. He picked up a deck brush and tossed it, too.

"Nelson," came Quinney's voice a second time.

Blake and Frank looked on sympathetically.

Nelson looked at the rubble on the cockpit sole. "You know, what I just did was incredibly sophomoric, but it sure felt good. We have plenty of mops. Maybe we should have a javelin throwing contest."

Nelson's humor was ineffective. The crew was not amused. "We should toss all this stuff overboard," Nelson continued. "Now, we gotta find that life raft. Quinney, wanna help me look through that disaster zone by the engine room?"

"Before you go tearing the rest of the boat apart, how about putting all this stuff back," Blake said.

Nelson looked at it, shook his head, and began laughing. "What a mess."

Fifteen minutes later the clutter was off the cockpit sole and the lazarettes were organized. Life vests filled two lazarettes. In the third lazarette were placed furled lines. Cleaning supplies and miscellaneous treasures went into the fourth.

* * *

Blake looked inward thinking, *What's happened to me? Have I become so reckless that my negligence could impact the lives of my crew?* He was already a deeply humble person, but reflections on his lack of attention to safety sent him into the pits of regret. Like any mariner, Blake knew the risks of sailing could eventually put him in harm's way with no escape route. He had made more than a dozen passages on the Atlantic, and he acknowledged that this passage had thus far been the most troublesome. He stared out to sea, envisioning his boat being rolled over by a rogue wave while he was at the helm, standing as best he could until the rest of the crew was off, allowing him to quietly go down with his ship.

* * *

Frank came across as a fearless seaman—always knowing what to do and when to do it. Being a commodore, he had to be the cool and competent captain around his swab trainees. It created a protective aura that defined his unflinching arrogance. Competency goes a long way in overpowering character flaws, and as much as Nelson disliked him and what he stood for, he respected Frank's ability and felt safer with him on board. If Frank were to fall overboard, Nelson felt he would "take it like a man" and simply go about the business of attempting to survive. When a person focuses on survival, there's no time for fear, rendering it ineffective. But Frank had climbed aboard *Momentum* assuming its captain with years of experience had made sure all emergency equipment was on board and working. With an overworked sailboat, a tired crew, and the ominous threat of a boat-crushing storm—even Frank with all his own skill and experience could suffer from Blake's negligence. His eyes said it all… whatever failed on the boat happened because Blake abandoned his duties as captain. Frank glared at Blake with his inattention to detail. To Nelson, Frank's body language shouted out his urge to tell him so.

* * *

Quinney sat listening as she attempted to piece together the deteriorating moment. She thought about the violent death that could come with an overturned boat. She fought the urge to panic and leap into the sea yelling, "We're all gonna die! We're all gonna die!" She thought about how Nelson's composure was reassuring but she was overwhelmed over the urgency to find a life raft. Her head filled with troublesome head talk. *Should I be worried?* She recalled a movie where passengers on a sailboat were huddled below during a dangerous squall and the captain jumped down the companionway and exclaimed, "You folks don't want to be down here if she starts to break up." While the seas were up, Quinney was confined to quarters until her ribs had time to heal. If there were truly a danger of "breaking up," Blake would not allow her to remain in her cabin—so she reasoned. She pictured the worst situation and became tearful at the thought that she might never see her family again. She could disappear into the sea, and none of them would ever know what had become of her. She pictured herself floating in a debris-laden sea and the dangers of being snared in lines that would drag her down as *Momentum* sank. She took a deep breath and muttered, "Put your big-girl pants on and stop whimpering."

* * *

Frank grew angrier and more agitated by the moment. He stood quickly and rubbed his head vigorously. Nelson watched, knowing Frank's frustration was about to boil over. His propensity to blame was a better fortifier of self-righteousness than Blake's remorse and regret. "Please don't go there," Nelson whispered repeatedly.

"I have a question," Frank blurted out. "I don't know who this Chaulee guy is. But from all I've seen, I wonder why this boat ever went out. Care to explain, Blake?"

"That sounds accusatory. Want to rephrase that?"

"I shoulda known something was wrong when I first came aboard. This boat wasn't ready for anything, not even island-hopping. I shoulda asked about emergency equipment, but I thought an experienced captain like you had already done that. Then I found the EPIRBs. You should have been the one to look for them, not me. You'd never make captain in my school. I have swabs who know more about boat safety than you."

"You're getting dirty," Blake said through gritted teeth. "You don't want answers. You want a fight."

"I'm just asking how a boat in such bad condition was ever allowed out of the harbor in the first place. The Coast Guard has some pretty specific regulations about things like radios, emergency communications, and safety equipment – such as life rafts. Why are we sitting on this boat with untested EPIRBs all loaded with dead batteries? Why are we hundreds of miles from land with a powerful storm looming down on us and just beginning to ask about life rafts? Can anyone explain this to me?"

"You're quick with the blame," Blake said. "Maybe you should ask other questions. Maybe you should learn about the conditions before pointing the finger."

"Fine. What conditions?"

"I don't have to answer to you."

"This is a safety issue. What conditions matter more than safety?"

"I had a weather window that was closing fast and a boat that needed another week before she was ready to sail. It was difficult getting crew, which is why you were brought in just before the call was made to scrub the passage. The boat owner was well aware of the regs but obviously scoffed at them. And guys like Chaulee represent the culture of the island."

"Blake, I get all that. But this boat was not fit, and you knew it, yet you did nothing about it. C'mon... dead EPIRBs, missing life rafts. There's not a single handheld UHF on the boat. Blake, that's basic. Even the swab here knows that. Why didn't you at least try to see or touch the safety equipment that should have been on this boat?"

"Like I said, I don't answer to you."

"Maybe you're not fit to captain this boat any more than this boat is fit to sail."

"You stepped on this boat nine days ago and haven't said anything until now. What are your motives here?"

Everyone stiffened. The sound of the sea, the engine, the wind in the sail—all became stifled with the tense brawl in the making. Quinney's head jerked from Blake to Frank and then to Nelson with a "do something" message in her eyes. Nelson stood poised to intervene should the fracas escalate.

"I know you don't agree with my decisions or how I choose to run my ship, but this is *my* ship. I'm the captain, not you."

"That can change."

Blake sternly pointed his finger at Frank's face. "Be careful what you say. Do that and you know the severe consequences you'll face. You'd better check your maritime law. If you want to take over the boat, make your first attempt count. You may be successful, but you'll never get another job crewing once you get out of prison, and you can say goodbye to your commodore job. You'll get farther if you want to have a discussion and do it without putting your nose to mine and trying to bully your way to what you want. You'd better think about your actions, mister, and you'd better do it fast. You're on the edge of making a very bad career decision. You want to conduct an inquisition about my skills and accountability? Do it in port, and then you can conduct all the investigations you want. My job out here is to keep this vessel going and keep us safe."

"Does that include compromising the safety of the people on it?"

"Right now you're the one who is compromising safety. You're the imminent threat. You're inciting an insurgence. I won't tolerate it. You know I can't and won't back down. Stand down before this becomes irreversible."

Blake's square jaw became more pronounced, and his steely eyes became more piercing. There was a threatening silence as the two glared at each other.

"Nelson! Do something! Please!" whispered Quinney frantically.

Nelson's body became rigid. He studied the two men as he weighed his intervention options. They began leaning toward each other like two testosterone-saturated titans trying to out-growl each other before the clash. Nelson's imagination went wild. *They leapt at each other like angry bulls. There was no fist throwing in the tight cockpit, but there was rolling around, shoving, grabbing, throwing. The more they engaged, the more violent the conflict grew. Frank lunged at Blake and the two fell backward and overboard. Before Nelson could attempt to turn the boat, the sea had swallowed the angry pugilists. As quickly as the fracas began, it ended, leaving behind a different kind of silence and the anxiety in Nelson's mind that he had instantly become a solo sailor on a vessel heading into a storm that had frightened even Blake.*

"Hey!" Nelson said. "My turn for a question."

Blake and Frank turned their heads slightly toward Nelson without taking their eyes off each other.

"Do you think Chaulee lied to us? And if he did, why would he do something like that?"

Blake and Frank looked at each other and back to Nelson. Tensions eased. It was plain that neither Blake nor Frank wanted a fight; otherwise the pushing, shoving, and cursing would have already begun.

"I'm standing right where Chaulee was when he pointed and said the ditch bag was there. Is this about right, Blake?"

Blake turned away from Frank and joined Nelson to re-create the scene with Chaulee. "Did Chaulee say it was in the lazarette or 'over there'?" Blake asked.

Nelson closed his eyes to visualize what Chaulee had said and how. He opened his eyes brightly. "He didn't say 'lazarette.' He said, 'over there.' Maybe he *wasn't* pointing to the lazarette. I wonder if he was pointing to the cargo hold behind the helm. It's in the same location."

Adrenalin had temporarily eradicated Quinney's pain. She darted below and returned with a flashlight. Nelson climbed behind the helm and opened an access hatch to a cargo hold. He stuck his head in for an initial look-see. It had the odor of fuel. The only light source was the opening. He climbed down into the hold and squatted to inspect the space. Like everywhere else on the boat, he was looking at another "junk drawer." Most of what was there was piled against the hull. There was little space to maneuver between the hull and the boat's steering mechanism and autopilot—the width of a foot.

Nelson emerged for air. "Would you believe it… I just came across another mop and pail. I can see the fuel containers, and there's even a stainless-steel barbecue at the far end. If our life raft is down here, we may have to pull all this stuff out of here to get at it. I want to verify that it's here before going any farther."

"There should be fourteen five-gallon containers of fuel," Blake said. "Check that out while you're there."

Nelson vanished into the hold. Frank and Blake stood near with their hands on their hips as they stared at the dark opening. Minutes seemed like hours.

"I guess it would be foolish to stick my head down there and ask if he found it yet, wouldn't it?" said Frank.

"I'm sure he'll let us know the moment he knows," Blake said while keeping his eyes on the opening.

"So what's taking him so long?" Frank asked. "There's only six or seven feet on that side. I'm gonna stick my head down there and see if he's OK."

The sound of Nelson's voice came up through the hatch. "Blake, I see a dirty old orange rectangular bag. Could that be it?"

Blake stuck his head down the opening. Nelson shined his light. "That looks like it. Let's pull the rest of this stuff out. We'll never get it out trying to pull it past all that. It's about fifty pounds of awkwardness."

They removed the fuel containers and everything else blocking clear access to the orange package. It sat in the dim light, pressed against the hull at the stern. Whatever newness it had had was long gone—it was covered with oil and fuel stains. It looked like a coveted treasure from an Indiana Jones movie. Even before they could verify what it was, tensions eased.

A line dangled down through the cargo opening. Blake called to Nelson, "Try to get this line tied to the raft, and then you get behind and push. We'll pull from up here."

Sweat squirted out of Nelson's head and down his face in the heat and squalid air. He carefully guided the package past the steering and autopilot mechanisms. It took the efforts of all three of them to squeeze it through the cargo hole.

The life raft had been found. They sat, staring at it. One by one they began giggling and their giggles grew to laughing until their laughter became uncontrollable and loud. Air hissed out of the cloud of tension. Eventually they returned to silence, transfixed on the single most important piece of equipment in a disaster.

Nelson sat to catch his breath and cool down. "What in the world were they thinking? Why would anyone put the life raft in the most inaccessible place on the boat? The ones I've seen were mounted on the stanchions at the stern, where they could be deployed instantly."

"They didn't see the need for it," Blake said. "To the owners, this is a party boat and having it accessible is inconvenient. I'd say the only time this boat sees blue water is when it gets transported from Chesapeake Bay to the Virgins and back."

Frank dragged the valise closer to him. "This is a four-person life raft. If we have to use it, we'll be packed in like sardines. The owner must've bought it *only* to satisfy Coast Guard requirements; otherwise he would have sprung for a six-person raft. Ever see one of these open? No? I'll talk you through it."

Frank gave a class on the fundamentals of life rafts—how they deploy, how to secure them, how to climb into them, and the kind of extra equipment they could expect to find inside. "When you deploy, it takes only about thirty seconds to completely fill the raft, supports, and canopy."

"OK… we have a life raft," Nelson said. "Let's hope we don't need it. How do we know this thing will even work?"

"Ah, we don't," Frank said. "That's why these go in for servicing every three years. Here's the service tag, but there's no date on it or information about who serviced it. That right there makes me suspicious. It tells me that it was last serviced by an unknown local establishment that may or may not have the certifications to ensure competent work. This life raft may not have been properly repacked. There are guys who offer bargain prices for servicing—less than five hundred dollars—and they do what's called a pirate pack. They don't test, inspect, or repair. Sometimes you get your life raft back without any of the equipment that was in there when you gave it to them. And unless you're certified, you should never open one to check on their work. The moment of truth comes when you pull hard on the painter. You can only pray it will open. Not too comforting, is it? That's where having a reputable service company pays off."

"Are we going to keep it on deck?" Nelson asked.

"The only place it could go is here in the cockpit, and that'll leave no room to move around. That could make the cockpit dangerous," Frank said.

"Let's make room in one of the lazarettes," Blake said. "Nelson, let's get these fuel containers back in the hold."

* * *

The matter of the life raft had been resolved. The altercation between Blake and Frank took time to reset. Blake, usually a man of deliberation and sure-footedness, showed signs of lingering irritation. He bounced from cockpit to cabin and back. When in the cockpit, his eyes darted around the boat and out to the horizon. He moved from one side to the other as if undecided which side might be more comfortable for sitting. He tidied up already tidy lines. He cranked on the sheet winch a couple of clicks and did the same with the jib. Nelson watched, careful not to exacerbate Blake's agitation. He attempted to determine if Blake's behavior was a result of leftover Frank or something the meteorologist had told him on the call.

Nelson preoccupied himself with helmsman tasks to stay out of Blake's way. He watched the sails and looked to the horizon even though there was nothing to check. "Pretty quiet up here, isn't it?"

Blake grunted.

"How long do you think this lull will last?"

"Until it's over."

"Anything I can do to help you?"

"Do I look like I need any help?" Blake replied, glaring at Nelson.

"No, sir."

"Then why did you ask if I needed help?"

"Just trying to be helpful."

"If you want to be helpful, you could get more fuel. We may not have enough. I looked at your logs. We're not even going to make a hundred miles today. That's the worst since we began."

"I noticed that, too. Are you concerned about weather?"

"I told you we'll run into storms. The big one just hasn't come yet. You want heavy weather? Just wait."

"Anything I can do?"

"Just keep doing what you've been doing," Blake said as he went below.

Nelson gave a half smile and looked out to the horizon. *Just keep doing what you've been doing. I'll take that as a compliment.*

Frank came up to the cockpit to begin his watch. Nelson moved away from the helm. "He's edgy about something," Frank said. "I wonder what's eating him."

"Other than your toxic comments earlier, I can't think of anything. We're light on wind and low on fuel. I think he's concerned that we may not be able to run around the storm. I think that's what he's worried about. How about you? Are you worried about the weather?"

"I never worry," Frank said. "If we changed direction and headed to the Stream, we'd avoid all that."

"Blake's decision. I need some sleep. See you later," said Nelson.

* * *

SHIP'S LOG—APRIL 28, 2010—1800 HOURS—33° 47'8"N, 070° 24'5"W

The seas had settled, and the general feeling of seasickness temporarily abated. Quinney took advantage of the opportunity and concocted something hot that smelled delicious. She brought a plate to Frank at the helm and served Nelson and Blake below. The smell of good food was like a hot lunch in grade school—it made everything better, and it loosened Blake's terse tongue. Quinney asked questions about his personal life and how he had come to be a lifelong sailor. She was good at getting others to open up, and it always softened tense moments.

"Hey!" came a shout from the cockpit. "There's a sunset up here you might want to see."

"You guys go up. I'll wash the dishes," Blake said.

The sky was blazing red. Behind the clouds to the west was a blast of rusty yellow that dominated the horizon. Higher in the sky and across the sea it was rosy. The glassy water was like a chameleon—instantly changing its color to reflect the sky. The bright spectrum became blue, then gray, until the junction of sea and sky was indiscernible. Moments later what was left of the sun pushed through an opening in the clouds. The water appeared silvery against a blue-black horizon. And then all was gone.

Additional entry from Nelson's personal journal—April 28, 2010

Momentum is nothing more than a speck in the sea—lost in the trillions upon trillions of waves that could instantly take her to the depths at the speed of a blink. Mother Nature is fickle. She gives no quarter. She is simultaneously uncaring and supporting. Why should she care? The sea belongs to her, and we're trespassers. It leaves me with a sense of smallness and dishonor. And humility. There is too much talk of danger ahead. Please, let's find harmony with one another to get through this.

UNRAVELED

Blake sat at the helm—frustrated. His eyes darted to the north and then to his watch. He shook his head and tightened his lips, seemingly talking to himself, only to become angrier with every utterance. His eyes became more piercing than usual. He fidgeted—acting more like a caged animal than the usually calm and competent captain that he was. Part of Nelson's career had been in conflict management. He watched Blake, hoping to find the source of his agitation. Blake was a master at disguising his body language. But now, there was a crack in his composure. Nelson wondered if it was linked to his altercation with Frank the day before but knew it would come out when Blake was ready.

"You seem troubled," Frank said as he came up to the cockpit.

Blake scowled. He waved his arm around the horizon. "Do you know where we are? I'll tell you where we are. We are right here—twelve hundred nautical miles from where we began thirteen days ago." He angrily pointed north. "Had we left when we were supposed to, we would have been in our weather window, and we'd be tied up in Charlestown right now. Instead we're more than four hundred miles and four days away. We missed our weather window. Am I the only one concerned about it? Doesn't anyone understand the importance of paying attention to it? Now I fear that all our routes to Charlestown are being closed off by the approaching weather front. It seems like all we've been doing is heaving to and drifting, heaving to and drifting. We're depleting our provisions and don't know how much longer we'll be out here. *Momentum* is getting tired. And now we're in the path of a dangerous weather front no matter which way we turn."

Nelson had the urge to assure Blake he knew the importance of the weather window, but Blake's question was rhetorical, not to be addressed.

"Don't blame me," Frank said. "I didn't come aboard until we'd already lost the weather window."

"Did you hear me say anything about blame?" Blake snapped. "Don't even think about it! If anyone's to blame, it's those guys in the islands who were hired to take care of this boat. They waited until cast-off day to begin preparing it for the passage. On the day we left, there were parts all over the deck from partially finished projects. They set those aside to start new ones. And now they're sitting in the bars getting drunk, saying, 'I wonder how the *Momentum* is doing.'"

"Did they know you were concerned about losing the weather window?" Frank asked.

"I don't know if they know what a weather window is, but there was no misinterpreting me when I said we had to cast off on April seventeenth when everyone agreed it was the day we were to leave. We went over the list of what had to be done, and Chaulee assured me the boat would be ready. He knew how important it was, but he is perpetually on island time. He has no idea what urgency is. None. No amount of pushing would get him moving."

"Well, we can't fix the weather window problem now. What can we do to help?" Frank asked.

"For starters, quit talking about blame. We need to stay our course until we turn north. If we're too fast, we'll have to turn back toward the Atlantic and hang out until it's safe. For all we know that storm could chase us all the way to Florida."

Quinney came to the cockpit. "I have cabin fever and I need fresh air. I know there are concerns about the weather window. I don't know as much about it as I would like, but I get that it's about the safety of this passage. Since I'm on this boat, I have a right to know about safety. I want to know about safety and emergency equipment so I can reach my family if I have to."

"Absolutely," Frank said.

"Let's say we get in trouble and need help. Who will come to rescue us?"

Frank and Blake looked at each other. Blake motioned with his hand. "Frank, you probably teach your students this stuff all the time. Do you want to respond?"

"Sure. Immediately, no one," Frank said. "Right now we're a hundred and fifty miles from land, and that puts us on our own unless another boat happens to go by or hears our call for help."

"We have a satellite phone. Can't we use that?"

"It needs to sync up with a satellite to relay calls, and satellites aren't just floating around up there. To use the phone, we need to know where we are and the timing of when the satellite is overhead."

"What about those EPIRBs?"

"We have EPIRBs, but the batteries are dead. They're useless. You already know that."

"Don't we have a radio?"

"Yes, but you saw with the *Adelia* that the range is twenty miles maximum. Radios are only good for short distances. If you can't see it, it's out of range."

"Well, we have emergency flares, don't we?"

"Good question." Frank looked toward Blake. "Do we? I don't know. Anyway, how far away they can be seen depends upon the type of flare. Some can be seen for about thirty miles away, and someone's gotta be looking in the direction we fire it."

"Do we have any spare tires?" Quinney asked.

"Spare tires?" Frank asked, chuckling. "No. Why spare tires?"

"I read somewhere that the black smoke from a burning tire at sea can be seen for miles."

Blake smiled at her astuteness.

"Well, have you checked the trunk?" said Frank.

"What *do* we have?" Quinney asked.

Frank opened the lazarette and pointed to the life raft.

"That? You said we would be packed in like sardines?" said Quinney.

Frank nodded.

"With the way everything else works on this boat, do we know if that'll work?"

"We hope it does," Frank said.

"Hope? We *hope* it works? So the only real piece of reliable emergency equipment is the PFDs that we brought but you didn't, right, Frank?"

Frank nodded again.

Quinney looked at Nelson. "What have you done to me? Why did you bring me out here in this… this… this scow? I asked if this boat was safe, and you assured me it was. Now I'm finding out that if anything goes wrong and we have to abandon ship, all we have is that, that life raft, and we don't even know if it works. My family warned me about coming out here with you. I should have listened."

Nelson reached out for her. "Don't touch me!" Quinney said as she pulled away. She put her hands over her face and wept. Nelson watched helplessly—feeling like a betrayer.

"You promised to protect me," Quinney said.

"That I did, and I will protect you with my life," Nelson said softly.

Her face wet with tears, she put her arms stiffly by her side and made fists. She took a deep breath and sat down. "OK, tell me about that thing," she said, pointing to the life raft.

"We already went over this. What would you like to know about it?" Frank asked calmly.

"Well, tell me again. Everything. Tell me everything. Why is it even up here? What do you know that I should know? Are we going to need it? Are you all hiding something from me? How do we all fit inside? What would it be like? Assure me it really is a life raft, not some flimsy rubber tube that the sharks will chew up before they get at us."

Frank took a deep breath and sat beside Quinney. "I can understand how you feel. When I looked at that, I asked the same thing. We might all be able to squeeze in there, but add any personal belongings, provisions, water, or other equipment, and it'll be really tight. Just getting into it requires crawling all over one another. Being in one while in high seas is like trying to find your seat in a moving roller coaster in the dark. Seasickness will come quickly as well as projectile vomiting, and the only place vomit can go is in the bottom of the raft where you're sitting, on you, or on others. You'll be peeing in your clothing and that will add to the discomfort. If the floor of the raft is not insulated, it can get very cold because the water will suck the heat out of your body twenty-five times faster than air will. There could be steep waves that try to turn us over, but there are water tubes under the raft that act like a keel to help prevent that from happening. As wretched as conditions inside the raft can get, I can assure you that it will save your life. You have to expect vomit, urine, and even blood in the raft, and it's very easy to become infected by the smallest cut. Included in the life raft is usually a medical kit, but prepared sailors will have their own in their personal ditch bag." He paused. "How are you doing with all this?"

"It sounds gruesome. Are you sure you're not sugarcoating it?" Quinney said nervously. Nelson sat quietly, taking in all that Frank said. This information was new to him as well.

"There are a few more things you need to know about these life rafts. Ready? OK. Let's talk about getting into it. The seas could be raging or flat. Let's talk about raging, because that offers the greatest challenges. If the boat gets knocked over…"

"Wait! What do you mean by knocked over?" said Quinney.

"Knocked over as in a huge overpowering wave comes from the side and breaks right on us. That could push us over. If that happens, there's gonna be a lot of stuff in the water that could tangle or trap us. You have to find a stable place to launch the life raft. You don't want it too far away from you but not so close that it gets snared in boat lines and rigging. If you're the first one on the raft, you won't have anyone inside to help you, but there's usually a strap for that. And when you step onto the rope ladder, it tends to go under the raft. Just be ready for that. Any questions?"

Quinney shook her head. "You talk like this is going to happen, not like you're trying to prepare us."

"There's nothing romantic about a life raft. Getting into one is exhausting. Sitting in one in a raging storm can be terrifying. You'll need every ounce of strength and courage you can find. If you're wearing your foulies, they will act like anchors trying to pull you down. An inflated PFD will constrict your moves even though it will keep your head above water."

Blake, concerned that Frank's explanations were too graphic and overwhelming, interrupted. "I think you get the picture. We get what Mother Nature throws at us. We rely on our experiences, and we have one another. Frank, anything else they might need to know?"

Frank reflected and began chuckling. "In the sailing academy, we spend one day simulating emergency evacuation. At first, the students are gung-ho about jumping off the pier and swimming out to the life raft, a good ten-minute swim away. We wear them out a little to increase the sense of urgency. About an hour later they have a completely different attitude. We don't tell them what to expect, and how they react to the training session can be amusing. There's always one kid who decides he wants to be in charge and proclaims himself the raft captain. We let that go for a while until there's a mutiny. Then we tell them no one's the captain and they must work as a team. Everyone in that raft brings a skill, so we have them go around, sharing with the others the skills they have that might be useful. The whole point of this is to emphasize that if we don't work as a team, our ability to survive the event is placed in jeopardy."

"This is way more than I bargained for," Quinney said, pointing to the life raft. "I don't like having to share the cockpit with a piece of equipment that reminds me of disaster. I'm not trying to be a Pollyanna, and I'm not closing my eyes to a dangerous situation. I just don't like it staring at me, but I guess I'll get used to it."

And with a disgusted look Quinney went below.

Frank spoke loudly down the companionway. "That's why we put it in the lazarette." He looked at Nelson and Blake as he opened his palms. "Did I do something wrong? Did I go too far?"

"You were somewhat graphic. I don't know if that was necessary," Blake said.

"We were all very nervous until we found the life raft," Frank said, "which tells me how important we believe having that raft is. I have never had to deploy one, but I have to keep up on all the nuances of it to make an impression on my students that this is serious business. Emergencies come quickly and take people by surprise. We don't have time to pussyfoot around. Events can happen so fast, there's no time to think. If you wait for an emergency to start planning your survival, you won't survive."

From the cabin belowdecks came Quinney's voice. "Frank, if you want to always be prepared, start by wearing a PFD!"

TORRENTS ON THE BULKHEAD

"Blake! Blake!" screamed Quinney from belowdecks.

"Now what," murmured Blake under his breath. Frank took the wheel as Blake dove for the companionway. "What's the emergency?"

Quinney stood in the galley and pointed. "There's water coming up through the floor, and it's pouring down the walls in your cabin. It's not like before. Now it's like a waterfall." He went to his cabin to inspect. Water was flowing in from the ceiling by the corner of the hull. Paneling disguised its source, but there was no question… The amount flowing in was significant enough to warrant immediate attention. He was unable to pinpoint where water was entering except that most of it was flowing down the bulkhead in his cabin. He checked the bulkhead in Quinney's cabin… Dry.

"Can you tell where it's coming in?" said Quinney.

"Not yet, but we gotta talk." Blake took a deep breath and looked into Quinney's eyes. "You screamed."

"I did, but I was scared."

"Quinney, there is no screaming in sailing unless you're winning a race. And today we are not racing. Screaming brings people, and someone could get hurt scrambling to get to you. Screaming can create panic. We don't want to panic. Panic is not our friend. We can't think when we panic, and that causes us to lose valuable time. Please don't ever scream on this boat again."

"You're right. I'm sorry. I screamed once on Nelson's boat when we were heavily heeled over, and he jumped all over me for it. I thought he was kidding, but now I see that he was serious. I'll try to do better."

"No, Quinney. Trying is not good enough. No more screaming. Now, if you'll excuse me, I have a leak to find."

Blake stood in the cockpit looking forward. Weather beat at them from the port side, and water splashed across the hull. Blake knew finding a leak in those conditions would be difficult. He knew that a crack in the hull or the beginning of a separation between the hull and the sole meant the structure of the boat had been compromised. Horrifying thoughts raced through his head. *If I find even so much as a hairline crack, and this boat goes into the Stream while there's a strong northerly wind, it will be the end of* Momentum. The implications of Quinney's discovery could be devastating.

Blake moved to the approximate position where water flowed into the cabin. He knelt, putting the deck within inches of his face—looking for any place water could seep through. Hairline cracks. Hull separations. Loose chain plate. Nothing visible. No telltale rust bleeds. He was puzzled. He kept searching for anything that looked suspicious, but nothing revealed itself. Water splashing and flowing over the bow only hampered his investigation. Unable to find the source of the leak, he thought he was either looking in the wrong place or not looking at the right thing. As he stood, he held a lifeline stanchion for support. It wobbled. He went to another stanchion toward the bow. It, too, wobbled. He inspected other stanchions but found only two that could be the culprits causing the water seepage.

"Find anything?" said Frank as Blake returned to the cockpit.

"I knew that sail was going to be a problem," Blake said, pointing to the bow. "Stanchions aren't meant to secure heavy, shifting, yanking cargo. Now it has managed to pull the mounting brackets out of the hull, and that's where the water's coming in."

"I secured the sail. It's my fault," Nelson said.

"No, I told you to use the stanchions because there was nothing else to tie to," Blake said. "For a short time, I worried that the deck sole was separating from the hull. Now, *that* would be a problem. We can fix this with caulking."

"We could just toss the sail overboard and tell the owner it got washed away in a storm," Frank quipped.

"That's a tempting thought," Blake said.

"I have an idea," Nelson said. "We have plenty of extra line and can retie the sail package with securing loops in each corner. Then we tie lines from the dock cleats to the loops. We'd crisscross the lines, so the left side of the sail is attached to the starboard cleats. Truckers do that when they attach cargo to flatbeds. If it works for them, it can work for us. I can make the line around the sail so tight it won't go anywhere, and there's no way the sail can pull out the dock cleat."

"Frank?" said Blake. "Your thoughts?"

Frank said, "Anything will be better than what's there now. I'm not convinced it will solve the shifting problem. The sail is tied around the mast, and it still shifted."

"It didn't shift at the mast. It shifted on the stanchions, and the line around the sail could have been much tighter," Nelson said.

"It's worth a try," Frank said. "I'll go below and look for some caulking. It'll be better if we heave to before doing this."

"As much as I hate doing that, we need to get this fixed now," Blake said. "Let's hove to, plug the leak, resecure the sail, give *Momentum* a rest, and empty the bilges."

Frank looked for caulking. Nelson pulled spare lines from the lazarette. Blake studied the waves for the optimal time to turn. Ten minutes later *Momentum* was hove-to and quiet.

"Years ago I worked for a man whose first job was in the shipping department of a typewriter factory," Nelson said. "They taught him how to tie twine around the shipping boxes so tight that it was difficult to get a finger under the twine. I remember how he did it. I could use the same technique on the sail."

"Show us the way," Blake said.

They stood the sail on end to get lines around it. They put in loops and intertwined the lines per Nelson's instruction and lay the sail back on the deck.

"How many years ago did that guy tell you about this?" Blake asked.

"About fifty."

Blake shook his head. "And you remembered how to do it after all this time. Even with a relatively soft sail package, it's hard for me to get my hand under the line. Good job!"

The sail package had been secured to the forward and amidships cleats. And, for good measure, they attached a second line around the mast.

Frank said, "I want to empty the bilges." He looked over the side where the bilge pump thru hull came, but there was no water. Down below, he flipped the breaker switches on and off without awakening the pump. He pulled up the floorboards, exposing the bilge. It sat, covered with water, and didn't respond to tapping, banging, or flipping the circuit breaker on and off. "Bilge pump died!" Frank called. "We gotta pump by hand."

Momentum was taken out of her hove-to position, and she sailed on the designated course to the southwest. Frank put himself on pumping detail.

* * *

"Anyone hungry? I'm fixing something to eat," said Quinney from the galley, looking up the companionway.

Blake smiled for the first time in days. "I'm up to anything you cook, but are you well enough for it?"

"I feel much better. I can do it."

"We're heeled over. Don't want you hurting yourself again," Blake said. "I'd strap myself to the stove using the harness."

"Is there a trick to it?"

Frank jumped to the rescue. The harness was nothing more than a leather strap fastened to both sides of the stove. When it was used, the cook stood between the stove and the straps. It would prevent

Quinney from falling away from the stove. With pan in hand, she was ready to proceed.

"Hey, guys… we just ran out of water," Quinney said.

Frank came back to the rescue. "I may have flipped the wrong circuit breakers when I was trying to get the bilge pump working." He returned to the galley, turned on the water, and heard the pump, but water still did not flow. He decided the problem was with the water-maker, a system that converted seawater to potable water. He pulled up a seat cushion and board, exposing the water-maker system. He jiggled some wires and looked for anything that would cause it to fail. "Try the water again." No luck. "Water-maker's toast!" Frank called. "The pump must have shorted out when the bilge filled up. Quinney, you'll have to wash dishes and pots in seawater."

Frank counted the number of filled gallons of fresh water and returned to the cockpit. "OK, boss. Seven gallons of fresh water. That's it."

Blake assembled his crew to discuss "new rules" for water conservation. "Losing the water-maker presents a problem. Our only remaining water source is what we have in gallon jugs, so we'll have to ration it. Seven gallons… Let's use one gallon per day for all of us. That's only a quart per person, and it isn't much. We're already battling the effects of dehydration. This is only going to make it worse. I figure we have five days to go, and that will leave us two gallons as backup. If we can capture rain, that will help. Quinney, you just made our last home-cooked meal."

* * *

"Quinney," Nelson said when he got to the galley, "I have bad news. In fact, it's really bad news."

Quinney's facial expression changed. "Now what?"

Nelson spoke low with a half-smile. "Having only seven gallons of water means you have to put up with my smell. This was supposed to be sex night for us, but you might want to ask for a rain check, or maybe just rain."

AUTOPILOT DÉJÀ VU?

"Blake, we have a problem."

Nelson was alone in the cockpit. With his hand on the wheel, he felt a faint yet momentary hesitation that snatched his attention. He disabled the autopilot and turned the wheel left and right. The steering fought back. It was as if someone was holding the wheel while he was attempting to steer. He put her back in autopilot and changed direction ten degrees. The wheel turned, but it growled and acted as if there were interference. He returned the heading to its original position. More grinding. More interference.

Blake, Frank, and Nelson stood over the wheel, experimenting as they attempted to define the problem. The grinding and interference persisted regardless of whether steering was in manual or autopilot mode. That told them their issue was not with the autopilot.

"I'm crawling down the hold to check the steering mechanism to make sure something didn't fall on it," Nelson said as he opened the stern hatch. Nothing interfered with the mechanism. Frank turned the wheel. It fought back, making a grinding sound that could not be pinpointed to anything in the hold yet was noticeable at the helm.

Nelson climbed out of the hold and pointed to the housing for the steering wheel. "Something is wrong in there. I could hear a little noise in the hold, but not like this. The problem is in here."

Blake and Frank stood watching as Nelson slowly loosened the bolts that held the housing onto the steering column. When they were a few threads from coming off, Frank leapt up and put his hands out. "Stop! Something's telling me that when we take the bolts out, springs are going to fly all over, and we'll completely lose steering. Let's think about this."

"Guys, there are no springs to pop out," Nelson said.

"How do you know?" Frank asked.

"It's a housing, a cover. All it does is protect the mechanism. It's not held in place with springs."

"Are you sure of that?" said Blake.

"The only things behind this housing are pulleys, a steering shaft, and the steering cable. The pulleys are attached to a bracket," Nelson said.

"Where do you get all this?" Frank asked.

"There are schools out on the West Coast that offer weekend seminars. I took classes in things like winch maintenance, anchoring techniques, diesel diagnostics, and troubleshooting electrical systems. One time they offered a class about the significance of displacement, but I chose to take the one on the maintenance and caring of steering mechanisms instead."

Frank shook his head and laughed. "He's quick. I'll give him that."

"Gentlemen, we need to get serious," Blake said.

"I'm going to experiment with one bolt," Nelson said. "One bolt is not going to make or break the steering. Hold your breath. Here goes."

He slowly unthreaded the bolt until it wobbled and was ready to come out. "See, if there were springs, the housing would be pushing against the bolt, and that's not happening. I think it's safe to keep going."

They agreed. There was dead silence except for the swooshing of the waves against the bow and wind in the sails. They all had their ears inches from the housing—listening for the *bear-r-r-n* or *sprong* of an escaping spring behind the housing. Nelson accidentally dropped a bolt. It crashed on the deck with a resounding thud that sounded like a shelf spilling all its dishes. Frank and Blake jumped like spooked cats. They flinched and their bodies stiffened. When Nelson showed them the offending noisemaker, they laughed. "Are we… jumpy?" said Nelson.

Nelson loosened more bolts. The grinding and resistance suddenly stopped. The steering returned to normal. Enormous sighs came from all three of them. "Let's not fix what ain't broke," Frank said. Nelson began tightening up the bolts, listening for the grinding to return. All was quiet. All was working. Nelson wiggled the housing after speculating that something inside of it interfered with the bearings on the steering shaft. They decided to not fully tighten the bolts. They tested the autopilot and shrugged—stymied by a problem that had solved itself. They were convinced they would make things worse if they attempted a "real" repair.

"It's a Chaulee and Zeke repair!" Nelson said, chuckling.

"I'm not comfortable with Chaulee repairs," said Blake. "I get a sense that they come back to bite you at the worst possible time. I can see this seizing up again just as we run into the storm front. If that happens, we'd have to cut the steering cable to steer manually with the emergency tiller. And a lot of bad things can happen while we go below and cut cable. I'm going to think on this a bit more before settling on it being repaired. Meanwhile, let's keep going and see what else breaks. Nelson, you'd better go on a hunt for the emergency tiller. It's most likely in the cargo hold."

"Everything that can break has already broken. What more is there?" said Nelson.

"There's always the engine," said Frank.

"Don't even think that!" said Blake. "That could be a real disaster."

Momentum moved along, leaving the mysterious steering problem unresolved to plague them another day. While the crew suffered from fatigue and debilitating seasickness, *Momentum* was also suffering from the passage, and per Blake and the meteorologist, the most difficult part was yet to come.

THE LITTLE RED ENGINE LIGHT

"Captain Blake! To the helm, please," shouted Nelson as he reduced the engine RPMs. He did not hear or see any movement coming from below. He would wait a few minutes before hailing Blake a second time. Blake always had a keen sense of the boat's movements and anything that changed—speed, direction, wind, sea conditions. Not knowing what else to do, he reduced speed again.

Frank was the first to appear at the helm. "What's wrong?"

"The engine warning light is on. And I smell burning oil," Nelson said, shaking an accusatory finger at a solid red light coming from the engine gauge by his feet. Burning oil meant a hot engine, which a precursor to a seizing engine or the potential for fire—a sailor's worst nightmare. No other tragedy on a boat could compete with death by fire. The thought of being trapped in a burning vessel with no escape tested Nelson's composure. The thought of falling overboard was frightful, but being trapped anywhere on a boat with the threat of incineration dwarfed that fear. The sail that the owner had asked them to transport blocked the forward hatch—the only alternate escape route if the companionway was cut off. Being trapped below and unable to escape while being pushed to the corners of the boat by fire would be terrifying.

Frank stooped to examine the engine light and shrugged. "That happened to me the other night."

"Did you smell burning oil?"

"A little."

"And you didn't say anything?"

"The red light went out. What's to say?"

Blake appeared on deck and looked around with his piercing eyes. "Engine light is on," Nelson said.

"How long?"

"Maybe five minutes now. I checked the exhaust pipe, and water is coming out."

Blake leaned over the stern to confirm flow, and then looked down at the engine warning light just as it went off.

"Did you get that burning oil smell?" Nelson asked.

Without a word, Blake went below.

"Frank, every sailor knows they can't ignore the smell of burning oil. I can't believe you just let that go."

Frank shrugged again. "The engine light went off, so the problem fixed itself. What's to do?"

Blake returned. "I think we have low or very dirty oil, or maybe the water pump impeller is going out. Nelson, keep an eye on that engine light. If it comes on again, slow the boat down some more. Call me if it stays on. How'd you happen to notice the warning light—especially during daylight?"

"That gauge has been bothering me since we began this passage. It's important yet out of the way. It's easy to miss something like that. I've become paranoid about watching it."

Frank and Blake went below. Nelson resumed his watch. *Momentum* crept along with her engine turning at lower RPMs to reduce its heat. Nelson remained on high alert, monitoring the warning light every few minutes. It remained off. He relaxed but sat vigilantly to ensure he could respond to Blake when asked how long it had been on should the engine light turn red. He chuckled at the paradox. The red engine light that had pulled at Nelson's curiosity and given Blake the impression that Nelson had fallen asleep at the wheel was the same one that could save *Momentum* or, more importantly, her crew.

An hour passed. *Momentum* did not self-destruct by fire. Nor did the engine seize. Nelson's anxiety turned to frustration and impatience. He realized he needed to keep his fretfulness under control. *Whatever is plaguing the engine needs to be repaired. Now!*

* * *

Blake stood in the cockpit scratching his chin as he began troubleshooting the engine's illness. "Nelson, increase engine speed." A few minutes later the engine warning light glowed. Blake stretched his head over the stern stanchions to check for water coming from the exhaust pipe. He looked aloft. "Nelson, shut down the engine. We're going to move under sail, even if the wind is pathetic."

Frank came to the cockpit and spread himself out on the lazarette. "What's the scuttlebutt?"

"Don't know," Nelson said. "He's checking things out in the engine compartment. I want to go below and see what he's doing. Mind taking the helm?"

"Sure," Frank said as he waved Nelson to the companionway.

Nelson stood behind Blake in the confined engine compartment. Blake assessed and inspected. "This will be a process of elimination." He searched around the compartment for replacement parts and fluids, expecting to come up empty-handed, since few things on the boat had thus far been available or locatable.

The oil level was low, and the oil itself was hot, dirty, and had a burnt smell. With fresh oil they started the engine. Just as they were convinced that they'd solved the problem, the engine light came back on.

They shut the engine down. They opened and inspected the raw water pump that pulled in seawater to cool the engine. Impellers have limited lives, and they hoped to find the culprit in a worn and chewed-up part. Under normal circumstances Blake would not have replaced it, but he pictured it failing in the middle of a storm. Since they had a replacement, they installed a new impeller. After motoring for ten minutes, the engine light returned. Not an impeller problem.

Blake maintained a calm demeanor, despite an annoying frustration with intermittent problems that would neither resolve themselves nor remain broken long enough to repair.

He once again poured over the engine. He discovered a cap on a supply pipe labeled "coolant." It took almost a gallon. They ran the engine. The light never came on again.

"Blake, I never knew engines had coolant. I thought they were cooled only by water."

"Some have it. Some don't. Apparently this engine does. What does it matter? The engine light is off, and *Momentum* is happy again."

But the recent problems were potentially threatening to the crew's safety. They could cope with water cascading down a bulkhead, and failed bilge and freshwater pumps, but seized-up steering and an overheated engine were another matter. Nelson began to understand Blake's assertions about *Momentum*'s state of happiness, but he began to distrust the reliability of the vessel… and for good reason. He thought, *Did we really repair the seized-up steering? What's to stop the little red light from coming back on? Momentum was not faring well. How can Blake say she is happy?*

STAY OUT OF THE STREAM!

"Nelson, change course to 3-2-0. We're heading toward the Stream."

"Aye. Turning to 3-2-0. Captain Blake, I thought you were going to call Peter before heading into it."

"Make the turn, Nelson. I know what I'm doing. All we're doing is getting in position. I'll call Peter as soon as we get into satellite range."

"Weren't we supposed to be concerned about square waves on the eastern side of the Stream?" Nelson asked.

"We're southeast of that danger. We'll need to know predictions about the waves as we head into the Stream. That's why I need to reach the meteorologist."

With satellite schedule in hand, Blake waited and kept an eye on his watch—1300 hours. Time to contact Peter.

"What's your position, *Momentum*?" came the greeting from Peter.

"Good to hear your voice, Peter. We are 33 degrees, 19 minutes, 2 seconds north, 76 degrees, 8 minutes, 8 seconds west."

"You headed south and around. Good decision, skipper. What's your situation?"

"We'll be easing into the Stream. Not encountering sharp waves. The seas are actually rather settled. I don't like that."

"That weather front has been consistent. It's moving as predicted.

Sea conditions are changing as we figured. What is your ETA east of Hatteras?”

“We’re about a hundred and twenty nautical miles south, southwest of Hatteras. If we jump into the Stream, we’ll be parallel with Hatteras in about twenty-four hours.”

“Blake, that’s way too soon,” Peter said. “Stay out of the Stream! You’ll catch up to the front. I told you yesterday that two fronts merged and intensified. You should make another course plan. You’d be doing well to heave to and drift around for another twenty-four or forty-eight hours. That’ll give the front plenty of time to go east and the seas time to settle.”

“Thanks, Peter; we’ll take that under advisement. What are the wave projections on the front?”

“Let’s talk wind first. That front is coming right at you, but we predict it will veer east once it hits water, and you should miss the worst of it. We’re already seeing that up at Chesapeake Bay. That’s why I recommend sitting tight for a few days. When the front gets to you, you’ll want to be far away from Hatteras, because you could find yourselves on a lee shore. You’re going to get strong waves from all directions, and things can get really sloppy out there.”

“So, we can expect the winds to pick up and shift sometime tomorrow?”

“Affirmative, *Momentum*.”

“Tell me about the wave predictions,” Blake said.

“With the shifting wind, you’re gonna get waves coming at you from all directions. Expect it and be prepared for rapid shifts. I’m not talking five or ten degrees. I’m talking ninety degrees. How’d your boat fare with those fifteen-footers a few days ago?”

“Some went to twenty. Larger ones broke over the stern, but we were able to handle the following sea when they weren’t breaking. Still, they were very dangerous,” Blake said.

“The significant wave field is predicted to be between twelve and fourteen feet, which is within the safety range of your boat. Forty-seven feet, right?”

"Affirmative, Peter. What are you predicting for the wavelength?"

"Ninety feet in front of the storm. You're in for some dangerous breaking waves. If you're in the Stream when the front hits, you will definitely be in square-wave territory where the wavelength can shorten to fifty or sixty feet. What is your projected ETA at your arriving port?"

"All things favorable, I'd say another three days. Once we get behind the front, we'll be able to tell better."

"You didn't sound too keen on my recommendation to heave to. What are your thoughts about running south toward Georgetown?"

"We've had a few problems with the boat. We lost our water-maker and bilge pump. We had an engine overheating problem, an undefined problem with steering, and a serious leaking problem we hope we repaired. We're exhausted, and hoving to sounds tempting, but we're low on potable water. We could be out of provisions before we reach Hatteras. We've been using more fuel than anticipated. It's possible we'll arrive at port on fumes or by sail. When we're in the bay, my plan is to stick close to the edge of the channel as a precaution in case we go dry and have to drop anchor. Running to Georgetown? I'm not favoring that option. You told me that our plan to keep away from the heavy weather seems to have worked and turning north will keep us behind the storm, but I agree we should slow down."

"How's your patient?"

"Doing much better. She's up and around. Thanks for asking."

"Fair winds, skipper."

* * *

"Nelson, bring your nav-tools." Blake cupped his hands around his mouth and yelled to the cockpit, "Frank, come on down so you can hear this."

They huddled around the salon table as Blake studied their options. He measured distances and laid out possible courses. "Where exactly are we?" Blake asked.

Nelson pointed to a position on the chart.

Blake said, "This might sound like a repeat of yesterday. I just want to get a starting point. Here's our situation. We're boxed in. The storm keeps intensifying and widening. Our efforts to stay south of it haven't worked. I'm beginning to think that damned storm's stalking us. Running north would be suicidal. Peter said that heading into the Stream would move us too fast and then we'd have to contend with the square waves—and we've been over that many times. We're low on fuel. We only have a few gallons of water. Any safe harbor we try to run to is beyond our supplies. We can't count on the wind to push us to safety. If we try to outrun it, we're sitting ducks if our calculations prove wrong. I don't like Peter's recommendation to hove to. Currents will push us north and back into the storm's path. Here's how I see it: We gotta slow down. We've got no wind, so we'll keep motoring at idle speed. Keep ourselves east of the Stream. Watch our speed over ground. If we exceed five knots, then we've stepped into the Stream and have to get out of it quickly. The eastern boundary shifts—we could be in it one moment and out the next. Watch for changes in the water. If you see it swirling, we're at the edge. Nelson, get a directional fix. Be quick about it."

After plotting and presenting Blake with a course heading at 0-3-0 degrees tracking parallel to the Stream, Nelson updated the ship's log with location and time. A rapid drop in barometric pressure warned them that the front was rapidly approaching. Even though there were no obvious indications of anything other than beautiful weather, it promised to be strong and dangerous. Blake had enough information to make informed decisions, but his comments sounded like his confidence in *Momentum* was faltering.

The western sky turned blood red with ominous clouds sweeping toward them. The water became the color of the sky, undulating in the dead flat calm that Blake warned would come before the storm.

Nelson and Quinney sat in the cockpit. She cuddled close and wiggled in his arms as if he were her comfort blanket. "Are we going to be OK?"

Nelson looked around and sighed. "Look at all this beauty, this incredible beauty. Water, clouds, sky. How much simpler can it be? Are we going to be OK? I don't know. I keep promising you that no harm will come to you as long as I'm alive. We're here by choice and fate, and it's a little late to change boats. Blake warned that we were going to have rough weather, and now it looks like we'll be meeting it tomorrow. A few days ago when he yelled, 'We must hove-to now,' I thought that was about as serious as things were gonna get. What's your stomach saying?"

Quinney's eyes welled up with tears. She pursed her lips to keep her fears from flying out. "I told myself I gotta put my big girl pants on, and behaving like a whimpering child won't help. I'm scared, Nelson. I'm trying to hold it all together, but I'm scared. We sat around the table talking like it's just another annoyance, but this is a big problem, and my stomach doesn't like any of this, not one bit. We could all die. Why is everyone so calm about it? What else can go wrong?"

Nelson pulled Quinney closer. "Who knows, tomorrow night we could be laughing about all this. When we first climbed aboard this boat, we accepted the reality that once we set sail, we might never see land again. I know this doesn't sound reassuring. I wish there was something I could tell you that would soothe you or make all this go away. As scary as our situation is, I look back at everything that's happened on this trip—and it looks like there's more bad than good—but I'd do it again with you in a heartbeat. And I think if you search your mind, you'd probably say the same thing."

Quinney buried her head deep into Nelson's shoulder and nodded.

"Quinney, you're gonna have to figure this out for yourself. You have to make peace with where we are. You came for adventure and experience. You're getting more than you bargained for. Remember the second time you went skydiving? You told me you remembered more than the first jump. That's because you weren't as scared, and you knew what to expect. Deal with your fear and drink up everything this experience has to offer."

"Says the man who signed up to deal with his fears," said Quinney. "Besides, that sounds like a line you pulled out of a movie. I was about to give you that speech, but you beat me to it. I'm not sure if what you said helped or hurt, but you turned my thinking toward something more positive. Kiss me good night, dear Nelson, and let me go below and think about all this."

ROGUE WAVE! ROGUE WAVE!

A blanket of clouds had sneaked in under the cloak of darkness. The star-crammed universe was hidden, and all perception of depth went with it. All that lay beyond the boat was an impenetrable wall of blackness. In the vastness and simplicity of the sea, it was easy to feel the enormity of the universe and appreciate being humbled by human smallness. Mariners at sea for days or weeks become accustomed to a sense of personal insignificance. Days are defined by never-ending tasks and vigilance. The sea keeps humble a mariner's pretentiousness, unpredictable his routines, and ready his anticipation.

Frank stepped out of the dark of the companionway and joined Nelson in the cockpit.

"You're here early," Nelson said as he checked his watch. "I have another fifty minutes."

"I couldn't sleep."

They sat in silence as *Momentum* motored north by northeast on a still night.

"We should be close to the Stream," Nelson said.

"Twenty or thirty miles. Too close for my liking, especially with what the meteorologist said. We gotta stay outside of it. Watch your speed over ground. If we start moving over seven knots, we're being carried by it and will have to steer away."

"I gotta ask you something," Nelson said. "When it comes to sailing, you come across as being fearless. You won't wear a PFD. You don't wear any kind of footwear. And you lean over the side like you're daring Mother Nature to take you. You're flirting with death. Why?"

"I've heard many times, and it's been mentioned several times on this passage, that sailors who go out to sea must accept the possibility of never seeing land again. My long answer is that I have no one to answer to. I am responsible only to myself. I hate rules so much that I'll break them just because they're there. I have been defiant with anyone telling me what to do, and that explains my many jobs and why I'm so hard to get along with. It must seem odd that as much as I detest rules—I rigorously enforce them in my sailing classes. As much as I don't care what people think of me, I want to be respected by the kids in the sailing academy. I'm an odd duck and I know it. I definitely live in the present, so preserving life for another day is unimportant to me. And when you think of it, that gives me a lot of personal power."

"What you said goes against what you told me about having your own boat. Or am I missing something?"

"The idea of owning a boat is a dream or a very stupid idea—depending, of course, on your viewpoint." Frank looked out into the dark and waved his arm. "You know, 'I dream that someday I'll own a boat and sail around the world.' That word *someday* is a dead giveaway for the future, and I just told you what I thought about that." He paused for a moment, then said, "This conversation is getting a little heavy and beginning to hurt my brain, so you should let me finish your watch and go get some shut-eye."

"You are definitely multifaceted, Frank."

"As in diamonds?"

"Could be glass." Both chuckled. Nelson headed below.

*　*　*

Nelson's personal journal—April 30, 2010

I have waited for fear to come, but it hasn't. Yet. Maybe the conditions have just not been harrowing enough. Just came off watch. Close to the Stream. The night is black as pitch. It occurred to me that we were motoring in the dark (duh), and I had no fear of it. Mission accomplished? I am ready to go home now, but we have three more days. Quinney was a saint for coming. No one has had more to complain about, yet not a word from her. I think we should marry when we get back home.

Perhaps I overcame my fear with small "baby steps." Maybe my fear just vanished. Maybe I was never afraid. Maybe I feared stories that were born out of my own ignorance. I think philosophically about the sea, this creature some believe has an intellect—one that can outthink man. I realize it would be easy to overintellectualize that which has no brain.

Nelson murmured, "I have more to write, much more, but not now."

Momentum glided over the sea. The sound of the motor sent a relaxing vibration through the boat. Nelson felt its gentle rise and fall over the waves. He closed his eyes for three hours' sleep. His watch would be on him soon enough.

* * *

THUMP! Nelson woke with a start. He sat up and rubbed the sleep from his eyes. Sometimes dreams seem so real that they commingle with reality. The rolling ride over the waves had changed. *Momentum* moved inharmoniously with the sea. She began to jerk. *Sea conditions must be changing. THUMP!* Nelson was not dreaming. *A sailor should know from the feel of his boat the conditions in which she sails,* he thought. Waves assaulted *Momentum* at a forty-five-degree angle at her port stern, slamming her, mocking her with their power, exercising their authority and warning *Momentum* not to get comfortable. Nelson realized that an experienced sailor could be equally or more connected to the sea by feeling it down below than by seeing it from the cockpit. *THUMP!* There was no chance that he would be able to fall asleep or miss the opportunity to experience something new.

Frank sat behind the wheel, leaning back with his arms draped over the stern stanchions. Ambient light from gauges lit the cockpit. The seas were up. Occasionally, a wave spilled its whitecaps near the boat. It sounded like pouring water into a bucket. Beyond vision, the sound of spilling waves could be heard all over. It was as though a huge pod of dolphins had discovered *Momentum* and they were taking turns swimming in the bow wake or breaching the water to get an inside look at the boat.

"I could feel a change in sea conditions when I was down below. Seems easier to feel it down there."

"That's because up here it's easy to get distracted," Frank said. "Close your eyes, lean back, and you'll feel the same as you did down below. It's like your favorite classical music. You get moved by what you hear, and when you close your eyes, you can feel what moves you."

"I felt thumping on the hull and the boat didn't move as smoothly," Nelson said.

"The waves are getting taller, and the wavelengths are getting shorter."

"Square waves?"

"No, changing conditions. Are you here for your watch?"

"Yeah. I couldn't sleep."

"We're doing OK. We're running two knots over ground, so we're still east of the Stream. Keep an eye on the speed. Keep us out of the Stream." Frank headed for the companionway.

"You OK?" Nelson asked.

"Yeah, why?"

"You're almost treating me like an equal."

Frank chuckled. "That's because you've stopped acting like a swab."

Nelson leaned back against the stanchion and closed his eyes. Like a miracle, he could feel the boat moving with the water. Each wave that slapped the side of the boat indicated its size, direction, and intensity. His eyes were like light switches. *Close eyes—be in touch with the sea. Open eyes—the sense of connection fades.*

* * *

SHIP'S LOG—APRIL 30, 2010—0525 HOURS—35° 09'06"N, 075° 13'04"W

The new day struggled to produce any tint of color through the thick blanket of clouds that covered the region. Dawn became day. Color changed from grayish black to blackish gray. Whitecaps kept pace with *Momentum* with the occasional thumping on the side of the boat. The air was noticeably cooler.

Quinney came to the cockpit and made a visual sweep of the nondescript landscape. "Well, I guess we're not in the tropics any-more. Br-r-r-r." She wiggled and squirmed. "When do you think we can get this duct tape T-shirt off me? I'm beginning to smell as bad as you."

"Sounds like you're feeling much better," Nelson said. "No broken ribs for you. Once the storm passes, we can cut you out of all that tape."

Quinney pointed to the horizon. "Is it my imagination or is it darker over there?"

"Yep. That's the big bad storm front."

Blake came up the companionway steps carrying the sat-phone. He climbed behind the wheel and sat next to Nelson. "The satel-lite is in position. I think I should call my wife. I'm sure she's been following the storm."

Blake pulled up the sat-phone antenna and, to improve reception, clamped it to the cable backstay with his finger. His conversation sounded pleasant and reassuring. Yes, she had been following the approaching weather front and was concerned. Blake explained how they had altered their course to go around the storm and slowed the boat to keep out of harm's way. He constantly assured her they were in no danger.

"Gotta go, hon. We're getting close to being out of sat-phone range. I'll call you in three or four days when we get into port. Love you."

When Blake finished his call, Quinney gave him the stink-eye. "Blake! You lied to her. Shame on you!"

"I've been delivering sailboats for over thirty years. Not a passage goes by where she doesn't worry and work herself into a tizzy. I'm glad she's concerned for me. It means she loves me. But her worrying is unhealthy. She can worry herself into being physically sick—as in, doubled over with stomach cramps and throwing up. I think it's better to fib than tell her the truth about our situation."

"Do we know the truth?" asked Quinney.

"You're in the middle of it. We're facing a very dangerous storm, and part of the danger is where we are on the map with the Gulf Stream, its currents, and a powerful northwesterly front blowing against it. Had we attempted to make a run into Chesapeake Bay, I'm convinced that we would have lost the boat. But we have a plan, excellent meteorological advice, and a boat built to handle rough weather. She's a tired vessel, but seaworthy."

"Why didn't you just tell her that?" said Quinney.

"Because I know my wife and how she reacts."

In the short time the three sat talking, the sea conditions deteriorated noticeably. The wind picked up. The swells were larger and closer together. Whitecaps began to take on the characteristics of breaking waves. Foam streamed with the wind on the ocean surface. Rain that began as sky-spit morphed into cold splats.

Nelson's demeanor changed. His movements became jerky and tense. He felt an urgency to scramble and prepare for heavy weather. With each wind gust came an escalation of the approaching storm—higher seas, shorter wavelengths, harder slams against *Momentum*. The sea looked angrier, and dirty. Nelson knew weather conditions could change rapidly, but he had never imagined they would change this fast. Almost too fast to react.

"Quinney," Blake said. "I think it's time you head below. It's going to get rough. The boat will jerk and buck, and I'd hate to see you get hurt again."

Nelson followed Quinney. "I think I'll go below and make sure everything is stowed."

Blake motioned with his head for Nelson to come near. "Nelson, as you secure everything, pretend the boat is going to turn upside down and imagine what will fly around. That way you won't miss anything. Secure Quinney in the lee cloth so if we heel over hard, she won't get thrown on the sole. And then come back here. I have something else I want you to do."

Nelson installed the lee cloth, a safety net to keep Quinney secure in her bunk.

"How come we didn't do this the other day when things flew all over?" Quinney asked.

"I don't know. Blake thought it would be a good idea now. If I had done this much sooner, I would not have rolled over on you whenever the boat heeled."

The thumping and pounding on the side of the boat became more forceful and came with greater frequency. It was like a haunting demon trying to get at them.

*　*　*

"Wow!" Nelson said as he returned to the cockpit. "Look how things have changed in the short time I was below." Wave heights had increased, some reaching fifteen feet. Occasionally a wave would break on the windward side, dumping enough water into the cockpit to fill an oil drum. The wind had whipped up to thirty knots and pressed against the mainsail already set at third reef. The front line of rain had begun. It was cold and felt sharp on Nelson's face. He shielded his eyes and looked windward. The "real" rain would arrive within the next ten minutes.

"Nelson, I have another task for you," Blake said. "I want you to go back below, collect all your vital papers—passports, identification, emergency contacts—plus money, medications, a knife, and a flashlight. Make an entry in the ship's log noting the time, our position, and a notation that we're at the edge of the Stream and the storm is about to hit us. Collect your journal. Fold up the chart and place as much as you can in ziplock baggies. Stuff it all in your backpack and hang it where it's readily accessible. Keep this to yourself. It's just precautionary. Before you come back, close all cabin doors except yours."

Nelson looked to Frank. "Don't worry, my stuff is secured down below," Frank said.

"Is Quinney wearing her foulies?" Blake asked.

"No. Should she?"

"Yes. They can provide thermal protection. Is your PFD the auto-inflate kind?"

"No. Why? Is that important?"

"Just being cautious. If she has it on and the boat rolls over, an auto-inflate would inflate in about four inches of water. You don't want that. What you wear to save your life could also endanger it."

*   *   *

Nelson sat at the navigation table and wrote notes in his journal and made an entry in the ship's log:

April 30, 2010—1630 hours—34° 30' 10"N, 075° 12' 10"W
Eastern edge of Gulf Stream—strong NNW front upon us

*   *   *

The sea pounded *Momentum* from what felt like all directions. Its vibrations and shock rattled her to her soul. At any moment Blake's commanding voice would be heard throughout the vessel: "We must hove-to now!" Blake had warned Nelson they could be at sea in violent conditions, and now they were attempting to avoid being caught in them.

Nelson sighed deeply. *I came to overcome my fears,* he thought, *and here I sit in the shadow of a big test. I'm not afraid. Am I not afraid because I don't know what to fear? Why am I not afraid? I feel a sense of peace. Does this mean it's my time or have I been given the wisdom to know that fear serves no good purpose to my judgment? Why am I even having this conversation? It's crazy head talk.*

Nelson sorted through their papers and protected them in ziplock baggies. The chart's bulkiness was a challenge, but he kept leaning on it, folding it smaller, and it gave in to Nelson's persistence. Into the backpack he stuffed the paperwork and everything else Blake had noted. Into a waterproof chest pouch he stuffed their money, passports, and other identification before hanging it around his neck.

"What are you doing? Why are you doing that?" came the frightened words from Quinney.

"We're just taking precautions."

"Precautions? What's happening? Tell me! I have a right to know," she pleaded.

Nelson sat on the bunk next to Quinney. "Quinney, we're close to the Stream, and you know from everything you've been hearing that things are gonna get dicey. Blake's anticipating very rough seas and doesn't want to have to think about safety when it's too late."

"Are you afraid, Nelson?"

"No… no, I'm not. I am concerned for you, though. That's always been my priority. I trust Blake. If I didn't, I'd probably be afraid. He's a good captain and has made this run a dozen times. He knows what he's doing."

"Are we going to turn over?"

"God, I hope not. Blake's gonna do everything possible to make sure that doesn't happen."

"Can one of those breaking waves sink us?"

"I'm not going to lie to you. It can, and that's why Blake wants all these things done—to be prepared for the worst. Heaving-to is our best protection. Blake knows exactly when to do it. We'll be OK,

Quinney. I have to go to the cockpit and be ready to turn. Are you going to be OK down here?"

"If the boat turns over and I'm down here, am I going to die?"

"Turning over doesn't mean death, Quinney." Nelson pulled her close and put his arms around her. His embrace said they would be all right. Quinney held him tight and rubbed his back and shoulders. They sat quietly, taking comfort in being together.

"Nelson, do you still doubt yourself?" asked Quinney without letting go.

"Funny you should mention that. I asked myself that same question last night while on watch. I thought about that stormy day when I almost lost *Ms. Sera*. I was so angry with myself and embarrassed for what I had done. I wanted so badly to prove I was a good sailor that I became a bad one. All that did was fuel my self-doubt. Blake and Frank now treat me as an equal, so there's no more reason for me to think differently. Yeah, I'm past all that now."

"Well, that's one good thing to come out of this trip."

"I gotta go up. I won't be far… just a few feet away."

Quinney nodded. Nelson kissed her cheek. Their fingers touched until he turned behind the cabin door. Quinney wore a lost look. To her, it was an awakening, and it occurred to her for the first time in the passage that she might never see Nelson again. But she had to let him go. He was part of the team that would keep *Momentum* afloat. Nelson looked back to Quinney and smiled. "We'll be OK." He gently placed his hand on his heart. She responded by doing the same.

* * *

"Did you close all the doors?" Blake asked as Nelson returned to the cockpit.

"Yes, except the one to our cabin, and the door leading to the engine room was wedged open with owner gear."

"Were you able to secure our drinking water?"

"The bottles are still under the benches around the salon table. There's no place left to securely stow them. They're the only things not battened down. Those and all that junk in the cabin outside the engine room."

"It'll have to do," Blake said. "We're too close to the Stream. Wavelengths are getting shorter, and the waves are getting too sharp. This is exactly what I wanted to avoid. We're turning east." Blake turned the boat and set a ninety-degree course. "Frank, tighten the sheets."

Rain pelted them from behind. Waves increased and began breaking, spilling water into the cockpit. "Nelson, close the companionway hatch!"

The seas continued to rise rapidly, and foam frothed the surface in long strips that rode up and down with the strengthening waves. Two waves broke into the cockpit. They were so close to each other that the first didn't have time to drain. A third wave broke and filled the cockpit to the threshold of the companionway.

"We can't outrun it," Blake shouted. "We have to hove-to now!"

Nelson clipped his harness to the lifelines and hustled toward the mast. The boat leaned as a large wave rolled beneath them, slamming him against the stanchions and then into the rigging. Wind whistled through the rigging, making a haunting moan as though the bow of a cello were slowly being pulled over a bass note. Nelson wrapped one of his harness lines around the mast. He readied the running backstays and waited for Blake's command.

"Helm's alee!" Blake turned the wheel hard to port and increased the engine speed. "Nelson! Let loose!" *Momentum* began to turn, taking the brunt of the steep waves. As she turned, waves bashed against her bow, slamming her back. She pitched and rolled in the troughs. The engine light came on, and the motor choked and died. The longer the sea came at her beam, the greater the risk. *Momentum* lost her momentum. Steering became ineffective. There was nothing to carry her through the turn. Without water moving over her rudder, she was at the mercy of the sea. She was adrift in an increasingly raging sea and unable to regain her command. Blake furiously turned the wheel hard to port and then to starboard, attempting to get her out of her stall. He stood at the stern with his legs far apart for balance. Rain blinded his vision. Frank held the mainsheet, waiting for the sea to give *Momentum* a chance to survive.

"Rogue wave! Rogue wave! Nelson! Hang on! Frank! It's coming straight at us. Hold on!"

Nelson hugged the mast with a death grip. There was no time for fear. Salt spray burned his eyes. His world became a helpless, surrealistic slow motion horror movie. At first, the wave gave hope that it would spare *Momentum* and roll under her, but it grew to a thirty-foot steepening wall of thousands of tons of raw, raging power. It became an inescapable beast sent by Mother Nature to punish. *Momentum* was no longer a seaworthy vessel, but fodder to the whim of the sea. She began surfing down the engorging wave. From the bowels of *Momentum* came the thunderous crashing of all things not secured. The wind in her sails pulled her to the breaking point. She screamed in agony. Overstressed rigging snapped and whipped like lightning. The mast moaned, buckled, and plunged into the sea. The wave crested and toppled forward, cascading with a deafening sound of destruction from its churning white force that slammed *Momentum's* beam and finished her off. She rolled over like a child's toy. The wave snatched Nelson from his grip, but his harness saved him from being cast away. He blacked out and went limp.

Momentum lay on her side. Silently. Defeated. Mother Nature had delivered a death blow.

In the midst of the destruction, there came a calm. The rogue wave came and passed in seconds. It rolled over *Momentum* as if she had never been in its path. Half-submerged, she lay on her side and abeam of the sea, but her position protected her as if she were hove-to. The violent sea went around her, and the slick appeared between *Momentum* and the oncoming sea.

Quinney's back pressed against the bulkhead as *Momentum* went over. She spread her arms and fingers to brace herself. She screamed in terror, not knowing what was happening. The bookshelf that was once by her side was now over her head. Paperback books began squirting off the shelves like a deck of cards being shuffled in her face. The sudden movements of the boat and being rolled around awakened the sharp pain in her chest. She listened for signs of life. There was no sound. Only silence. *Momentum* rolled with the sea, but the violent pounding had ended.

"Nelson!" She listened. "NELSON!" She yelled frantically and pounded on the bulkhead. She searched for anything that resembled a voice, a knocking, a movement. Anything. But there was no reply. She knew the boat had been pushed over. *They've all been washed away. I'm the only one left. No one's coming for me.* Aloneness seeped through her body. Wrenching aloneness. The kind that turns a stomach inside out and makes a person feel gut punched. *I'm all alone. No one's coming.* Her breathing rate increased. She felt lightheaded. She could not catch her breath. Her mouth became cotton dry, and she began belching profusely. She knew she was hyperventilating and needed to bring her breathing under control. She grabbed a blanket and placed it over her head. Slowly, her breathing returned to normal, but she was certain she would soon die by drowning in a sinking boat. She lay in a fetal position. Waiting. Waiting for death to come.

Nelson regained consciousness. He opened his eyes to confusion and chaos. He lifted his head. Then his arm in an attempt to prop himself up, but his harness, only moments ago his lifesaver, had shackled him to the mast. He coughed and gagged. He unclipped his harness and knelt up straight, panting. He looked into the water—a spaghetti bowl of lines, cables, and debris floating out of the half-flooded cabin. The companionway hatch had been torn away, leaving jagged splinters and sharp edges guarding the entrance.

Momentum lay like death. What was left of the mast was unsalvageable. It clung to *Momentum* by unsevered cables. If she could right herself, as sailboats are designed to do, she could do so only if she were free of the broken mast.

Gone were the sounds of a sailboat—the sound of wind in the

rigging, luffing sails, and the constant creaking of lines gripping winches. All that remained was the sound of breaking waves—out there—beyond the boat.

Although her hove-to position fended off breaking waves, the sea was merciless, relentless, brutally cruel. *Momentum's* keel lay exposed to windward with the wreckage of her broken body to the lee. Even with the protective water slick, rolling waves forcefully assaulted the downed vessel, sending water up and over the hull and gunwale as if it were a sandy beach. She was listing slightly to port—toward the keel, which was keeping the torn-open companionway above water and *Momentum* afloat.

Hove-to boats remain in place by sail and rudder angles. *Momentum* had neither. There was nothing to stop her from drifting from her hove-to position and scooping water into the boat instead of pushing it away.

The water was April cold. It ran down Nelson's back and filled his foulies, weighing him down and adding to the fatigue of his already spent body. The cold water was like thousands of stabbing knives, but partially anesthetized by adrenaline. Cold rain smacked his head and stung his eyes.

Then came the shivering.

"Blake! Frank!" Nelson stood high. He held the stanchion for balance while looking out over the waves for his lost crewmates, but then he stared at the boat's hull as if looking through it.

"Quinney! Quinney!" he yelled as he pounded his fist on the side of the boat near their cabin. No response. He called her name repeatedly. It was miraculous that *Momentum* had rolled to starboard. Quinney was trapped, but in her portside cabin she would be above the waterline. Nelson's tension increased. His heart raced. Panic gave him strength. Stories sprinted through his head—she had been knocked out or killed.

The chilly water became an enemy. It sapped his energy, dulled his senses, weakened his muscles. He slid down the companionway. Even with his efforts to secure the cabin before being struck by the wave, retreating water from waves pulled unsecured debris into his path, obstructing the passageway. Empty gallon water bottles bobbed around like toy ducks. As he was pushing it all aside, he came across his backpack floating among the debris. He clipped the pack to his harness and continued.

Nelson's muscle memory knew the boat layout when it was upright. What was once a deck was now a wall. He had to navigate irregularities—nooks, shelving, galley equipment, and cabin entrances. An error in footing could bring serious injury. The day was fading, and he was running low on light. One moment he had his footing, and the next he had none. He used the galley sink for a step that put him halfway through the doorway to their cabin. A bookshelf gave him handholds as he climbed up. Quinney, hidden in the bedding, cowered in the corner of the bunk in a fetal position. He slowly pulled back the blanket and stroked her face. She looked at Nelson. "Hey, Quinney, how's it goin?'" he said softly. She looked at him, saying nothing. Her body was shaking. She was in shock. He crawled beside her and held her. She looked straight ahead, only occasionally blinking her eyes.

"Why am I sitting on the wall?" Quinney asked quietly in a slow, coarse voice.

"*Momentum* is on her side. She was knocked over by a rogue wave."

"Are we all going to die?"

"Not today," Nelson said. "We have to hurry, though. *Momentum* is afloat, but she could eventually go down. Getting out of here is only a few feet away, but everything's disoriented, there are some jagged pieces of the companionway, and the water is cold."

"We haven't sunk?" said Quinney as she grasped Nelson's arm.

"No, we're floating. We're on our side. We gotta get outta here."

Nelson looked into Quinney's eyes. She looked into his. "Do you trust me, Quinney?"

"Why do you ask me that?"

"The hardest part of getting out of here is getting to the companionway."

Nelson looked over the cabin opening and into the water in the galley below. He studied how they would have to maneuver to get out. "Come here, Quinney. You need to see this." She crawled over and looked down and through the doorway. She slammed herself back to the wall and screamed, "We're all gonna die! I knew this would happen."

Nelson tried to put his arms around her, but she violently shoved him away. "You brought me here. You talked me into coming. Now I'm gonna die, all because of you."

Nelson made another attempt to hold her. "Get away from me!" She held her hands up. "Don't touch me!"

Nelson forced his way past her flailing arms and held her close. Her screaming turned into sobbing. Her rejecting arms grabbed him and held him tight. Tears rolled down Nelson's cheeks as he rocked her back and forth. They embraced in silence. A wave hit the boat. Quinney jumped and grabbed Nelson hard. "C'mon, Quinney. We have to go."

Quinney lifted her head off his shoulder and looked at him. "You're bleeding!"

Nelson felt his head for a wound. "It's not gushing. Not a problem."

"How are we going to get through the door?"

"I'll go first. Watch what I do carefully, and when it's your turn, do as I tell you." He inspected her foulies and tightened her PFD. "I'm going to put the backpack on you. It has all our important papers."

Nelson climbed around the cabin door, wedged himself between the door and bookshelf, and slid down until he reached the cabin threshold. He stretched a leg and felt the side of the galley sink two feet away.

Pisssschshshshshshshshshshshshshshshshshshshshshshssh came a startling half-minute hissing that fizzled and stopped. It reminded Nelson of an air compressor when the pressure tank was purged after it was shut down.

"What's that noise? What's making that noise?" Quinney screamed.

"It's OK, Quinney. Blake! Is that you? Frank! Are you up there?"

"But what was that sound?" repeated Quinney.

"Someone inflated the raft. C'mon, Quinney."

Quinney's legs were too short to reach the cabinet. She tried to reach it but slipped. *Splash!* Nelson quickly grabbed her and pushed her toward the partially submerged companionway.

"What's that smell? What's in the water? Nelson! It's all over my hands. It's all over you. You have it on your face and hair. What are those dark blobs and that brown stuff?"

Nelson put his hand to his nose to smell the slippery substance. "It's oil and fuel from the engine. It's all over us and probably down into our foulies. It must have started to come up after I climbed into the cabin. If something sparks this, we're in real trouble. Come on, we gotta go."

"Why? What does it mean?"

"Fire. Not a good way to go."

Moments later they were out of the cabin and standing on the side of a lazarette, waist-deep in water. The life raft had been inflated and its painter tied to a stanchion. Blake sat on the dry side of the steering column. Nelson wiped the stinging rain from his eyes. The two looked at each other and nodded.

"Quinney, we gotta get out of this water. Hypothermia can kill us. Climb up there and sit on the port holes." She hiked up and wrapped an arm around the stanchion in case a powerful wave sneaked up from behind.

Blake sat with his head down and wet hair draped over his face, still trying to catch his breath.

"Do you know what happened to Frank?" Nelson asked.

Blake feebly pointed downwind and said in a hoarse voice, "I saw him… that way."

Nelson squinted and shielded his eyes from the rain and salt spray as he looked leeward. It would be a lucky accident to see Frank. He could be thirty feet away from *Momentum* and hidden in a trough. To be seen, Frank would have to be on top of a wave without any taller ones between him and Nelson. And if that happened, Frank would be visible for a second at most. The fading day stole valuable light, and the rain obscured all there was beyond a hundred feet. Waves hit and rolled over *Momentum*, making an unstable platform. Floating debris appeared and disappeared behind waves. Each item looked like it could be Frank, but most were empty water jugs or duffel bags that had escaped from the owner's cabin. Suddenly, Nelson spotted a flailing object. He squinted and waited for it to reappear.

"I see him!" Nelson shouted as he pointed. "He's directly to lee. He's trying to swim toward us."

Without lifting his head, the strength-spent Blake said, "How far back?"

"A hundred feet. Maybe a little more."

"He's gone, Nelson. There's no hope for him getting back. He has the wind and sea against him, and he's already been in the water half an hour. When he runs out of strength, he'll give in to the sea."

"There must be something we can do."

"There's no way to reach him. Let it go, Nelson."

Nelson shielded his eyes from the rain, continuing to search for Frank.

"Nelson, that's all we can do. I'm sorry."

Nelson looked around, futilely searching his imagination, hoping to find anything that could help. The life ring at the stern was gone. Running rigging was made from material not meant to float, and there was none accessible that would be long enough to reach him if it could. It was too far to toss a line. Nelson stood in anguish and frustration. There was a man out there, a mere one hundred feet away yet unreachable. One hundred feet, the length of Nelson's driveway—a distance that could be walked in less than a minute but was impassable at sea in a storm.

"Life vests! We have life vests!" Nelson shouted and pointed. "In that lazarette." He stepped down to a submerged lazarette, opened the one holding the life vests, and pulled them out. "If Frank can't come to us, let's send these to *him*. Maybe one will get to him." He tossed one to Blake and threw the rest high to catch the wind to be carried beyond entanglement. Nelson watched as the bright orange life vests bobbed and floated away from *Momentum* and directly toward where he'd gotten a glimpse of Frank.

Nelson cupped his hands to his mouth and turned leeward, yelling. "Frank, life jackets… coming your way!"

Nelson had done all he could for the man who swore he would never wear a PFD, and there he was, a hundred feet away, battling for his life and destined to drown. With luck, one or two of the life vests might reach him.

Nelson climbed up and sat beside Quinney. Both were shivering. None of them was safe from hypothermia. The constant sheets of cold rain kept them soaked. The wind made the cold feel colder. The fading light promised a drop in air temperature.

"If Frank can catch a life vest and swim toward us, maybe he can get close enough for us to toss him a line," Nelson said.

Blake ignored Nelson's attempt to rescue Frank. "Get Quinney in the raft. She could die if she's out in this cold much longer. She has a better chance in the raft. Same for you. Can't bring it any closer to the boat. Sorry. Too many loose cables with sharp ends. When you get her in, come back. We have to find the cable cutters. Be quick. If *Momentum* shifts, we won't be able to go back into her."

Nelson slipped into the water and activated his PFD and then Quinney's. "Grab the painter and pull yourself out. Don't kick or you could get tangled. Just pull. I'll be right behind you."

"It's a long way," Quinney said.

"It's twenty feet. It'll be like walking across the living room. Don't try to talk or look back or you could swallow water. Go!"

Quinney pulled herself, hand over hand, over the painter. It was impossible to avoid swallowing seawater. She groaned with pain from her ribs. She faltered. She put her head down into the water and came up gasping for air. "I can't do this! My hands aren't working!"

She screamed as she flailed her arms and plunged into a panic that began dragging her under.

Nelson pulled her close. "Quinney! We're almost there. Hang on to me. Look at the raft. Look how close we are. Try, Quinney, try!" Nelson tugged on the painter, doing the work of two—pulling himself and pushing her. Cold water and the strain punished his hands.

Nelson reached inside the life raft and unrolled the canvas ladder. "When you get up the ladder a little, you'll see a strap by the opening. Use it to pull yourself in."

Quinney struggled. "I can't do this. My legs keep going under the raft. I don't think I have the strength."

"Yes you do! You're almost there. You have the strength. Try to pull yourself up. I'll push. Just one more step and you'll be inside."

Quinney crawled inside the cramped quarters and poked her head out. She choked, and vomited seawater.

Nelson fought for air. "You're safe now. More protected here." A wave slapped his face. He breathed in water and gasped for air. He coughed convulsively. "What's in there?"

"I can't see anything."

"Feel around."

"Nelson, there's nothing here."

"Nothing?"

"No. Nothing. It's empty."

"Gotta go back."

"Don't leave me here!"

"Have to find the cable cutters. *Momentum* can sink if she stays over. You're better here."

Quinney continued to choke and vomit.

"Do you understand? I have to go back," Nelson shouted over the waves, wind, and pelting rain.

"Don't you go dying on me, Nelson!" Quinney knelt in the life raft and squeezed his hands. Then she watched Nelson pull his way back to *Momentum*.

The return trip to the boat was far more challenging than going out. Nelson's energy and strength were nearly gone, and the elements mercilessly pushed against him.

Blake pulled Nelson out of the water. "It was harder to get back here," Nelson choked out.

"The boat's shifting. Raft's out of the slick. No more protection from the boat."

"The water… feels like it's getting colder."

"It's hypothermia, not colder water. It's hard to swim, especially with foulies. Don't be tempted to take them off. They weigh you down, but they give some thermal protection. Did you get your ID papers?"

Nelson padded his chest. "Right here. In a waterproof pouch. Boat papers in backpack. With Quinney. There's no emergency equipment on the raft."

"Nothing?"

"Nothing," affirmed Nelson.

"Figures. We have to get fresh water and find something that could work for a paddle and to catch rainwater. Cutters first."

"Is *Momentum* lost?" said Nelson.

"Only if she sinks. She can't come up with the broken mast. We have to find the cable cutters. They're somewhere below. We gotta go back inside and search around."

"How do you want to do this?"

"We'll take turns," Blake said. "You go first. Look for cutters but grab what you can."

"Aren't you cold?"

"Gettin' there. Home is New Hampshire. I'm used to the cold. Let's get what we can."

Nelson floated down the companionway. He returned with water-soaked sleeping bags, a sweatshirt, and a canvas bag with tools, utensils, knives, and his binoculars.

"No cutters?"

Nelson shook his head.

"We gotta keep trying," Blake said.

"I need a rest."

"OK. I'll go."

Nelson watched as Blake held his breath and dove into the submerged cabin next to the engine room. He came up gasping, hyperventilated himself, and dove again and again and again. He returned to the cockpit—empty-handed.

"No luck?" Nelson asked as he tried to see if Blake had anything in his hands.

Blake shook his head, shivering. "Where's that sweatshirt?"

They sat on an unsubmerged part of the cockpit. The rain and wind only added to the coldness.

"That rogue wave came so fast, I didn't see what happened," Nelson said. "I whacked my head on the mast, and the next thing I knew, I was out cold. What happened with you and Frank?"

"I got knocked windward. Frank went leeward."

"Any ideas how we're gonna get out of this?"

"She sure took a beating, but she's taking the waves. We did the right thing… closing the cabin doors. She's leaning the right way. God! If we could only find those damned cable cutters."

"Then what… after she comes up?"

Blake shrugged. "Who knows, we could get knocked over again. If we can keep away from those breaking waves, we might make it. My wife thinks we'll be in port in four days. The Coast Guard won't initiate a search until someone reports a missing vessel or spots all this stuff floating around here. We're near one of the world's busiest shipping lanes. Someone will surely be by within a day. We're gonna be OK, Nelson."

"I gotta clear something up with you."

"What's that?"

"I wasn't asleep at the wheel."

"What? Our boat just turned over and you're thinking about *that*? Nelson, you can crew on my boat anytime. Now, forget about falling asleep at the wheel and go below and find some water before it's too dark to see anything."

Blake watched as Nelson struggled down the companionway, past floating bags and duffels. A few minutes later Nelson came through the companionway pushing three jugs of water.

"Nelson!" came a shriek from Quinney. "I'm floating away. Nelson!"

Blake jerked his head around and pointed. "Jeez! It *is* drifting away. Nelson! The painter… just behind the stern. Don't let it get away or you'll never catch it. Go, Nelson! Go!" Blake cupped his hands and yelled, "He's coming to you, Quinney."

Nelson lunged and swam fiendishly to catch the painter. His PFD snagged the boom and tore. When he was out of *Momentum's* protective shadow, he suddenly felt the full force of the ocean with its breaking waves and confused sea. The life raft had become a sailboat. Each time the bitter end of the painter was in his hand, it was jerked away by a wave tugging at the raft. He swam up the backside of a wave and surfed down the front, trying to keep up. At times, the sixty-foot painter was the only evidence that there was a raft beyond him. He found himself in one wave trough with the raft in another, with a cresting wave in between. Daylight had become a dwindling dusk. Rain continued to bombard him, and the sea tossed him about like a stick. He heard a faint, distant call. He thought it was Quinney, but maybe it was his imagination. His exhaustion was playing tricks on him, but the idea of her voice gave him strength. He slid down a wave and found the painter with enough slack to loop around his hand. The sea tugged on the raft. And the painter tugged on his hand—tightening its grip on Nelson. Without his strength, he knew he would not reach the lifesaving raft. He fought the urge to give up. Pulling his body the last fifty or sixty feet would be nearly impossible. But if he let the painter go, he'd be letting go of his life.

The painter wrapped around his hand reminded him of the navy maneuver to pick up survivors after their ships had been sunk during World War II. A few days earlier, he had shown his crewmates how to tie a bowline knot with one hand. What saved sailors during the war could save him now. *I need ten feet of line behind me to make this work.* He pulled on the painter—struggling against his water-filled foulies and a bulky PFD. He pulled hand over hand, stretching to move up another foot of line. His hand stung from the strain as the painter tore his flesh. Salt burned his wounds. *I need just nine more feet behind me. Come on, hands! Work! Pull!* He screamed with pain. He cursed as Mother Nature played with him. He heard her laughing. "Come on, Nelson. You've struggled your entire life. Don't tell me you can't do one more foot. Pull, you swab, pull!" He shouted angrily and cursed as he lunged for another foot until he had enough behind him to make the bowline knot.

His hands were cramped and stiff. His palms were skinless. He screamed as the painter chewed through his skin to the layers of meat. His hands became numb. The pain ceased. They shook. He began to doubt if he could even make the bowline.

He made a coil in his left hand to start the knot. With his free hand he reached behind him for the loose end. *The rabbit came out of the hole, around the tree, and down the hole again.* After he pushed the painter "down the hole again," he had to let it go—allowing the bowline to self-tighten, securing him. If he formed the coil the wrong way, the knot would fall apart, and he would have to begin again only if he were quick enough to grab the painter before it got out of reach. In all the turmoil, he could neither visualize nor see if the important loop was correct. *If I tied it wrong, I will die. This is it… my moment of truth.*

He opened his hand. The bowline knot tightened, and the loop around his body was large enough for two people.

Nelson could feel himself being towed—a sign that he was securely tethered and only fifty feet from Quinney. He could rest. At times he could see the dwarfed shadow of the raft, but mostly his saving painter lifeline vanished behind a wave.

His attempts to look back at *Momentum* were futile. He floated in darkness with too many wave crests and troughs between him and the boat. Whichever way Nelson looked, he got a face full of water, pummeling rain, or an overpowering wave. Being dragged by the painter helped keep him afloat. Nelson held his breath to keep burning salt water from finding his lungs. His throat felt scorched. The salt water he swallowed was nauseating. His lips were burned and swollen and bled from small cuts made by the water.

He lay on his back, motionless, waiting and hoping for strength to return. He imagined the fifty feet between himself and the raft. If he were walking, it would take only twenty-five steps, only seconds. He pulled on the painter. Lightning bolts zapped his raw hands. Cramping in his arms and legs punished all movement. He felt a rapid falling. He looked up to see a breaking wave about to pummel him. He pressed his fingers to his nose and covered his face. *CRASH!* When he opened his eyes, he saw an approaching boat—a white dory with a curved-up bow. Blake leaned over the bow with an extended hand. Nelson reached for it. Another wave broke over Nelson, and the image of Blake was gone.

With the painter tied around him, Nelson decided to dump the torn PFD. He fought with its buckles and straps and entanglement with the painter, and it drifted away. His foulies continued to pull him down. He decided to ditch them—he would float better and regain his strength faster. Blake's words echoed in his head: *"Don't be tempted to take off your foulies."* His thermal protection would be gone, but the raft was only a few seconds away. *It'll take only a few more minutes to reach Quinney and a half hour for hypothermia to take me. I'll risk it.* Nelson wasted precious seconds and dwindling energy struggling to remove his foulies without losing his tether. He lay in the water. Spent. The vision of Blake and the dory faded, and so had his will.

Waves continued to wash over him. He let go of his struggle with the sea. A sense of peace flowed through him like a hot dye injected into his blood. Through his salt-parched throat he whispered, "I'm trying, baby. I just need to rest for a little while more." He bobbed on the surface, riding over waves and into the troughs. Sounds came from breaking waves, but no longer near him. *So, Lord, is this how it all ends? Methinks it's so. It's all so quiet. So beautiful. So peaceful.*

Two people had signed up for a journey many said was reckless. Two lovers, only fifty feet apart, lay in a forbidding world ruled by indifference and unpredictability. The wind blew harshly. Rain came in sheets. Thunder rolled through the clouds. The sea was tall and menacing. They were mere specks. Insignificant specks. It was no place for humankind.

MOMENTUM LOST

FIVE DAYS LATER

Aboard the tanker *Moley Ann*
May 5, 2010

The ship's engine hummed. The infirmary was library quiet. Medical Officer Stevens' patient opened her eyes, looked around without moving her head, and whispered slowly, "Where am I?"

Her last memory was of being bashed around in a life raft. Her eyes darted in search of clues. Confusion loomed. The room was dim. Except for the blankets covering her, it was monochromatically white. Cabinets ran along one side of the room. Several had locked glass doors that revealed a small cache of medical supplies. Under a bare-bones countertop were more drawers and cabinets, each labeled to identify its contents.

"Where am I?" she repeated faintly.

She tried sitting up. A stabbing pain reminded her of an injury. She gripped her chest and moaned her way into an upright position. Her efforts were welcomed by a pounding headache and lightheadedness. She pressed her fingertips hard against her temples, trying to suppress the large metal ball she felt inside her head as it crashed from one side to the other. Her vision vacillated between foggy and out of focus. She squinted, trying to see through her confusion. She fell back in bed.

She examined her strange clothing and the IV tube taped to her wrist. "I must have died," came a semiconscious whisper. She looked around the cabin. "Where's Nelson? Where's my Nelson?" A lone tear rolled down the side of her face as her eyes morphed from confusion to the desperate thought that Nelson would never be by her side again. Had he survived, he'd be there next to her.

Stevens came into the room. "You're awake! Welcome back!" He placed the backside of his hands on her forehead and cheeks. He checked her pulse, heartbeat, and breathing. He wrapped a blood pressure cuff around her arm.

"Who are you?" she asked quietly. "Where am I?"

"Shh. Hold still a minute. I'm trying to get a reading. You've improved a lot. My name is Stevens, Third Mate Stevens. I'm the medical officer. I've been taking care of you since we found you yesterday."

"Where am I?"

"You're in the infirmary on the oil tanker *Moley Ann*. We were en route to the Port of Philadelphia when we spotted your life raft. Can I get you anything?"

"Got anything for a real bad headache?"

Stevens reached into a half-size refrigerator and retrieved a bottle of water.

"How long was I out there?"

"We don't know for sure, but we're guessing three days. Maybe four."

"There were two of us in the raft. Nelson. Where is he?"

"Who was Nelson to you?"

She choked out, "He was my fiancé. You asked who Nelson *was*, not who he *is*."

Stevens frowned and his eyes softened. She studied his face, then put her hands over her eyes. She fought the urge to cry. It was useless. The pain was overwhelming. She began sobbing.

Stevens stepped back, giving her time to let it sink in. There were questions—many questions. "Ma'am, I want to give you all the time you need, but I need to ask you some things." He handed her a tissue. "Your name is Quinney, right?"

She nodded. "Yes. How would you know that?"

"You were wearing a backpack. We recovered the ship's log. On one page of the log there were four names listed, and yours was the only female name. Can you confirm there were only four on the boat?"

Quinney nodded with her head hanging. "Yes, only four."

"Can you confirm the names of the others?"

"Besides Nelson—Captain Blake and Frank." Quinney looked inside her blanket. "How did I get into these clothes?"

"You were wet and soiled. I cleaned you up. You were in the advanced stages of hypothermia. Another day on that raft and you would have perished. We had to warm you quickly. Do you know what—"

"How'd I get here? Last I remember, I was in that smelly raft."

"We launched an FRB—sorry, a fast rescue boat—and raced to your raft. We pulled you out and transported you here. You were unconscious the entire time. Do you know what happened to the other two—Frank and Captain Blake?"

"Our boat went over in a wave. Frank got thrown into the water. I never saw him again." Quinney hesitated and mentally drifted off.

"And the captain? What about him?"

"I don't know. He survived the wave. They talked about finding cable cutters to clear away the broken mast, and he said the boat would come back up. After Nelson got me into the raft, he went back to help Blake find cutters."

"What happened to the boat?"

Quinney stared off as the details drifted back into her head. Her emotions tried to take over, but she fought the tears. "They were trying to get the boat to heave to. I heard Nelson and Blake yelling to each other when a huge wave hit us broadside. The boat jerked to the side. As we rolled, the books in our cabin flew off the shelf and right at me. There were terrible noises. Crashing everywhere. Waves slammed against us, knocking the boat sideways. I covered my ears, but I still felt the pounding. The boat creaked as it twisted and turned. I was sure it was coming apart. I heard lines snapping and the mast creaking, and the wind sounded like it was trying to pull the insides out of the boat. Water poured down the companionway, and I knew it was all over for me.

"Then suddenly, it got quiet. The boat was on its side. I was on the wall. Nelson called for me, but I couldn't answer. It was like I was no longer in my body. Somehow Nelson climbed up from the galley and helped me out. They put me in the raft because I was shivering badly, and Blake thought I could die. I thought I was going to drown getting to the raft. It was hard to swim with all that stuff on. I think it was harder for Nelson. He went back. The boat seemed like it was not going to sink, and I don't think Blake ever considered abandoning it. The raft tugged on the painter. Then the tugging stopped. I looked out. I was floating away, and I called out. I heard Blake yelling to Nelson, 'The painter! Grab the painter!'"

Quinney coughed and choked on her tears. Stevens gave her a few moments. "I'm sorry you have to relive this nightmare."

Quinney sighed deeply. "I have to get it out. I need to talk about it. I had plenty of time to think about all this in that raft. I was hoping it was all just a bad dream. I thought I'd be safe in that raft, but it was scarier than being trapped in the cabin. I never warmed up. I was seasick and kept throwing up even when there was nothing left to throw up. I knew without water I might not survive. I tried to sit up and look out the opening for Nelson, but I didn't have the strength, and it was getting dark. It was pitch black in the raft except for a little light coming in the opening. I kept drifting in and out of sleep. Sometimes it felt like a wave was going to turn the raft over.

"I kept crying out for Nelson—I knew he was out there somewhere, and I couldn't help him. It seemed to take forever for him to get to me. Then he climbed onto the raft and zipped up the opening.

I reached for him, but he just crawled over me and lay quietly while breathing heavily. At first he didn't say anything. He must have swallowed a lot of seawater. He kept throwing up and coughing. His voice was parched and gritty. It didn't sound like him. I could hardly hear him through the noise of the breaking waves.

"Water inside the raft kept sloshing around. It was cold and filled with vomit. He kept me calm and talked quietly to distract me. He told me we had to sit on the side of the raft where the waves were coming from so a breaking wave wouldn't flip us over. It was like he had been in one of those things before. He kept reassuring me. He even sang that Bob Marley song, 'Don't worry about a thing, 'cause every little thing gonna be all right.' Then he stopped talking…"

Quinney hesitated and looked ahead vacantly. "When he stopped talking… When he stopped talking… I knew I had lost him. I knew he was gone. That song… It's the last thing I heard from him. When I realized he was gone, I just gave up. I didn't care anymore." Quinney lay back in the bed and stared at the ceiling. "I just can't believe it all ended that way. There were so many things we planned to do—sailing the Exumas… scuba diving… walking on secluded beaches… watching sunsets. You know, if that painter hadn't come loose, things would be different." Her voice was soft. "Do you know if Blake made it? Has anything been found?"

"You may be the only survivor. Maybe your boat didn't come back up as Blake thought. That front brought a lot of wind, rain, and high seas. When a boat is lying on her side, she's vulnerable. There's only so much pounding she can take. So you were belowdecks when the boat went over?"

"Yes. A few days earlier, I got slammed against the steps during a different storm and Blake thought I cracked a rib. He confined me to quarters until the seas settled down. Every breath hurt. Nelson put me in a T-shirt and wrapped me tight with duct tape. It helped a lot. When we went over, I couldn't believe how fast it all happened. There was no time to react."

"The duct tape answers some of my questions. Does it still hurt to breathe?"

"It was getting better but feels worse now. I still feel like something is stabbing me."

"That's because I took off the tape. When we found you, you were in foulies and a deflated PFD—uh, personal flotation device. Nelson wasn't wearing either one. Do you know why not?"

"He wasn't? That's strange."

"The only foulies and PFD we found were the ones you were wearing."

Quinney rubbed her face, looked at Stevens, and shrugged. "I don't know. I just don't know. It seems so long ago."

"Do you know if your boat had any emergency locator beacons?"

"EPIRBs? It did. Frank found them scattered all around the cabin—stuffed wherever they could fit. One was in a drawer. They found another in a cabinet. They found one big one and several smaller ones. None of them worked. All the batteries were dead."

"No one checked them before you left?"

"We didn't even know we had them until Frank found them. I'm not a sailor. I wouldn't know what to look for. The first time I knew about EPIRBs was when I saw them on the galley table after Frank found them. That boat was a mess. Everything was broken. It shouldn't have been allowed to sail."

Stevens looked down in disbelief. "There will be an investigation. At some point you'll be meeting with the Coast Guard to discuss what happened. They'll ask you to write down anything you can remember. What happened with all the equipment in the life raft?"

Quinney shook her head. "There wasn't any."

"Nothing?"

"No, nothing."

"Usually, all that is clipped or tied to a ring inside the safety raft. But that will come up in the investigation. Who kept the logs?"

"Nelson. He was the navigator and kept track of where we were. Where is he? Is he on this ship?"

"Yes, he is."

"Can I please see him?"

There was an authoritative-sounding knock on the door, and the captain walked in. "Well, it looks like you've made good progress."

Stevens made introductions.

"Do you need anything?" the captain asked.

"I'm pretty thirsty. Could I have some more water?"

Stevens grabbed another bottle.

"Why do I have this throbbing headache?"

"You were severely dehydrated," Stevens replied. "We gave you two liters of fluids, but it could take a few days to fully recover."

The captain said, "I came to see how you were doing and let you know that you'll be our guest for the next few days until we make dock at the Port of Philadelphia. Your condition has improved so much, the Coast Guard took you off the watch list. When we get to port, there'll be an ambulance waiting. You'll be taken to a hospital and officially checked out. The Coast Guard will open an investigation. You'll be extensively interviewed. Then… you will be taken home by your family."

Quinney's eyes and face lit up, and tears filled her eyes. "My family? Coming to meet me? How did they know?"

"A list of emergency contacts was among travel papers we found in the backpack. You were the only female listed in your ship's log, and we matched your name to a name on the emergency contact list."

"You said I could see Nelson. Could we do that?"

* * *

Stevens wheeled Quinney down a passageway to the galley. He stopped at the entrance to a walk-in cooler. "Are you sure you want to do this?" he asked. Quinney nodded. He opened the cooler door and brought her to Nelson's side. He lay on a table covered with a blanket.

Quinney began sobbing in anticipation of seeing her fiancé's body. Stevens slowly pulled back the blanket, exposing Nelson's face, and stood back. "Quinney?" he whispered softly.

Quinney lifted her head, hoping that by some miracle Nelson would wake up, but when she saw his face, she paused, confused. She leaned over, looking at him intently. She squinted, rubbed her eyes, and looked again, and then looked at Stevens. "This isn't Nelson. This is Frank. Where's Nelson?"

Her voice trembled. "What's happening? Help me understand. Where's Nelson?"

Stevens quickly covered the body and wheeled Quinney out of the cooler.

"Quinney," Stevens whispered. "When we picked you up, we had no idea who anyone was or what you were doing out there. The documents in the backpack gave us names. It was you who told us that the man in the raft was Nelson. I'm as stunned about this as you are. How Frank came to be in the raft instead of Nelson, I can't even guess. Let's leave that for the Coast Guard. They're thorough and will be able to piece together a plausible story, if not the actual one."

Stevens wheeled Quinney down a narrow corridor to a small room. "*Moley Ann* is going to be your home for the next few days until we reach port. You stay here for a while. I'm going to collect some fresh clothing and put together a dopp kit. You can collect your thoughts and be alone as long as you'd like. Feel free to venture around the ship. There's always someone walking around, so if you get lost, just ask."

* * *

Stevens returned to the bridge and resumed his duties. He peered out to the horizon and pondered the trauma of Quinney's experiences. He searched deep within himself to fathom the gut-wrenching sense of helplessness and aloneness, and the acceptance of an inevitable end.

Stevens brought medical paperwork for the captain to sign. He was explaining the medical requirements when the captain spotted

Quinney outside on the bridge. He motioned with his eyes. Stevens looked over. "That's one extraordinary woman," said the captain. "She has a strong will to live."

Quinney stood by the rail on the bridge, looking out to sea. She wore a shirt with sleeves rolled up to her elbows and jeans rolled up until she could walk without tripping. She carried a jacket about six sizes too large, but it would keep her warm.

"We picked her up yesterday when we took her for dead," the captain continued. "Look at her… She's getting around pretty well. She's been through an ordeal, and only a handful of people on this earth could appreciate the horror of it all. You brought her back from the brink. That reflects your quick thinking and medical skills."

"Her body seems to be recovering well, thanks to the IV," Stevens replied, "but she's been through acute trauma, which could turn into a hefty case of PTSD. I'm not a doctor, though, and not qualified to diagnose it. I can't even mention it in my report. I just hope they pick up on it when she's taken to the hospital. I think she's got a long road to recovery ahead."

* * *

A chilly early evening breeze found its way through Quinney's clothing. She tightened the jacket around her and gazed back out to sea, watching sky glow from city lights and her first glimpse of land in weeks. She stood—just staring out over the water.

Stevens watched with concern. He grabbed his jacket and approached Quinney on the bridge. She was completely focused, unaware of his presence, and appeared startled when he spoke. "Quinney, evening will bring cold temperatures and icy dew. We've come a long way in your recovery, but your body is still vulnerable to hypothermia. It would be wise to get you inside. I want to take you to the mess hall for some good old-fashioned ship's grub so you can get some hot, solid food in you."

Quinney looked at him and back out to sea. "Nelson wanted to take me sailing in the Exumas. Did you know there are three-hundred and sixty-five cays in the Exuma string, most of them not much more than a sand dune? One for each day of the year. Nelson always talked about sailing south to the remote cays. He said we'd drop anchor in the lee sand, sip mint juleps while watching the sun set and the moon rise. We'd have the world to ourselves." She dropped her head. "That's not gonna happen now."

Quinney continued, "Let me look out at this one more time before going in. I'll meet you inside." She turned to the east, where they had found her only a few hundred miles away. She tried to imagine how far she had drifted and the point where *Momentum* had gone over.

She coughed and choked on her faint words – words that vanished in the vast sky and hidden by the breeze on her face. "Nelson. Nelson. My Nelson. My dear Nelson. Where are you? Have I abandoned you? Have you not been found yet or are you really gone? I was sure that was you tied to that line trailing the raft, but was it Frank all along? Did you rescue him by throwing the life jackets into the water? Maybe you're still out there, clinging to a floating something. Someone will find you and bring you back to me. Nelson, oh Nelson. I can't say goodbye. Please don't leave me here alone. Please come back. Come back. Please."

Quinney gripped the handrail and slumped over, sobbing. She looked around as she tumbled helplessly into the agonizing, tormenting pit of grief. "Nelson! Nelson!" she cried out repeatedly, looking up and into the darkness. She doubled over and clenched her stomach. She slowly slid to the deck like a marionette whose strings were being cut one by one. Bitter weeping brought no relief. And none would come that night.

Stevens watched from inside the bridge. He wanted to mend her fractured soul – to fix what was neither his to fix nor something he could. He waited and watched. A lone tear snuck past his resolve to remain dispassionate. Her hurt was his. He stepped out of the warmth of the bridge into the damp and chilly evening and stood nearby, searching for something to say while realizing anything he could utter would be empty words. She lay motionlessly slumped against the railing. And emotionally drained. Stevens put a gentle hand on her shoulder, helped her up, and escorted her to her quarters.

* * *

Four people had set out on what was to be a nine-day boat delivery. They were at sea for fifteen. Nelson went to prove his worth as a mariner, so noted his sailing résumé found amongst the recovered documents. Quinney went to tick off an item on her bucket list, so said hers. The actual route of the sailboat, painstakingly recorded on their water-stained chart and ship's log, told a story of mariners attempting to flee the worst of Mother Nature. What the crew had attempted may have appeared to be haphazard decision-making, but sometimes a person finds himself in the wrong place at the wrong time even with the best information.

The *Moley Ann* headed to the Port of Philadelphia, where Quinney would be met by a grateful family and a rigorous Coast Guard investigation. And… she would have a profoundly intense story to tell.

EPILOGUE

The US Coast Guard investigated the disappearance of *Momentum*. They searched the area around the last recorded GPS coordinates from the ship's log and found neither wreckage nor floating debris. The investigative report concluded she had succumb to the forces of nature.

The bodies of Nelson Sharpe and Blake were never recovered.

How Frank made it to the life raft was never answered. Quinney's testimony was sketchy and speculative as she was certain the person who joined her was Nelson.

Quinney returned to California with her family where she attended extensive therapy for PTSD. In 2012 she resettled in the US Virgin Islands, purchased a 37' sailboat, and opened a charter business offering island-hopping adventures. Since its inception, Quinney has grown her fleet to six sailboats.

THE END